WHAT THE FLOWER SAYS OF DEATH

DANIELLE KOSTE

ISBN 978-91-984252-2-2

Edited by Autumn Lala

Cover design by Divine Michelle © YONDERWORLDLY DESIGN

TO MY MOTHER,
and all the other

beautiful,

brave,

brilliant

women in my life.

Mothers, daughters, sisters, and friends

who make me a better human being

Acknowledgements

Special thanks go out to the following wonderful women, my creative midwives, who without, this publication would not exist.

JORDAN, for being Jack's number one fan—officially—and my word-of-mouth Queen.

LAURA, for being my comic relief, my apathetic twin, and, too often, my therapist.

DIVINE, for making my creative visions ten times more beautiful, even while fighting a tropical depression.

AND AUTUMN, for reaching out to me when I needed you the most.

I

My grandparents' estate was not how I remembered.

When I was young, the rolling acres seemed never-ending against the forget-me-not horizon, and the modest, victorian-style manor felt stately and royal, like a palace. I recalled playing in the technicolor garden, violets in the air and grass stains on my tights. Feeding the sheep and goats, their fuzzy lips tickled my palm. Going on horseback rides along the ocean with my grandfather, salt tangled in my ashy hair.

I spent many summers there as a child. Whenever my mother felt stifled by my incessant needs, I visited my grandparents for a few weeks. As I grew older and became more capable of taking care of myself, the trips waned to once in a blue moon. It had been eight years since my last stay.

Returning was underwhelming.

Unlike the warm, dewy summers, fall in Newport was desaturated and still, making my grandparents' oceanside residence appear foreboding. The white fence surrounding the property had faded to a cinder gray. The house's exterior, once a vibrant yellow, was now sun-bleached and dulled with dirt and grime. Maple trees lined straight and neat on either side of the dusty road leading to the house, their old age showing with patchy autumn leaves and skeletal silhouettes. I was akin to them, spindly fingers gripping tight onto the last of their beauty as the winter threatened to strip them bare.

I'd once remembered this place having so much life, but Death had touched it since then. Fitting that I was spending my next few months here, as I'd also recently been touched by Death.

I tucked a bitten fingernail under the bandages binding my wrist, scratching at the forever itchy skin beneath. If I'd known I would be caught, I wouldn't have slit my wrist. I loathed the idea that I now had to live with the scar.

Battle wound, I tried reminding myself. A scar was what my mother called it while expressing disappointed in my now tarnished skin. Something unsightly, something to be covered up and hidden, like why I did it.

"Remember, Vi. You're to do as your Nan says. You'll help with the chores, and take care of Grampie."

I rolled my eyes. "Grampie's in a coma." What care could I possibly provide?

My mother opened her mouth, her frosty gaze saying she was about to snap at me, but she found the willpower to hold her tongue. I smirked to myself over the minute victory.

I wasn't looking to start a fight, but I was bitter and she knew I sat on a short fuse. Rightfully so, since she was ditching me two hundred miles from home only ten days after a suicide attempt. I guess her daughter's troubling desire to kill herself wasn't enough to make my mother wake up and smell the fragrance of her own neglect. I gnawed at my lip, my annoyance itching as violently as my stitched up wrist. I was angry that she was running away again, but maybe it was for the best. I didn't want to be around her for a second longer.

I opened the car door before my mother brought it to a complete stop, forcing her to slam the breaks.

She followed me out of the car with an exhausted huff. "Violet, please. I just need some time to think. To figure out what to do. I don't know how to handle all this. I'll be back for your birthday," she reasoned, always stifling a note of frustration when talking to me.

I retrieved my duffle bag from the backseat and slammed the door closed, sending a sharp glare at her over the hood of the car. As a teen filled to the brim with unnecessary angst, everything came out of my mouth far more poisonous than intended, so I committed to the toxicity. "Why do you only seem to be able to think when I'm not around?"

My mother stared at me, a deep wrinkle appearing between her brows, like I'd wounded her. She was about to reply, but the front door of the aging house opened, and my grandmother stepped out onto the veranda. There was a smile on her face, but it shrunk a fraction when she felt the heat from the conversation she'd interrupted.

I turned back to my mother, shutting my eyes to settle my anger. "I'm sorry. Just do what you need to do." I always ended up apologizing. Every time. Because a small part of me always hoped she'd change. That she would suddenly see the errors of her ways, tell me to get back into the car and take me home, and we could resolve it like a real mother and daughter.

My apology just gave her permission to not feel guilty though.

She sat back down into the driver's seat and took off with little more than a goodbye.

I watched her drive away until the dreary gray swallowed our silver sedan in the seaside fog. Once released from the paralyzing disappointment, I turned, slipping past my grandmother as she held the door open. I avoided her gaze so she wouldn't be forced to hold her sugary smile anymore. I knew she was doing it. She was so much like my mother and me.

I glanced around the entryway instead; it was as I remembered, yet hauntingly different. It wasn't the warm, welcoming home away from home it used to be. Now, it felt cold and quiet, smelled of stale air, just as in the hospital. The comparisons made my mouth dry and my skin itch, as if my wrist wasn't the only part of my body covered in uncomfortable gauze.

"The spare room is tidied up for you. I left some boxes in there so it's a bit cluttered, but I don't expect you to be spending all your time in your room while you're here anyway."

Her frigid tone suggested she was as apprehensive of me being there as I was. I didn't blame her; there was enough on her plate with taking care of the estate and my grandfather by herself. I guess I understood now how she might need my help, even if it was simply one of my mother's weak excuses. But did she *want* my help? That curiosity didn't have such an easy conclusion. I felt like nothing more than a burden, only there on suicide watch. Another unresponsive body for her to tend to.

"Let me know if there's something I can help with," I answered.

I didn't exactly want to do anything, and I wasn't sure how the offer would hold up if she ever decided to take me up on it, but I didn't want my grandmother sore with me before even making bed. All I wanted to do was curl up and sleep through the winter. But if she wasn't going to allow it, then I might as well try to help make our time together as painless as possible.

"I'm making dinner at six," she said, locking the front door and heading upstairs without another word. I heard the beeps of a heart monitor before she disappeared behind a closed door at the top of the stairs, leaving me alone.

II

The spare room was almost exactly as I left it eight years previous, apart from the addition of a few stacks of boxes filled with old, moth-eaten clothes and books. By the looks of it, the room had gone completely unused since I stopped visiting: dust accumulated on the window sill, pluming in the air as I opened the curtains, and an old chestnut vanity tucked under a white sheet hid behind boxes. The linens on the small, single bed were new though, and the wooden dresser was emptied, dusted, and free for me to use.

I dropped my bag to the floor and sat down on the bed, the springs squeaking under my weight. It wasn't as comfy as I remembered, but it would do fine. Hopefully. I was always either sleeping too much, or not at all; the bed never made a difference.

I sighed as an overwhelmingly heavy sensation threatened to lure me under the covers and keep me there. I pet a thumb over my bandages, the wound still tender, then got up.

I didn't want to waste my time any longer. I only had a bit of it left, after all.

I unzipped my bag and rummaged for my leather journal. I'd

wrapped it up tight in a pair of leggings so my mother wouldn't find it when I packed. I couldn't let her see it; she'd tell her shrink and they'd send me to a hospital instead of just my grandparents'.

The journal was my diary, but also my day planner, and my therapist, since I refused to keep a real one for longer than a few weeks. I told it everything through drawings and jotted notes. Most of what was written or doodled inside would have no meaning to any prying eyes.

The incriminating content was my newest installment: my "to-do" list.

I started it the day of my failed suicide attempt, after deciding I'd have to try again. I had already written a goodbye note; it was folded up and tucked into the secret pocket I made in the binding at the back of my journal. I titled it for the day I'd attempt again: January fifth, my eighteenth birthday.

After the note, I started a list of all the things I wanted to do before the date came. None of it was mandatory. Rather, they were simply ideas to keep myself busy as I passed the time. I wanted to try sushi and go to a concert. I wanted to make a snow angel like I did as a kid. I wanted to kiss someone, one last time. When I had a thought, I'd write it down. I hoped the list would keep me from indulging myself and sleeping away the last few months of my decidedly short life.

Along with my list, I started writing down new ways to take my life as they sprung into my head. Most of them were foolish. Some were considerable. I hadn't decided yet how I wanted to do it this time, so the notes helped me keep track of my options.

I knew it was morbid. I knew it was sick. I knew it was dirty and wrong and dangerous, and that's why the journal was a secret. That's why everything was a secret. I didn't want to get caught this time, especially after being caught the first time. My mother finding me, my wrist butterflied and bloody, was a moment I regretted, but she ended up just delaying the inevitable by coming home early that night.

Nothing changed. I still wanted to die more than ever. I'd have do it right this time.

I decided I would unpack later, or eventually, but for now I had to get myself up and doing something or else I'd root to the room and start growing into the walls like the foreign weed I was. I tucked the worn leather book into the waistline of my jeans, skin to cold, dead skin, then laced my arms into a heavy, wool sweater. The book hid snugly against my hip, concealed under my oversized clothes; with all the meals left skipped or forgotten, I was swimming in my wardrobe lately.

I closed the bedroom door behind me and followed my fingers along the old wallpaper back to the entrance. On the way, I passed the room my grandmother had disappeared into. It seemed she had left, the door remaining ajar. I paused, hearing the monitors again, beeping with heavy, dreadful intention. I placed my palm on the varnished wood of the door, opening the crack a little wider. I saw the crisp sheets of the bed and I froze, then retreated. I only caught my breath again when I was halfway down the stairs.

I stumbled upon my grandmother in the den, doing a cross stitch, her reading glasses balanced on the tip of her nose. She turned her attention to me when I approached the doorway.

"I'm going to take a walk."

She nodded, requiring no further explanation, and I had to conceal my surprise. I'd forgotten how it was to not undergo an interrogation every time I made a move. Just before leaving for the drive up, my mother made me take a shower with the bathroom door open. The lack of trust stifled me more than I realized, and when my grandmother didn't question my intentions or motivations, a small weight lifted off my shoulders.

Would she regret the freedom she was allowing me? Would she

wonder if she could have changed something, if she'd only kept watch on me like a jail warden? Like my mother?

I ventured to the stables first, but the barn was locked and boarded up. It seemed the horses, sheep, and goats were sold long ago. The upkeep was probably too expensive, and too tedious, when my grandmother was taking care of it all alone. I wasn't surprised, but found myself disappointed anyway. One of the horses, Marvin, used to nip sweetly at my sweater as I brushed his neck, and I felt a sudden deep regret that I never got to say goodbye to him. Or anyone, really. Last time I was here, I had no idea it was going to be so long before I returned again.

Next, I checked the garden, and I was disappointed a second time. The wrought iron gate was locked with a chain and padlock, both showing the first signs of rust. I climbed up the fence to see inside, but the plants were overgrown and uncared for, so there wasn't much to see. The garden possibly lasted longer than the animals, but it had still been at least a few years since someone tended to it. Weeds overtook the delicate undergrowth, and the hardier plants engulfed the other, more particular ones.

I continued on, heading for the coast, assuring myself the sea had not changed in its luster since I'd been gone. I hiked up to the cliff where my grandfather and I would often eat sandwich lunches, and though it was more gray and cold than I remembered, this location did not let me down.

I sat on a rock, folding my knees up to my chest and sucking in the salty air like I'd been drowning all this time and was finally catching my breath. The ocean was choppy, peaks of white speckled against the dark green. I retrieved my journal and drew the coast as I saw it, then the branches of the maple trees outside the front of the house as I remembered them from earlier. I wrote: *Hang from the thickest branch. Jump from the cliff and let the ocean swallow me.* I added to my list: *Go horseback riding, smell the Newport violets, swim in the ocean,* even though I knew the last one was impossible in the time I had left without risking hypothermia. I scratched out the sentence, changing it: *Go swimming in December. Let the cold take you.*

After an hour I headed back, not wanting to take too much advantage of the freedom my grandmother allowed me. I cut through the sparse line of woods on the property, taking the same path I used to with my grandfather. After years of neglect, the trail was now colonized by bushes and hanging branches. Because of the overgrowth, I found myself winded once I emerged from the trees to the backyard of the property, fifty yards from the house. I felt out of shape in this environment; New York had broken me like a bridle on a wild horse.

I circled the house to enter back through the front door, but as I turned the corner, a shadow caught my eye. My steps faltered as I checked, catching another glimpse of a dark-haired boy dressed all in black, raking leaves from under the near-naked maple trees.

So far, the property was hauntingly empty and devoid of life, I'd almost forgotten other human beings existed. His presence took me off guard, as did the unwavering stare he sent back at me. I directed my eyes away and hurried forward to the entrance, but snuck a second peek as I closed the door behind me. He had bent down, returning to raking.

My grandmother was in the kitchen making a cup of coffee. As I crossed the threshold, she offered me the mug she held and turned to prepare herself another. I used the mug to warm my chilled fingers, the smell reminding me of quiet, early mornings before heading out with my grandfather.

"Who's the kid?" I asked as subtle as possible. I was still bewildered by his presence, considering the lack of any other people at the estate, and I think it leaked out with my question.

When I visited as a child, there were always lots of people

around. My grandparents had a maid for the house, groundskeepers, and stable workers to help with the animals. Now the place was little more than a graveyard, besides that thin boy who looked like he could have simply broken off from the very trees he raked under.

She spooned a bit of sugar into her drink. "Right. He came by a few days ago offering to help tend to the grass. I've given him some money to rake up the leaves, they were becoming a hassle. He's from town I believe. I can't remember the name." She paused her rambling to take a sip from her coffee, then turned towards me with a glint in her gaze. "He's about your age, I think."

I scoffed, and she snickered before leaving the room. I let her believe I was embarrassed by her suggestion, but really that was nowhere near the truth. I had laughed because the thought of conversing with another human being, for romantic purposes or otherwise, was the furthest thing from my mind considering my coming plans.

Nonetheless, I shifted over to the kitchen window and sipped on my coffee while spying on him, pulling the orange and red leaves into neat piles, his movements smooth and willowy like the sway of tree branches above him.

III

I got up with the sun the next morning, having the fleeting motivation to try and battle my oversleeping for once. I knew by the afternoon I'd be desperate for a cup of coffee or a too-long nap, but for now, while the determination struck me, I'd try to seize it. I tucked my journal into the front pocket of my pull-over hoodie and left my borrowed room to greet the day.

On the balls of my bare feet, I crept towards the kitchen, but found myself pausing outside my grandfather's door as I passed. It was closed again, and as I held my breath to listen, I could hear my grandmother on the other side. At first I thought she was humming, but after listening longer, I placed her steady, gentle rhythm: she was reading to him.

Shaking my head, I continued on as quietly as possible. I had no intention of bothering her, so I'd just get a bowl of cereal and mind my own business. As I searched the kitchen I realized there was no cereal in my grandmother's house though. Actually, there wasn't much of anything to have for breakfast, besides coffee. I considered surrendering and starting a brew, cutting to the chase and dosing myself up on caffeine immediately instead of waiting until the inevitable exhaustion set in, but my stomach rumbled fiercely in protest and I knew I'd need to make something.

If I was going to be baking, then I was going to go all out. I pulled out my journal and set it on the counter, flipping through to a recent doodle I'd sketched along with a jotted down note: *Make this!* The drawing was poorly done—my limbs were still weak from the blood loss at the time—but recognizable: a plate of Belgian waffles stacked up with a spoon of ice cream on top. A replica of the magazine photograph I'd drooled over while at the hospital. When I saw it, I knew I had to have something similar before my birthday.

It was on my list, and I was sure making breakfast would help keep me on my grandmother's good side, so I scratched a line through the words in my journal to check it off. Then I scoured her cookbook collection for one on desserts, managing to uncover an appetizing recipe for Belgian waffles.

As I expected, my grandmother kept a full stock of baking supplies just as she used to; I had everything I needed. About thirty minutes later, when she shuffled into the kitchen in her night robe, I'd already put my dirtied dishes into the washer and was taking the first waffle off of the steaming iron.

"I didn't expect you up so early. Aren't kids your age supposed to be awake all night and asleep all day?" She shifted past me and filled the kettle with some water; it was tea for her in the mornings, it seemed.

"How do you know I've even gone to bed yet?" I joked, ushering her to a seat at the bay window and placing the waffle and a fork in front of her. "Let me know if it's good."

"Oh dear. Dessert is not for breakfast." Her words objected but she raised her fork and cut off a corner to taste it regardless. "Get me the honey, would you, Flower?"

I had already turned to gather it for her before she asked, but I paused when my old pet name escaped from her lips; it had been so long since someone called me that. I thought perhaps she'd forgotten all together. She pretended as if she didn't noticed what she said, but when I handed her the honey she smiled and something in my chest fluttered, just barely.

"Who taught you to bake?" she asked. She could never admit it was good, that was not the style of the women in our family. I knew the question was her way of confirming it was delicious though.

I made sure to conceal my smugness, returning to the iron to start my own waffle. "You did."

"Oh yes. That's right. It certainly wasn't your mother."

I snorted at her sass.

When the kettle whistle assaulted the silence, I retrieved her tea for her and then settled down across the table. She was nearly done with her plate and had unfolded the newspaper to start doing the crossword as she finished. The lull between us made me thoughtful, and as I watched her read over the paper, I recalled her voice reading to my grandfather only a little while before.

"When I got up earlier, I heard you reading to Grampie," I noted through a bite of delicious waffle, swirling my fork through the whip cream on top as I let the comment sit briefly. "Why do you talk to him?"

She tensed, and I was worried I offended her. I knew my grandfather was still a sore subject for her, especially when neither my mother nor I came to visit when he first fell into a coma. She took a sip of her tea and let her shoulders relax again, settling her eyes back down to the paper before answering.

"The doctors say it's good for him. They say he can hear everything still, so it's good to keep him stimulated. That it might help."

I nodded, leaving it there. I didn't want to prod further when I realized how careless I'd been with my first question. Next time, I'd tread lighter. She finished her waffle and dismissed herself shortly after, bringing her tea and the newspaper with her to the den. When she left, I retrieved my journal again to add to my list: *Talk to Grampie.*

My grandmother entered my room later in the afternoon while I was unpacking, asking if I needed anything from the grocer. I requested only cereal and milk, not wanting to be too much of a bother. She took note, then explained that she would be back in a hour, and drove off in my grandfather's beat up old farm truck, allowing me to be alone again for the second time since arriving, and since the "accident."

The house was too quiet. In the way that a graveyard is hauntingly silent despite the countless bodies. Or like a hospital room, when everyone's trying to avoid talking about the elephant between them. I could hear the old radiators clicking as they warmed up, the ticking of the big grandfather clock in the entryway, and the distant beeps of the monitors, confirming there was still life besides myself there.

I played with the zipper on my sweater, up and down, just to hear a noise, to overpower the beep, beep, beeping. It didn't work though. The sound consumed me. I took a deep breath, exiting into the hallway.

Talk to Grampie, I had written. What better time than now, when I was given some privacy? I followed my hand along the wall to the other end of the hallway. The door was ajar again, the stale-air smell growing stronger the closer I got. It reminded me of sterile linens and bandages and stitches. It reminded me of coming back to life. I picked uncomfortably at the wrap around my wrist before stretching my hand out and placing it flat on the wood of the door.

The door creaked as it parted from the threshold, slowly, and I saw the corner of the bed, and then the blankets covering stiff feet, and then the monitor screen, blinking and refreshing with each tonal heart beat. I could hear mine in my ears now, wet and alive, deafening. I took a deep breath and inched the opening wider.

He slid into view; I saw the tubes wrapped around him, in his nose and arms, his skin gray like a corpse, and I felt the panic grab at my lungs, a pair of hands, crushing the wind from me. I retreated, my back hitting the opposite wall hard, before I ran down the stairs to the entryway and then out the front door. I was suffocating, drowning when I wasn't even underwater. The cool October air shocked my lungs into working again, and after escaping from the house I was able to catch a hard, painful breath.

I braced my hands on my own knees as I tried to work past the anxiety attack that assaulted me, willing myself not to faint, negotiating my wild heartbeat down to just a jackhammer. This was not a new experience for me, but the attacks weren't often this bad. I had medication I was supposed to be taking for them, but the pills made me feel even more suicidal than the depression and anxiety did.

The tunnel vision faded away and I was able to stand up straight again, feeling as though I'd just ran a marathon. I combed my fringe back from my forehead, damp with a cold sweat, and scanned the area with clear, albeit sensitive eyes for the first time since leaving the house, only to find a shadow across from me.

I caught the gangly boy's gaze as he watched, standing perfectly still a few yards away. The panic grasped my throat again as I realized he must have been there for my whole, dramatic scene.

The overwhelming embarrassment froze me solid in a silent stand-off with him, until he shifted to take a step forward. I bolted like a scared animal, swiftly turning back to the house and escaping behind a locked door.

Once I determined it was safe, I peered through the frosted

glass detail on the entrance. He stared after me for a moment, before reaching up and tossing his hood over his hair, going back to tending to the leaves.

IV

That evening I picked a book from my grandfather's dusty library and joined my grandmother in the den as she worked on her cross stitch. I thought it might be awkward, sitting quietly with her, and it almost kept me from coming down from my room. With my mother it was always uncomfortable, like she couldn't help but fill the silence with words, complaints, or judgements, overstimulating my already wild brain and forcing me towards solitude.

My grandmother was not my mother though. She was exactly how I remembered, sans the additional stress that wore on her features in the lines under her eyes and the droop at the corners of her mouth. She appeared older than she was, but her nimble fingers stayed young. She was already nearly finished with the project she started the day before.

It was as comfortable as it used to be when I was a child. I remembered staying up late, enjoying the cool summer evenings, so still I could hear the wash of the ocean waves in the far distance, beyond the moan of the old house flexing and the taps of the needle against my grandmother's thimble. It was the same now, only I was older and my heart beat a different rhythm; the stitches on my wrist itched when I turned the pages, and the wind screamed as it billowed around the aging house.

"Your mother called me today."

My grandmother interrupted the silence as I started chapter eight. I flinched, the metaphorical walls springing up around me at the mere mention of my mother. Obviously, right when I'd let myself be vulnerable.

I tried to act like I wasn't already in a panic, turning a page I hadn't read. "Checking if I was still alive?" I considered waiting until my mother came to pick me up to try and kill myself again, just so maybe she'd realize it was mostly her presence that made me wish I didn't exist.

"She seems worried about you," my grandmother responded, trying to hide her skepticism. I mirrored it with a sarcastic hum.

"She wasn't concerned about me until I 'made a scene.'"

I rolled my eyes, then placed them back on the pages of the book, but I couldn't return to reading. My throat was tight with frustration and I had to focus hard just to keep breathing normally.

A heavy silence lingered as my grandmother considered her words. She started speaking again, more careful this time. "I wasn't sure about having you here at first. I was worried I couldn't give you what you needed. We haven't seen each other for so long and… I don't fully understand what you did. Why you did it. I can't comprehend, with so much life ahead of you…"

She stopped. Maybe she felt my guilt in the air and thought it best to leave her further judgements silent rather than vocalized. I didn't blame her for not understanding. I barely understood myself. At the time it felt like the only thing left to do. Like there was nothing else. No other option.

Instead of continuing, she tried to insert some positivity. "Maybe this place is a better environment for you, though. For now at least. Maybe with a change of scenery, you can leave the dysfunction behind." With a sigh, she put her cross stitch down and stood, coming over to set a hand on my shoulder and place a kiss in my hair.

I didn't know what to say in response, but I tried to smile as she left the room, heading back to my grandfather. My heart fluttered again in that weird way, like when she had used my nickname over breakfast, or when the paramedics had resuscitated it with an electric shock in the back of a speeding ambulance.

It wouldn't change anything, but it sounded nice regardless.

My grandmother needed to go out again the next day. When I pried, she seemed apprehensive to share, but explained that she needed to pick up some supplies for my grandfather. She was a retired nurse, which was why she was able to tend to my grandfather on her own, but despite saving money on paying for in-home care, she still had to pay for the expenses of his life support, which were clearly adding up from the state of the aging house.

She didn't go into details, and I didn't ask further, knowing I was already treading in sensitive territory. I couldn't help but wonder about how much money was already spent on my grandfather's care though. He'd been in a coma for almost three years now. Was my grandmother in debt yet? I remembered hearing my mother argue on the phone with her years ago, about expenses. Grampie's accident had put an even bigger splinter in their relationship.

I knew my mother would never say it, but she had already mourned her father and wanted to end things cleanly. My grandmother adamantly refused when the decision to stop life support first came though. My mother didn't understand why my grandmother put herself through the suffering of caring for him, but then again, she didn't understand a number of things. The women of our family had a lot in common, but empathy was never something my mother excelled at.

I think I knew why my grandmother held on. It was because sometimes the pain reminded her she was still alive. She was in that room every day, seeing him lying there, and her heart ached, but at least she felt something. I imagined being alone in this house, which had once been a home always filled with my grandfather's warm laughter, eventually made my grandmother feel like she was the one who died. The one lingering where she didn't belong. A ghost in a place long since dead.

I wondered, if she could understand better what I did, if she knew that was the existence I was trying to escape. A never-ending nightmare of barely existing. I knew too well how it felt, because I had been there also.

Maybe I still was.

Maybe I was so scared to go in my grandfather's room and see him because I might feel something too. I'd grown used to being a walking corpse, avoiding reminders of my autonomy like the plague. I wasn't sure how it would be to feel alive again. The thought itself scared me. Like coming back to life.

I opened my journal, taking the cap of my pen with my teeth and underlining, three times: *Talk to Grampie.*

Before she left for town to get the supplies, she took out some cash from her purse. Two fifty dollar bills. "Can you pay the boy today? Fifty for him. The other one is for you. You can go into town and see a movie sometime if you'd like. Or buy yourself some new clothes. If you need more, let me know."

She was being too sweet, a glint in her eye; I knew what she was doing. Setting me up to talk to the living was a sneaky move fit for my mother. There was something different about the way she did it though. I knew her actions were for my own good, rather than her comfort and reputation.

I pretended to be annoyed, but I couldn't muster the emotion convincingly. I knew her intentions were honest and I couldn't be mad. She didn't realize what handing off that money meant for me though. I had, after all, thoroughly embarrassed myself in front of him just the day before.

I watched out the kitchen window as my grandmother left, disappearing into the desaturation, leaving me alone again. Since arriving the atmosphere seemed to only get more gray, and I wondered what happened to the sun that shined so bright here when I was younger. Had it forgotten about Newport as I almost did?

He arrived not long after. I didn't notice him walking down the path to the house. It was as if he just appeared, trimmer in hand as he got to work clipping the shaped hedges around the perimeter of the house.

I zipped my sweater up and slipped my flats on, realizing immediately upon stepping out that they wouldn't be appropriate footwear for the Newport winter. The wind confirmed my thought, its bitter chill as I exited the house hinting towards the frigidness of the coming season. Maybe I'd ask my grandmother if I could buy a pair of nice boots.

I approached him, trying to muster an indifferent expression even though I could tell a flush was already warming my ears. He turned to greet me with nothing more than mild curiosity. His eyes were a stormy gray, like the sky since I'd arrived; the heat grew unbearable under my collar.

I buried a hand into my pocket and withdrew with one of the bills. "My grandmother told me to give you this."

He glanced down, then smiled politely, straight teeth peeking out from behind his lips. "I don't need payment. I'm—"

"Listen, I don't need to hear your good samaritan excuse. Let's stop beating around the bush here. Just take it and say thank you and we can get on with life." My overwhelming embarrassment came out as hostility, and I threw my gaze to the ground to avoid his reaction, and so he couldn't see me mentally kicking myself.

He didn't say anything else. Instead he reached out and took the bill, folding it up and putting it in his back pocket. With my obligatory errand dealt with, I turned on my heels to retreat.

He called after me. "Are you alright?"

I stopped, glancing back at him over my shoulder, wearing a questioning scowl.

"I meant, after yesterday. You seemed shook up about something. I was just wondering if you were ok," he clarified, eyes shining with a sincere curiosity.

I wanted to be annoyed, wanted to say it was none of his business and that he should mind his own. I couldn't be angry when he looked so innocent though.

"I'm fine," I replied sharply, hurrying back to the house to avoid further interrogation.

V

It was a phone call with my mother that brought me out to the seaside the next evening as the sun was beginning to go down. After talking to her I always felt stifled, more so than ever now, since getting a glimpse of what it was like to breathe again while being away from her.

"You're tending to the stitches?"

"Yes, Mom."

"Make sure to get some cocoa butter. You know you're prone to scars."

"It's not even healed yet."

"It's good to use it early. It'll help. How are you sleeping?"

"Fine."

"You're not oversleeping anymore, are you? It's not good for you."

"I know."

"You really need to start trying, Vi. How's Nan?"

"She's fine."

"You should talk to her about Grampie if you get the chance."

"I don't have anything to say to her about Grampie."

"You know what I mean. This has gone on too long. Just try and make her see some reason. You understand."

"I have to go, Mom."

"I'll see you on your birthday."

"Sure."

My throat was tight, painful, and choking, a knot in my esophagus that throbbed with every pound of my pulse. I escaped the house to try and breathe again, and my wandering feet followed the pull of my aching heart, like a bird drawn to migrate south without a sense of why.

The stormy waves frothed foamy white far out in the violent waters, but calmed as they approached the coast, reaching out to caress the sand like a lover's fingers across a cheek, then pulling away. A forever unsatisfying romance between the water and the land. I could taste their romance in the air, misty and moist, salt on my tongue and tangled through my hair.

I sat there for hours, letting the sound of their love calm me. The clenching in my throat released as the sun dipped under the gray clouds and touched the horizon. A chill set in when the rising water threatened to kiss my feet; I shivered and wrapped my sweater tighter around me, wondering what it would be like to keep sitting there and let the ocean take me away with it as the tide retreated again in a few hours.

I stood, watching the waves approach my toes, teasing close then drawing away, a curled finger beckoning me to follow. I kicked off my runners and discarded my socks, then took a step forward, meeting the water with its next approach.

It was freezing, biting at my bare skin like knives. The pain only lasted a moment though, then my feet were numb and the caress became bearable. Is this how it felt to disappear into the water's embrace? Briefly painful, but with a blissfully numb conclusion? It seemed nice. Tolerable. I gripped my bandaged wrist, squeezing and making the wound ache. Slitting my wrist had hurt more than I anticipated. I knew I didn't want to do it that way again.

I stood there until the ocean's frigid advance wrapped around my ankles and soaked the hem of my jeans. I stood there until I couldn't feel my toes any longer, digging them into the sand to test them. I stood there until the soft lullaby of the sweeping waves was interrupted by the assaulting noise of someone clearing their throat.

I twisted towards the sound, stricken with panic, pin pricks over my hot skin, which dissipated into annoyance and embarrassment as I found a familiar shadow behind me.

"What the hell are you doing here?" Profanity unintentionally escaped with my surprise. I thought to apologize, but my offense from his intrusion kept me silently scowling instead.

He let his hood down and swept his black fringe back out of his vision. The low light casted shade on the contours of his face, making the lines of his cheeks and jaw skeletal. His gray eyes flicked down to my bare feet, submerged in the water.

"I could ask the same thing."

I shot a glare at him as cold as the water I stood in, then turned away, determined to ignore both him and his question. It wasn't any of his business anyway.

When I didn't answer I heard him shift and I peered from my peripherals as he bent over to roll up his jeans and untie his boots. In no time he was barefooted also, and I stared at him unabashed as he stepped towards me.

His expression stayed smooth and emotionless, even as he stepped ankle-deep into the freezing waves with me. I was far less discreet with my reaction, and when I continued to gawk, he answered with a curious look.

"What are you doing?" I asked sharply, when I was finally able to shake off my confusion and find annoyance again.

He shrugged, admiring the brightly painted horizon. "You tell me."

"I came here to be alone." I deflected the question again. I didn't like the idea of admitting to some weird, skeleton kid that I was indulging in fantasies of killing myself. "Did my grandmother send you?"

He shrugged again.

"Are you stalking me?"

This garnered a response from him, but it was nothing more than a grin in my direction. Then, he put his hands in the pockets of his jacket, letting his shoulders fall into a relaxed posture.

"Fine. I was just leaving anyway," I said, stomping my wet, frozen feet out of the water and back to my shoes. I dusted off my soles messily and threw on a sock, not caring about the wetness making sand stick between my toes. I wanted to get out of there as quickly as possible.

Before I had my second sock on, he was following my lead and returning to his footwear. I glared at him again, but he just smiled sweetly back at me.

I knew he meant to come with me, so I fled to the woods, thinking to lose him on a path he was unfamiliar with. Unfortunately for me, I misjudged the amount of sun left, and as I reached the dense tree line, barely any light made it through to me. I tripped over roots and stones, unable to properly see where I stepped. It slowed my pace significantly, and he caught up to me in a matter of moments.

While trying to keep my pace to lose him, I stumbled, going over on my ankle and collapsing. It wasn't a necessarily rough fall, but it was enough to make me admit defeat to the battle I was fighting. I sighed and sat on the ground until he covered the few yards between us, carefully avoiding the obstacles I had so much trouble with.

He reached into his jacket to retrieve a small pen light as he approached, shining it on the ground near me to help give us both some vision. He didn't say anything in reply to my sheepish embarrassment. Instead, he simply held out a hand and helped me get back on my feet.

He directed the light to the ground in front of me so I could see where I was stepping and we continued at a slower pace. I refused to speak to him, and he seemed fine with not talking, so the walk was filled with a silence that was only awkward from one side. It gave me time for my previous frustrations to dissolve though, so when we finally exited the woods, I felt slightly more humbled.

When we approached the entrance to my grandparents' estate, I lingered with my hand on the doorknob. "Thanks for helping me back."

He smiled again, nodding once. "Bring a flashlight next time."

His inflection never changed, but I could tell he was teasing me. Despite myself, a grin of my own twisted at the corner of my lips as I entered the house, closing the door behind me.

My grandmother was hanging up the phone as I entered the kitchen, stress causing her frown lines to harden. "There you are. I just about had the police coming out to look for you. Your mother told me you spoke today. I was concerned."

I lowered my gaze in shame. It was the first time in a long time that I hadn't meant to make someone worry. "Sorry, Nan. I was down at the water."

"I don't want to demand you tell me where you are at all times, you're almost a grown woman. But you need to at least tell me where you're going, when you'll be back. For the sake of my already high blood pressure."

My grandmother seemed genuinely concerned by my disappearance, and it made me feel even more disappointed with myself. My mother always bickered at me when I ran off alone, maybe because she assumed I was going off to hurt myself, but my grandmother didn't react as such. It was as if she was simply aware that any number of things could happen to me, and she was concerned for all of them, not just worried about what I'd do to myself.

"It won't happen again. I promise," I said, bringing my eyes up from the floor to make the oath to her.

She sighed, not in frustration but in relief, and bridged the space between us to give me a gentle hug. The tenseness in my muscles, put there by my mother and lingered in my joints all day, released as she held me. It had been so long, I almost forgot that I had a body, that I wasn't just a ghost.

I sighed also.

As she withdrew, I tried to loosen the knot in my throat with some lightheartedness. "And besides, even if it does happen again, you can always send that kid after me again. He did a pretty good job of finding me."

She screwed up her nose. "The boy? I never told him I was looking for you." Sensing my confusion, my grandmother smirked. "Maybe he followed you. Maybe you have an admirer."

I grimaced. "Stalker. That's what we call it nowadays, Nan."

She scoffed playfully at me.

&a.

With my feet still frozen, I wore three pairs of socks to bed that night and sat up with a lamp and my journal, a cocoon of blankets wrapped around me. I spent a while reading over the things I already had written. I added a few notes to my list: *Go to the movie theater. Watch the stars. Stay up all night to see the sun rise.*

I looked at my drawings from the days before, what I'd jotted down, my list of ways to kill myself. *Go swimming in December. Let the cold take you.* I scratched out December and substituted January, then marked a star next to the sentence, for future reference.

I fell asleep drawing the way the fiery sunset had chiseled into his features.

VI

Still feeling guilty for disappearing the night before, I decided to hang around the next day to show I meant my promise.

I thought to clean the house as I used to do for my mother when I was desperately trying to win her praise, but unfortunately there wasn't much cleaning to do since my grandmother kept an already immaculate home. I tidied up the boxes in my room to make a little more space for myself, then moved my motivation to the rest of the house, dusting off surfaces and sweeping the floors. I cleaned up the kitchen last, putting away dishes and cleaning out the fridge of expired produce.

As I glided around the room, finishing my tasks, I kept peeking out the bay windows. When I noticed, I forced my attention back to my actions, but they'd return to surveying the front yard once I let my mind wander again.

He wasn't there today, under the maple trees. The last of their leaves trembled in the wind, like they were alone and cold without his company, scared to fall all the way to the ground and not be collected with their friends by his rake.

I frowned, a line creasing between my brows as curiousness

stuck in my skull. It was strange I never saw him coming or going. Even down by the ocean, I hadn't heard him approach. He was just there, at the most inopportune time once again. It was unsettling. There was a twist in my stomach about it that wouldn't unwind.

When I was finished in the kitchen, I slipped into my shoes and exited the house with a garbage bag in hand, ready for a stroll down to the main road to discard the trash and collect the mail. I tightened the fabric of my sweater round my neck to shield from the chill of the wind, all the while discreetly searching for a gangly shadow boy. There were no signs of life though, besides my own heartbeat and the call of a crow off in the distance. There weren't even footprints in the mud at the edge of the road or tracks from a vehicle besides my grandfather's old truck. Any evidence of the boy's existence seemed to disappear and reappear as easily as he did.

I discarded our trash in the bin at the end of the road, then unlocked the mailbox and collected the delivered envelopes. I stood there for a moment, peering out across the lawn, down the road in either direction, and then into the great, gray sky. I could see pretty far. The fog covered my vision before any obstacle did. How had I never seen him approaching the house? How did he even get there without some transportation? If he walked the whole way, wouldn't I have seen him on the road?

I scolded myself, shoving the thought aside, annoyed that it still plagued me. It didn't matter anyway. I didn't care. There were other things to worry about besides how some creepy kid got around. I turned on my heels and headed back to the house, folding my arms across my chest against the cruel wind and my frustration.

As I approached the estate, I briefly dragged my attention away from my surroundings for the first time since leaving the house, inspecting the letters in my grasp instead. Credit card offers and other spam mostly, but there was one envelope from the bank that felt weighted and important. Suspicion twisted up my stomach.

"Morning."

I dropped the letters in a startled mess, clutching at my chest to ease the heart attack he'd just induced.

A smile tugged at his lips. "I'm sorry, I didn't mean to scare you."

"Are you sure?" I was skeptical. His sudden appearances seemed intentional. "Where did you come from?"

He pointed to around the corner of the house. "I've been here for an hour now. I'm pulling the ivy off the side of the house. If you let it crawl too high it can work its roots into the chimney cement, and then you have a fire hazard."

I narrowed my eyes. Why hadn't I seen him arrive? I sidestepped to follow up on his gesture, noting the ladder propped up against the side of the house and the ivy hanging from the brick chimney. So his story fit, yet somehow it also didn't.

I turned back to start picking up the letters, and he followed, helping me.

"I really am sorry."

"You're a little unsettling, you know that?" The comment came out more callous than I intended.

He didn't take my words badly though. Instead he just chuckled, as if he knew something I didn't, the gray of his gaze shining like silver. "I've been told." He handed off his half of the envelopes, then stood with me. A bunch of his black fringe fell out of place and he tucked it aside. I felt my ears grow hot.

"Your feet didn't fall off from the cold, then?"

I looked down at my shoes. "No. Neither did yours."

"Nope."

The heat was spreading to my cheeks now. "I should get this to my Nan," I said, tapping the stack of envelopes against my knuckles.

He nodded, smiling. "Say hi to Mrs. Holt for me."

Desperate for an escape from my embarrassment, I shifted towards the house, trying to smile also but managing only a small, awkward quirk of my mouth.

He stopped me once more with words. "I'm Jack, by the way. De'Morte."

I glanced back at him, one foot on the step up to the door, slightly taken aback. For some reason, a name made him feel much more real. Shadows don't have names, do they?

Ghosts do, though. "Violet."

He nodded again, another easy grin. "Like the flower."

❧

I found my grandmother in her office at the back of the house, a calculator in hand and her reading glasses perched on her nose again, looking over something that seemed important. Stacks of papers and boxes filled with binders surrounded her. The office used to be cluttered like this when I was younger; my grandfather preferred to keep hard copies of all his expenses. Since then though, the amount of free space had greatly declined. Even with no longer having the expenses of owning animals or paying house-workers, it was obvious my grandfather's medical bills added to the piles. I placed my steps carefully to make my way over to my grandmother sitting at the desk.

"I picked up the mail," I said, reaching to hand her the stack of envelopes. She flipped through them quick, pausing only briefly on the letter from the bank that I was curious about. If it meant anything to her, she concealed her reaction well.

"Thank you. I completely forgot." She tried to smile but it was strained.

"Maybe you should take a break, Nan. You're tired."

She chuckled. "I'm always tired. Thank you for the concern. Maybe I'll take a nap once I'm done here."

I nodded, not wanting to fight it. "Do you need anything?"

She sighed, rubbing the bridge of her nose, then gave another defeated laugh. "A glass of wine."

My answer was coy. "I'd offer to go pick up some from the store but, underaged."

A genuine grin replaced the stress on her face, and I turned to leave when she waved away my thought. I lingered at the threshold, adding a last question.

"Nan?" I waited as she peeked over the stacks at me. "Do you have the key to the lock on the garden gate?"

She lifted her gaze to the ceiling, thinking. "All the keys should be in the top drawer of the cabinet, right by the front door. Why?"

I shrugged. "I haven't been inside the garden or the stables in a while. I'd like to check them out."

She hummed with approval, and I dismissed myself.

I passed by my grandfather's room quickly and into mine, snatching up my journal. I wrote: *Get really drunk on expensive wine,* then spent the evening drawing ivy crawling up old, broken brick walls. I wished I was like the ivy, with the instinctual need to dig my roots into everything; clinging to life, solid and stable. Instead, I was more like the leaves, alone and ready to fall away at any moment.

No. I was a small, lonely violet. Fragile and short lived. The winter would have its way with me, and I would let it. *Like the flower.*

VII

The next morning I ate my breakfast before setting out towards the garden, a handful of mismatched keys in my pockets. Hopefully, I could save at least one, tiny violet from the winter chill setting in. I knew it was a long shot, since it was late in the season and the garden hadn't been touched in years, but I was hoping for a small miracle.

As I passed, I noticed the ladder that had been propped up against the house the day before was put away, the ivy pulled from the chimney, just as he said he was doing. There was no sign of him again though. Not that I was looking.

A short walk brought me to the wrought iron gate of the garden, and I buried my hands in my pockets to search for a key to match the padlock securing it shut. I tested keys for a while, a number of them fitting ill or not twisting in the hole. Any that didn't work were returned to my pocket.

Finally I found a key that slid into the lock smoothly. When I turned it, the mechanics clicked with success, but as I tried to open the lock, it wouldn't budge. The rust had gotten to it more severely than I thought, and the lock simply refused to give.

It took me a moment to come up with an alternative plan, leaving the gate and returning to the backyard of the house where the tool shed sat. I was curious to know whether or not my grandparents owned a bolt cutter.

Just as I was about to enter the tool shed, Jack emerged, a push lawn mower in hand.

"Good morning, Violet."

His sudden appearance was strange enough, but hearing him say my name was even stranger. All I could manage was surprise.

"When did you get here?"

"Just now," he answered, putting the mower aside and opening the door to the shed again, holding it for me as I entered.

I stepped past him, curiosity brewing. "Do you have a car?" I asked as I glanced around the shed, attempting to subtly interrogate him.

"No. Are you looking for something?" The way he asked his own question to avoid elaborating on his answer seemed almost too convenient.

I searched for a bit longer before admitting defeat. "A bolt cutter."

"Planning a breaking and entering?" He inquired teasingly, following behind me and shifting a few things out of the way to collect the tool of my request.

I watched him stretch over a shelf to where the bolt cutter hung on the wall. "Nothing nearly that exciting," I said, taking the heavy metal cutters as he handed it over to me. I chose to purposely omit the details just as he had. I could be annoyingly evasive as well.

"Do you know how to use that?" he asked, holding the wooden door for me again as we left the shed together.

I scoffed a little. "I'm sure I'll manage." How hard could it be? Besides, what kind of help would he give? He was probably weaker than me, with his spindly, tree branch arms. "Thanks," I added, the words intending to dismiss myself, but with my retreat I heard his boots shifting the gravel walkway as he followed me.

I slowed my pace, glancing over my shoulder at him. "What are you doing?"

"Helping." He gave me an innocent look.

I laughed, but the tone of it was clearly sarcastic. "I don't need any help."

He shrugged. "Ok, well, either way." His response implied he was doubtful, but his tone and expression never showed anything besides sincerity.

He was being ridiculously frustrating, but it felt inappropriate to get angry because of his politeness. I kept walking, deciding to let him follow if he really wanted to so badly.

We trudged together in a silence again, a trek that was awkward for me but seemed perfectly comfortable for him. I was relieved to get there, ready to prove I could break the lock open on my own so he could go away. It was when I arrived at the sealed gate that I finally realized I had never used a bolt cutter before and wasn't sure how to go about it.

I paused in front of the gate to assess the situation, painfully aware of his gray eyes watching me. When I glared at him, there was no sign of judgement, but I couldn't help but feel embarrassed regardless. I cleared my throat, and stepped towards the gate, setting the clamp part of the tool around the rusted lock. I tried hauling the handles together and realized immediately that my arms were not going to be strong enough for this particularly robust lock.

"Need help?"

His honest intentions were so sugary sweet it made me sour.

"No," I snapped, sending sharp ice his way.

He smiled in response, putting his hands in his pockets as he waited.

I turned back to the lock, trying again to press the handles together and snap the metal wedged between the sharp clamp, but failed once more. I huffed, flustered from the expended energy and from the embarrassment of his audience, witnessing me fail so terribly.

As I started my third attempt, an extra set of hands grabbed the tool with me, higher up on the handles. He pushed them together as I did, and with his extra strength, the cutter finally snapped through the metal padlock.

I let go of the handles, clearing my throat. "Thanks," I offered, looking anywhere but at him to avoid his smugness, even though I knew such an expression would probably never cross his gentle features.

"No problem." He removed the cutter and set it aside. "What is this place?"

I had gotten to work on removing the broken lock and unwinding the rusting chain that held the wrought iron gate closed. "It's my grandmother's garden. I used to spend a lot of time here when I was a kid. It hasn't been tended to for years though."

"Why not?" he asked, following me through the gate as I entered into the overgrown garden.

I turned to peer at him; he was completely unaware his questions could be considered prying. The fact that he was honestly curious made it a little easier to be truthful. "My grandfather is sick. My Nan doesn't have the money for extra expenses right now."

He admired the area, but with my admission, he turned his gray gaze back to me. There was no smile this time. Something somber sat in its place instead. "That must be hard for you."

His seriousness surprised me. I cleared my throat and waved the comment away. "There are worse things." Self-conscious, I tugged my sleeve down over the bandage around my wrist when I realized it had ridden up.

"So why are we here now then?" he pried further, tapping an old, wrinkly tomato dried on its stem.

I stared, unsure what to make of him using a plural pronoun like "we." I never asked him to join me. He was imposing. This wasn't a group activity. I was visiting one of my favorite places, and he was following, again.

"You ask too many questions," I said, sarcasm on my voice as I resisted the urge to tell him to mind his own business like he ought to have ages ago.

A laugh played on the lines around his eyes.

I went about my business, roaming around a high wall of crossed fencing covered in climbing plants, searching for any violet that had managed to stay alive this long. He lingered back, allowing me my space, occupying himself by checking out the overgrown vegetable crops.

Despite myself, my attention drew back to him, watching discreetly through the small gaps in the fence separating us. He buried his fingers into the dirt and pulled a bunch of weeds out from the bottom of a pepper plant, tossing them to the side, not even brushing his hands off after. Satisfied, he strolled over towards the berry bushes, out of sight.

I continued to the flower bed, hoping for the best, but I was sorely disappointed. Most of the plants had been taken over by dandelions, which died and smothered the other, more fragile flowers. Some of the late bloomers still hung onto their petals, but there were no violets in sight. I brushed aside a few overgrown bushes to be sure, before sighing and admitting defeat.

I rejoined him at the blackberry bush, his hand maneuvering around a thorny branch to gather a few dark berries from the depth of the plant. Despite it being a few weeks late for blackberry season, there seemed to be a few still ripe.

"You're not supposed to pick blackberries after October eleventh," I said.

He glanced at me, then at his handful. "Why not?"

"The Devil gets in them on October eleventh. That's what my Nan always said." I took one from him, testing its plumpness between my fingertips.

Coyness passed his lips. "I picked these ones special though. They were hiding all the way down, past the thorns. I don't think the Devil saw them." With his words, he popped the rest of his handful in his mouth, smug with satisfaction.

I couldn't help but laugh this time. "Well in that case..." I ate mine as well. He was right. It was still sweet, a kiss of summer on my tongue.

"Did you find what you were looking for?" he asked, tilting his head towards the direction I had disappeared to.

I shook mine. "The violets are all dried up."

"Violet looking for violets." He found humor in that, a tease of teeth behind his spreading lips as he shifted off towards the flower bed himself.

I hung back. "I already looked."

"A second time doesn't hurt." He glanced back at me, his expression sincere again. I rolled my eyes, pretending to be annoyed, but the joking had left a smile lingering on my lips, revealing the bluff.

I watched him through the fence again, strolling slowly among the dried up flowers, inspecting each and every one of them carefully. He tore out some weeds as he searched, like he did earlier, not caring about the dirt caking under his fingernails.

He stopped where the violets were, taken over by other plants, their old petals dead and dried up from the cold. He bent at the knees and lifted the overgrown bushes as I had, meticulous in his hunt. Unlike me, he didn't stand right away. He stayed leaned over, his hand buried in browning leaves so I couldn't see. Then he shifted his gaze to me, as if he knew I'd been watching all along.

I followed his silent beckon, and he turned back to the spot he'd discovered, holding up the bush to show a single, tiny violet sprouted in a pristine patch of dirt.

I was dumbfounded. I got down on my knees right next to him for a closer look. "I checked here though." I was certain. Just a moment ago the area was all dried up.

"You must have just missed it," he said simply, smiling that sugar smile.

I turned away from the flower to stare at him, catching his gray gaze and seeing the sincerity flicker briefly.

"I guess I must have."

That evening, with my journal propped on my knees and a sketch of blackberries started, I peered over at the violet, now sitting in a pot on my bedside table. I bit the end of my pencil.

"Where did you come from?" I whispered, staring down the flower as if my intimidation would break its silence.

You must have just missed it.

I hadn't though. I was positive.

VIII

The house was always quiet, but that morning it was particularly noticeable. I woke to the tapping of the old water heater coming to life, the house sighing with the new warmth.

I needed a second pair of socks and a hooded sweater over my long sleeve tee-shirt just to get myself out of bed. The cold was in my bones though; it had nothing to do with the approaching winter. Today was simply a bad day: one where my heart slammed in my skull and made my head hurt. Where my skin felt like an ill fitting sweater, itchy and tight around the collar, pulsing under the wrap on my wrist. Where I wanted to sleep away the hours and starve myself so I could feel the emptiness inside me.

My grandmother wrote me a note, left on the fridge. *Went to the bank.* I knew it was coming; she spent the last few days reviewing expenses, over and over. Something was going on that I wasn't seeing. Rather, I was seeing it and didn't want to.

I turned on the kettle for some tea, hoping the liquid warmth might revive my insides. The house was so quiet, it was growing noisy again. I could hear the clock ticking and the wood frame flexing and the chirp of my grandfather's life support. An artificial heartbeat that wouldn't stop beep, beep, beeping to the painful rhythm of my own.

A-live. A-live. A-live.

The panic drowned out everything, even while the kettle was screaming at me.

I turned the heat off, gathering my shoes and escaping the deafeningly quiet house, but my heart, caged in my chest, was forced to follow. As the door shut behind me, the wind blew and the maple trees shivered for me, filling the gaps in my skull with fuzzy white noise that muffled the protests of my restless pulse.

"Morning, Violet."

Startled, my heart hammered even harder against my ribs. I clutched at the front of my sweater to ease the ache of the panic attack still gripping me. "Stop doing that." The demand came out harsher than intended.

He laughed regardless. "Sorry." He only seemed mildly apologetic.

I glanced back at the house, unsettled by the idea of going back inside. He must have read my body language or the look on my face because his chuckle faded to concern.

"Are you alright?"

I turned to him, seeing the sincerity in those gray eyes again, and I considered lying as I usually did, but somehow I couldn't muster the energy. "No," I said instead. The truth. People didn't like the truth.

I braced for his retreat. For an excuse. I was used to them.

"Do you want to go somewhere?" His reply took me off guard. No questions asked.

I felt something uncoil inside me: relief. I sighed, like when Nan hugged me, and nodded.

He took my wrist, the one stitched up and tender, wrapped in gauze, and led me away with him as if it was nothing. As if he was used to guiding people away from their problems, and I followed like it was the easiest thing in the world.

We walked for a long time, until my legs were sore and I felt my stomach groan with hunger pains. Until my seized lungs were coerced into working again, and my deep, tired breaths refreshed my body and cleared the fog from my head. We walked until we neared the edge of my grandparents property, finding a sparsely wooded alcove.

"Where are we going?" I asked finally.

He stopped briefly, then shrugged. "Wherever you need to go."

"You don't know where you're going?" I stared in disbelief, my stomach twisting, with regret this time instead of hunger.

He shrugged again. "I thought you knew."

The panic wasn't as settled as I thought it was. It rose like vomit in my throat in reaction to his flippantness. "I've never been here before. Are you stupid? You got us lost!"

It was unnecessarily harsh. I regretted the words immediately, and groaned with frustration and embarrassment with my outburst, but I couldn't shake the anger so easily, even if I knew it was unwarranted. It was never so simple.

Instead, I stomped off, searching the area for a place to sit because my throat was tied up in painful knots again, and I was starting to feel lightheaded. I settled on the soft moss at the base of a tree, sitting and putting my hood up to cover my eyes. Even with the sky a gray overcast, they still ached with overstimulation; I leaned forward to bury my face into my knees instead, forcing some deep breaths of the musty forest air.

It worked. I swallowed my frustration back down past my swollen throat, clenched my fingers to stop their shaking, parted my lips to suck back more cool, fresh air, and I felt the building pressure wane.

Being in nature always helped me calm down. In the city, the brick walls seemed to close in on me like a cell. Sometimes all the noise helped; it drowned some things out, but more often than not, it just made the bad things even louder. The toxic thoughts. The spiraling. The sound of my ragged, tired lungs and strained, heaving heart. Like they were all battling to be heard.

New York was never the place for me. Even after years living there, I never adapted. I was always the same tiny flower, trampled down and covered with cement. My mother was a city girl; she said the buildings had a pulse, but when I tried to feel it, all I could hear was my own.

A-live. A-live. A-live.

I barely noticed him as he wandered over to me. He stepped so delicately, even in those combat boots that looked too big for his feet. Even with the leaves crunching under his gait. It was only when he spoke that I was hauled out of my head and back to reality though.

"You'll catch a cold in just a sweater."

He peeled his jacket from his thin shoulders, then plopped himself down on the ground next to me and held it out. I watched, trying to read his intention, but his expression was easy and earnest, as always.

I took the jacket and wrapped it around my shoulders, leaning forward to hug my knees again, folding myself up under the new warmth. I couldn't help but notice the smell on the cotton: woody and fresh like the air around us.

His silence unnerved me. I felt self-conscious, painfully aware of how strange I was in comparison to his simple smiles. I sniffed, discreetly swiping at my eyes when I realized they'd been watering.

"I'm not crazy," I blurted out, unable to hold back my nervousness any longer.

He focused his gray gaze on me, nothing but a kind laugh shining in them. "That's good. Neither am I."

I stared at him. "That's what you think, isn't it?"

"Why would I think that?"

"You've seen me come running out of the house hyperventilating twice now. You found me standing out in the ocean in my bare feet in the last week of October. That's grade A, mentally unstable shit you've witnessed."

It was all true too. He'd seen me at the very worst moments since I arrived. Indulging in my most morbid fantasies. It didn't even seem to faze him either.

I felt the need to explain it away, to say all my usual excuses when people caught my strange behavior and asked questions. *I'm fine. It was nothing. I'm just messing around. I'm totally OK.* Because the truth was inconvenient. I'd learned that a long time ago. People would rather believe my smiles and lies than admit to seeing me falling apart and take on the responsibility of putting my pieces back together.

I didn't even blame them; most of the time I pretended to believe my lies too.

"Aren't you curious?"

He was curious about everything else. Yet, he didn't seem to mind at all that I was always showing him the ugly, broken shadows seeping through the cracks of my poorly put together mask. He looked at me with the same sincerity as always, no pity or concern, no judgement.

It was weird. It made something twist inside me. Or maybe... Unwind.

"Do you want me to be?"

The meaning behind his question surprised me, and I had to stew around in it for a second to grasp its full intention. I needed him to ask questions, so I could explain away my insecurity as I always did. Without his curiosity, I was stuck in my head with my own doubts. I needed my excuses as much as everyone else did. When I told others I was ok, a part of me believed it too. Until I wasn't, at least.

"I dunno. Maybe I do?"

He nodded, agreeing to play my game. "OK. Why are you in Newport? Not enough room in the psych ward?"

The joke could have been offensive, but something about his delicate delivery was nonabrasive. A giggle crossed my lips briefly, letting my head fall into my knees again. I thought to joke back, because that's what I did to ease people's minds. *The doctors said I was only a danger to other people. I'm not crazy, the voices in my head are.* Make fun of it, make light of it, don't show people it's serious. Hide it. Nobody wants to see.

I played with the sleeve of my sweater, tugging it down to my palm, the stitches on my wrist begging to be scratched. It was so hard to lie to him. I opened my mouth to fib, but the truth came out again.

"I tried to kill myself."

I didn't know why I said it. Certainly not for attention, as I already had his. Maybe I wanted to shock him. To wipe the kind, teasing smile off his face. He was being nice, but nice was easy when you didn't really know.

A line appeared between his brows. It was as drastic a reaction as I'd ever gotten from him, and for a moment, I thought I had proven myself right.

After a pause, he reached out for my wrist, as if just now remembering the gauze he touched while dragging me behind him. I flinched, almost pulled away, but he was so gentle. His thumb glided over my wrist until he touched the skin under my sleeve, and I felt a hot fire flare up from under my collar.

"Why?"

It was the simplest question and yet, when I opened my mouth to answer, I realized I didn't know what to say. No one asked me that before. Not really, at least. My mother had once, but she didn't really want to know *why*. She wanted to know why I did it *to her*. Why did I have to be so difficult? Why did I have to cause a scene? Why did I have to have meltdowns and panic attacks she could never understand because I barely understood them myself? Why now, when she was trying to make her relationship with her boyfriend work, or trying to get her promotion, or just generally dealing with "a lot?"

The doctors didn't ask why either. They asked questions about how I thought, what music I listened to, what books I read. They asked me if I was nervous sometimes, then gave me pills that numbed not only my anxiety but also all my other senses. The pills made me want to hibernate the days away even more.

"I dunno," I said finally, feeling as if I needed to speak but not having the words. It wasn't entirely true; I knew why I did it, why I still wanted to, but to explain would take a lifetime, and even then, I still felt like my reasons might not be good enough.

Because none of it made any sense. I knew that. No reason would ever be "good enough." But thinking about fading away, about disappearing, about finally not existing to take up what little space I did in the world, it was the one thing that helped me feel as if everything wasn't spinning completely out of my control.

It felt like peace. The only peace I knew.

He allowed me my limb back, the skin of my hand slipping through the warmth of his palm as I withdrew. As if he heard my previous thought, he sighed, turning gray eyes up to mine to give me a somber look as he said, "I'm sure it was justified in the moment."

I didn't understand why it was so easy for him to accept. Like telling him I'd tried to kill myself was as simple as telling him I got up every morning and ate breakfast and brushed my hair and did all the other things any normal human being did.

It was frustrating, that it didn't shake him, that he barely even reacted. When someone says they tried to kill themselves, it's the type of thing that should make a person run. The kind of thing that... Makes a person dump you in the middle of nowhere with your aging grandmother and comatose grandfather.

He wasn't allowed to accept it so simply, like it was the easiest thing in the world. So I pushed further, to see what I could say to scare him away. Because I would scare him away eventually. It was inevitable. I scared everyone away.

"I'm going to try again."

I wanted a reaction, and with my words I got it. His fingers, which were digging through a pile of crunchy leaves between his legs, stopped fiddling.

"I'm going to try again, and I'm not going to mess up this time."

He looked up, and I was prepared to see the shine in his eyes that showed the first sign of discomfort, but it never came. There was something else in its place.

Sadness.

"Why are you so eager to leave when you just got here?"

Those words came out strange, like he meant something else besides what he said, but I was lost to their true intention. I felt my heart twinge terribly in my chest, regret twisting in my gut for trying to play with his emotions. I never intended to hurt him; I just didn't want my vulnerabilities to betray me. Like they always did.

"It's not about Newport..." That wasn't enough though. I needed an explanation. I needed to say something. "My whole life has felt so out of my control. I need to know, that I have this one last thing. I die when I choose to. No sooner or later. It just needs to be this way."

Vocalizing it made me realize how stupid it sounded. But I still believed every word.

He watched me for a really long time. Until I felt small and silly and the heat crawling up my neck assaulted my face with an embarrassed flush, and I tried to hide deeper in the collar of his jacket. There was never judgement in his expression though. Not a single time. His stare was simply one of trying to figure something out. Like he was attempting to bore into my skull and assemble the pieces of my thoughts into even a fragment of understanding.

He sighed when he finally averted his gaze. I don't think he found what he was searching for in my head. "I guess there's always a chance you'll change your mind."

It was my turn to stare, because he didn't argue or deny the legitimacy of what I'd revealed to him. He didn't say it was stupid or foolish or that I was crazy. He didn't tell me I should want to live. That something was wrong with me. That it didn't make *sense*.

He just accepted it, in all it's ridiculous, illogical foolishness.

I couldn't help the breathy laugh that escaped me. He was unbelievable. But then again, maybe I was too.

"I guess so."

There was no chance though. I was positive.

IX

I sat at the bay window in the kitchen the next morning, with a blanket around my shoulders and my journal opened in my lap. I hadn't slept well that night, and I was trying to treat the lingering anxiety from the day before with comforting things like tea and drawings.

Jack was outside, up on the ladder pulling debris from the gutters, stretching his thin arms and gathering a gloved handful of big maple leaves, tossing them away to let them float down to the ground. The gentle beauty of the falling leaves was nothing in comparison to the way his black fringe fell into his vision constantly. Not like I was watching, or drawing it.

I wasn't sure who was the stalker anymore. Sure, he literally followed me on multiple occasions without invitation. Perhaps that put him one point ahead, but my curiosity was getting so out of hand I was beginning to consider following him around to satisfy my taste for a bit of knowledge about him. I was always glancing out windows, watching him, wondering. I still had yet to find out how he arrived every day, how he was always around when it was

55

least opportunistic, or how he discovered that tiny damned violet now sitting up in my room.

I tried to be discreet about my prying, but I wasn't sure I was acting as well as I hoped. Even through the window, I could tell he knew I was watching him. There was something satisfied in the look on his face, too satisfied for just clearing gutters of muck. I thought to open the window and ask him what was making him so smug. I thought to go out there and grab him by that stupid jacket he'd wrapped around me the afternoon before and…

Something heavy and solid hit the glass of the window I sat by, shaking me hard out of my thoughts and forcing my heart into an angry pound. When I searched out the window again and there was nothing in sight, not even Jack, I untangled myself from the blanket and hurried outside to find the cause of the commotion.

I found Jack, no longer on the ladder but crouched down outside the window I'd been sitting at. My reaction at first was annoyance, assuming it was him, banging on the glass then hiding to play a prank on me. As I approached though, he reached down into the bushes, retrieving a mass of black.

"He hit the window. His wing is broken."

The crow's mangled appearance made him barely more than a bunch of tattered feathers, but as I neared I could see its chest, grasped in Jack's work gloves, moving in and out rapidly as it tried to gather air. The bird struggled, flapping its good wing once, but gave up immediately, not having the energy. He adjusted his hands, folding the bird's wings down again, both the good and the broken one, so he could hold the whole of the animal's body securely.

"Is he ok? Can we help him?" I asked, feeling an unsettling illness roll in my stomach. Jack stood and I inched closer, reaching out for his elbow as I neared, locking a tight grip around the joint. From over his shoulder, I watched the bird, its breathing rapid.

"He's suffering," he said, a somber inflection on the words.

"We can bring him to a shelter. Or a vet. They'd know how to help." I looked up at him. His gray gaze wasn't satisfied anymore.

"He's dying, Violet."

The words hurt for some reason. Like a hard punch in the gut. He turned back to the bird he held in his hands, and I watched, swallowing something hard in my throat.

Jack removed one of his hands from around the bird's body and placed it on its head instead, covering its black, blinking eyes with his palm. The bird's rapid breathing calmed down, and I felt a brief second of relief, before the dread fell into the pit of my stomach like a heavy rock as the animal stopped breathing altogether.

The hyperventilating migrated to my lungs instead. "Did you, did you just—" It didn't make sense, because he hadn't suffocated the bird or snapped its neck, yet with one movement of his hand, Jack helped it succumb to death.

"Violet." He reached for me but I was already withdrawing away from him and the death he held. I didn't know where I was going or with what purpose, but something had me fleeing. It was the same thing that kept me out of my grandfather's room and why I was never able to slit open the second wrist. For someone so ready to die, staring it right in its unsightly face was terrifying.

I marched away, until the winter chill seeped into my bones, freezing my muscles and joints. Until a shiver took over me and I had to hold my teeth together to stop their chattering. I'd forgotten a coat again in my anxiety and was paying the price once more.

I stopped, wrapping my arms around myself, and waited for the sound of his heavy boots to catch up with me. He was following me silently the entire time, and it was really only the gentle pace of his steps behind me that helped calm me down at all. As he reached my side, he shrugged off his jacket and held it out for me, just like the day before. The cold that stuck deep under my skin seemed to barely affect him.

I laced my arms into the sleeves of the jacket and wrapped it around me, trying to hold in the last of my body warmth. Surrounded by that woody scent again, my lungs took their first real breath since fleeing, sighing it out along with the tightness in my chest. When the shivers stopped, I finally found the nerve to look at him.

He smiled, his expression gentle and passive. I shook my head, red embarrassment creeping up my neck, still amazed that even after all this, he was able to stand there and not judge me. Anyone else would have let me leave, left me to deal with my crazy by myself. He was still there though, as if he almost understood, or at least wanted to. As if he wanted to help.

I glanced down at the hand hanging by his side, the now dead bird still tight in his grasp.

"Violet." He called my name to get my eyes back up to his. When he caught me in his gaze, he tilted his head to the side a little. "Come with me? I want to show you something."

I returned an apprehensive grimace, but he had yet to lead me wrong, so I willed my frozen joints to follow. He took the glove off his free hand, and when I was within reach, grabbed mine in his warm grasp. My numb fingers thawed in his grip.

He brought me back to the woods, starting down the trail I had stumbled along the night after he found me by the water. He quickly diverted from the path though, leading me carefully through overgrowth, pushing aside branches and holding them away as I passed.

I thought to ask where we were going, but I knew he wouldn't tell me. That wasn't his style. So I kept my mouth shut and let him lead me deep into the woods, trying to assure myself that if he tried anything funny, I could at least easily defend myself against the spindly boy. My clothes might as well be wearing me, but little more could be said for him.

He stopped finally, waiting for me to crawl over the trunk of a fallen tree and reach his side again. "Stay here," he said, turning away again and continuing on. I wondered briefly if he was going to ditch me out here, lost in the woods, but he didn't wander far. I could still see his black hair through the bare trees.

He leaned down, placing the deceased animal he held onto the ground then turned and started back. Half way, he stopped at a thick tree and beckoned me towards him again.

I followed, my feet crunching through the bed of fallen leaves on the floor of the forest; he put a hand up to halt me. "Slowly," he said, waving me towards him again.

I nodded, watching my step and placing them carefully this time. As I neared, he reached out for my hand again, helping me over a tangle of roots until I was settled steady next to him.

Growing desperate for an explanation, I eyed him expectantly. He offered a tilt of his lips and leaned back against the tree, then nodded his head out towards where he'd discarded the crow's body. I sighed, slightly annoyed with his crypticness, but followed his gaze and peered out into the forest as directed.

I was unsure of what I was supposed to be seeing. The forest seemed still as ever. I was almost ready to give up and beg him to explain himself, when there was movement within my vision. I blinked and focused onto where I saw the shifting shrubbery, catching a flash of fire orange disappear behind a tree.

I shifted onto my toes for a better angle, and caught sight of the orange again, swishing from side to side: a tail. Through a bush and under a tree root, the fox came into full sight, sniffing the ground as it approached the crow.

Once deciding there was no threat, she picked up the bird in her mouth and started back in the direction she came. I noticed her awkward gait as she went though, the way she hopped on one of her back legs to keep weight off the other.

"Her leg is broken. She'd be unable to hunt until it healed, possibly risking starvation. Along with her pups," Jack explained in a low tone as the fox returned to the forest growth.

I turned to look at him, dumbfounded. How was it possible, for him to have known about the fox, known to come to this exact spot, even though it was evident that this direction through the woods had been untouched before today? "How did you…?" I didn't have the words to express my confusion. "Why?"

He smiled, shrugging as he took the other glove off to put them away in his pocket. "I wanted you to see. I felt like maybe you needed to. To understand. Sometimes death is just a small piece of a bigger picture."

I surveyed the forest again, still and silent yet somehow full of a new life I hadn't appreciated before, and I knew that what he showed me was somehow just what I needed. I wasn't sure I completely comprehended its meaning yet, but it was there, planted in the slush of my skull, working out the cold in my bones.

I leaned back against the tree with him and sighed, pulling his jacket closer. We stood there for a long while as he let me sort through my emotions. Finally, I turned to him and broke the silence. "You're not going to explain all this to me, are you? How you knew about the fox, or what you did to the crow."

A shine of sympathy passed his eyes before he glanced away. I knew what that meant. As long as he was silent, he didn't have to lie to me. Curiosity brewed in the pit of my stomach, but for now I was content in letting him keep his secrets. I still had a few of my own after all.

✦

I settled into bed that night next to my violet, with fresh drawings of forest animals riddling the pages of my journal. New entries were added to my list: *Feed bread to the birds. See if the fox survived. Fall asleep in the forest and never wake up.*

I buried myself under the blankets, turning the light off and getting comfortable on my pillow. As the quiet night engulfed me, I put my thin, always cold fingers to my lips and tried to remember how warm they were in his grasp.

Beyond my fantasizing, in the silence of the old house, I heard my grandmother reading to my grandfather again. The sound of her voice was comforting at first, and I let it lull my heart to a resting patter. I realized soon that she wasn't reading aloud again though. She was talking, a quiet whisper, and when she stopped talking, she was crying.

The good sleep I almost found evaded me once again.

X

I exited my room around lunch the next day, journal tucked in the waist of my jeans. My grandmother wasn't supposed to be out, but the house was silent as if I was alone. I set out to search for her, and it didn't take long to find her. She was still in the room with my grandfather; she must have stayed with him overnight.

When I peeked into the room, I could see her leaned over in a chair next to his bed, sleeping with her head on his arm. I knew I had to move her to her bed, she'd hurt her back sleeping like that, but something kept me hesitating at the threshold of the room. There was a panic in my chest keeping me motionless. I let out a heavy breath, forcing the feeling away. Putting my eyes to the floor, I pushed the door open slowly and entered.

The air in the room was stale, and I could smell the intravenous fluids and the sterile linens. It burned my nostrils like acid, turning my nose up. I tried to ignore it, but the anxiety gripped my lungs tight, forcing me to hold my breath. I hurried over to my grandmother, wanting to get out of the room as soon as possible.

I touched her shoulder, shaking her a little. "Nan." As she

stirred, I stroked her arm gently. "You fell asleep. Let me help you to bed, ok?"

Her eyes fluttered open, only half conscious and confused, then nodded to me and allowed me to help her up. I noticed as she stood with me, a piece of paper was folded up in her grasp along with her rosary. Despite being just woken, she held onto both objects with a firm grip.

I led her to her bedroom and helped her under the covers. It was best she slept in for the day; I knew she wasn't getting much of it because of all the worrying she was doing over the bills. She reached out for my hand and squeezed it to thank me, settling herself under the blankets. I circled around the bed to close the curtains, hoping a bit of proper darkness would help. I wasn't sure it was necessary, since when I returned to her side, she had already drifted away again.

I took her reading glasses off her face delicately and set them on the nightstand, then turned to remove the paper and rosary from her grasp. I coiled up the rosary and set it next to her glasses, but lingered with the paper in my hand. My curiosity had become impossible lately.

I unfolded it as quietly as I could, turning towards the hallway to catch enough light to read. I didn't need long to recognize what it was, and I felt that anxiety from before shift into a full blown panic attack.

The paper fell from my hands and I exited the room, fighting hyperventilation. The urge to run was overwhelming, but somehow I managed a careful pace as I headed for the kitchen. I picked up the phone and dialed my mother's number.

"You got the notice then, I assume." She answered her phone with a callousness, thinking I was my grandmother.

"Is it true?"

"Violet?"

"Is it true, Mom?"

She paused, sighing in frustration. "It's time your grandmother lets him go."

I felt my mental state bending. Even from so far away, she was putting pressure, pushing and pushing. I knew I wouldn't stand it for very long. It hurt already, trying to keep myself together as my lungs screamed for air.

"Maybe so, but is this really how you're going to do it?"

"She won't see reason."

"So you're taking her to court? You're going to take Nan to court over him?" My voice cracked at the end of my words, and I cut them short to hide my emotions from her. I knew she heard them regardless.

"It's not fair to me, or you, what she's doing. We're not able to finish mourning him. He was my father, and he was practically a father to you as well. We need her to let him go so we can let him go."

"You didn't seem to care about what he meant to me when he first fell into a coma. You didn't even let me see him!"

"You wouldn't have wanted to see him like that."

And there it was, the breaking point. My bending patience snapped violently, and I felt the pain swell in my throat like someone had gripped my neck too tight for too long. Like hard bruises blooming under the skin. "You have no idea what I wanted! You never cared about what I wanted! I wanted to see him! I've always wanted to see him, but you kept me from him and Nan for so long. For what? Because of some stupid disagreement?"

There was a long silence on the other end, and I thought maybe my broken, teary reaction had finally gotten to her. She replied with a cold, level tone. "You haven't the faintest idea what you're talking about, Violet."

I resisted screaming at her over the phone, biting my lip so hard that I thought I'd tasted copper on my tongue. When I got a hold of the anger and sniffed back the tears of frustration escaping my eyes, I replied, "Maybe I don't. But I do know Grampie loved you, and he would hate to see you fighting with Nan. I wish you could just stop being so selfish for once and look at what you're doing. She needs you right now, Mom. She needs you here. I need you."

I couldn't help the tears, swelling big and terrible, dripping from my eyes wet and out of control. I couldn't help the sob that escaped my chest, violent and convulsive, my lungs having trouble taking in air around the pain deep in my sternum. I had held back those thoughts for so long, they came flooding out like a broken dam, unyielding and destructive. I'd hoped they would sweep her away somehow, but perhaps I was wrong.

When the silence on the other end of the line lasted too long, I cursed and hung up. I knew what was coming, because it was always the same, and I didn't have the emotional strength to deal with another one of her excuses. I couldn't do it. I ran for the door.

I remembered my jacket this time, the keys to all the places on the property heavy in its pockets, but I didn't care. I just needed to go somewhere so I could breathe again. The jarring pain in my chest told me to do things — *run, scream, cry, disappear* — but when I exited the house, I knew there was only one thing I needed to do.

Find Jack.

It should have been easy, since he always seemed to show up on his own when I was making a mess of myself. This time though, when I knew I needed him, he was nowhere in sight.

With my lungs working overtime to try and catch a breath, I hurried around the property, searching for him in all the places he'd popped up previously. I checked the shed and the bushes and the tree line and even out by the garden. There was no sign of him. Like the ghost he often seemed to be, he had disappeared completely.

Frustrated, and with more fat, wet tears threatening to spill from my eyes, I admitted defeat. I gave a stifled scream into the silence of the property. Not for anyone to hear, but rather just to let it out from being caught in my throat. I knew it was loud and echoed through the fog, but I could barely hear myself past the panic. *Run, disappear, run, run.*

And I did.

I ran fast and to nowhere, for a long time, until I started sweating under my jacket and I collapsed on my weak knees. Desperate for oxygen, my lungs were forced into functioning again, sucking in cold, ragged breaths that made my head split with pain and dizziness.

When the tunnel vision dissipated and I was able to see again, I tried to identify where my panic had brought me. I found my bearings eventually; I recognized the lone tree, which my grandfather and I used to called The Grim Reaper's Tree because it never grew leaves yet still stayed standing. It was overlooking the stables, so if I headed towards it, I should see the building right on the other side of the hill I sat on.

The wind picked up wickedly as I approached the building: a storm calling out its arrival. The only way to avoid it would be to head back right away, but I didn't want to have anything to do with the inside of that musty old house, and my legs objected with every step I took.

I fished through my pockets for the stable key. It took a while, but eventually I found it. I remembered it because it was an old style key, big and long, for the ancient keyhole on the door. It took a little effort, but somehow the key still worked. The old mechanism unlatched and I entered, escaping from the cold wind.

The stables were left mostly as I remembered them. Immediately upon entering was the tack room; my grandfather had decorated it with unvarnished wooden furniture and the antlers of animals he'd hunted over the years. We used to spend most of our time here, if we weren't outside. My grandfather worked on his designs, a hobby that was once a career, and I would copy him, drawing butchered versions of his detailed architecture, a passion for art blooming in my baby fingers with every messy sketch.

I distracted myself from the bittersweet memory by looking around, only to dive deeper into my dark thoughts. The place was dead in comparison to what it used to be, and it reminded me of how lifeless my grandfather was now also. Frozen in time, him and this room.

And now me.

Most of the items had been removed, like saddles, bridles and brushes, along with my grandfather's drafting table, leaving the place bare and forgotten. A few little things from the past remained though. There was a mirror, which had always been broken, still hanging on the wall, covered in dust. The rug, now far dirtier, was still on the floor, softening the tread of my feet as I wandered the room. To the left of where my grandfather's drafting table used to be was a stack of wooden drawers, repurposed since leaving the main house from a storage space for clothes to a place for an assortment of small tools and animal care products. I opened each one, but they were mostly empty now. I found only dirty pencils and rulers, some paper clips and pins, an old notepad with water damage, and an unused checkbook.

I opened the bottommost drawer last, and at first it looked empty, but as I closed it again something shifted. I took a second peek, reached into the back past dusty cobwebs, and retrieved a bottle.

I nearly laughed out loud, remembering the stash of whiskey my grandfather kept out here with his drawing equipment. My grandmother wasn't a fan of him drinking before dinner, not that he did it often. To avoid an argument, he snuck a bottle out to the stables and took a swig every now and then during our drawing sessions. Nan always knew because the alcohol flushed his cheeks and nose in pink.

My amusement shifted to watery eyes, the tightness returning to my throat.

"It's not expensive wine, but I guess if this is all you're going to give me it will have to do…" I spoke to myself, or maybe someone else who wasn't there, lifting up my jacket and sweater to pull my journal out from its hiding spot against my stomach. I flipped it open and stole one of my grandfather's old, unsharpened drawing pencils to scratch out the words I had written a few days previously. *Get drunk on expensive wine.*

I unscrewed the cap and took a whiff. It was strong, burning my sinuses, but something long since dead inside me stirred with the nostalgia of the fragrance. Woody and sour, laced with a smokey undertone. I wondered briefly if the years hidden away in the stables had given it some age. Was that how it worked, or did it only age in the barrel? Was whiskey made in a barrel? Regardless, I knew it probably wouldn't improve the taste for my virgin palette. The only alcohol I ever tasted was the sangria my mother made during the summers, and even then she watered it down with cranberry juice for me.

I shuffled over to the wooden bench that always had a bit of a wobble to it, sitting down to mentally prepare myself. Before I could convince myself not to, I took a large swig. I reacted immediately, almost spitting it out as the harsh taste met my tongue, but I managed to hold it in my mouth and swallow it down. It burned my throat like fire on its way, then warmed my belly once it settled.

The sting of the drink numbed something else I was feeling for a brief moment, something hopeless and hurt, drying my leaking eyes and easing the ache in my chest. When the numbing effect disappeared, I went back for more. I managed another mouthful down my throat, this one a little easier. The burn wasn't so bad, and the numbing lasted a second longer. Rinse and repeat, until half of what little was left in the bottle was gone and the numbness stuck.

Being inexperienced with alcohol, I didn't realize it could take a while for the full effects to really kick in. I definitely drank more than necessary, but it didn't feel like it was doing much of anything at first. It made me warm and cozy in my jacket, calm as the approaching dark clouds loomed in and the storm tapped raindrops on the roof. Then the minutes passed and I felt my vision swim and my head grow heavy.

It wasn't so bad. I couldn't remember why I had even been upset in the first place anymore. The tears on my face were just sticky salt lines now, and the warmth in my stomach had cleared my stuffy nose. My anxiety was long gone, smothered by the thick, warm honey currently in my skull. It was lovely. This golden brown liquid was magic medicine for a broken soul. A bit of liquid life for a ghost like me.

I wasn't sure how long had passed. Time was already so distorted for me, sometimes it disappeared completely. I might have taken a few more sips, but then sitting upright began to feel wrong. My head spun and laying seemed to help. Closing my eyes helped even more. I wouldn't sleep though, that was a bad idea, wasn't it? I'd just shut them, for a second, to stop the spinning from making me feel so sick.

&

I was laying in the grass under the bright summer sun, just like when I was a child visiting Newport. It was so warm on my skin it almost burned. I could smell the wildflowers and the sea in the air, an intoxicating fragrance that brought me to life. It was absolutely beautiful. When I sat up and put my hand above my eyes to block the blinding light, Jack was suddenly next to me. I smiled as he did, his hand reaching out to pet a tangle of my ash brown hair aside, leaning towards my ear to whisper to me. His words were warm on my cheek.

"Not tonight, Violet."

It went dark, and then it was cold. Like someone had thrown me into the ocean. A thousand daggers plunged into my skin. I was somewhere pitch black and freezing. I couldn't stop shaking. I couldn't get up. I couldn't move at all. I heard water, could feel it soaking into my pores and petrifying my veins. My heart didn't want to lead the blood through my cold limbs. I couldn't feel my fingers. Were they even attached to my palms anymore?

I mustered my strength and reached out for something, out into the blinding darkness, hoping my trembling digits would find their grasp. Just as my arm was about to collapse from the painful cold, something took my hand and pulled.

XI

I woke to my stomach flipping upside down, and the bile was already on its way up my throat when my grandmother handed me a bucket. It had been a long time since I was sick last. I forgot how terrible it felt. My whole body convulsed to rid my stomach of the poison in it, and afterwards, every muscle felt weak and sore from being overworked.

Luckily, I felt just terrible enough to not care about my grandmother watching me retch out my insides. As I tried to gather my strength and breathe again, she pet my forehead with a warm cloth, which fought off the chill that threatened to shake my bones. Once I was sure it was safe, I put the bucket down and yanked the blanket back up to my shoulders.

"How do you feel?" my grandmother asked, handing me the cloth so I could tend to myself.

I groaned.

"Yes, well. Remember that next time you find yourself wanting a drink."

She was disappointed, but there was a smugness in her expression as well. As if she was well aware I was receiving enough

73

punishment for my actions already. She left the room to dispose of my sick. I thought to call after her with my appreciation, but I was scared that opening my mouth might tempt another round.

I was in my bed with an extra quilt on top of me. The dark sky outside my window suggested it was well past evening, and I could feel the alcohol still lingering in my blood, but the sweet numbness of before was long gone and was replaced with a pulsing, spinning illness in my skull and stomach and veins.

When my grandmother came back into the room I mustered a voice. "How did I get here?"

My grandmother's smugness became even more noticeable. There was a glint in her gaze. "The boy found you."

I sat up in surprise. "Jack?" I regretted the movement immediately, laying myself back down as my gut protested. I remembered him from my dream, his voice in my ear that seemed almost too real to be just imagined. *Not tonight, Violet.*

She nodded, then the glint grew stern and motherly again. "Out in the stables in the middle of a storm, blackout drunk. Where did you even find the whiskey? What were you thinking?"

I groaned again, feeling thoroughly foolish and embarrassed. I buried my face in the pillow to hide my shame. "I wasn't."

It hadn't been like the day I slit my wrist, when I was strangely calm and calculated with my decision. When I was already dead anyway. This was a mistake made in hysterics. One that had almost killed me before I intended.

She scolded me with her gaze. "Well, you're lucky he found you. God forbid you were left out there to freeze."

Her tone hurt, but I knew she was only concerned about me. From under the blankets, I reached out my hand and took hers. "I'm sorry, Nan."

The frown on her lips eased up. She reached out to the tall glass of water she had prepared by the bedside. "Drink this. I'll make up some soup for you to eat, it will help get rid of the alcohol faster if you eat something. And come down when you're feeling alright. He's in the den waiting for you and won't leave until he knows you're OK."

I sat up quickly once again, surprised a second time. "He's here still?"

As she turned back, the glint had returned. "Has been all afternoon."

I downed the water as quickly as I could, drowning the ill feeling in my stomach. It helped, but my body still felt weak and feeble from the lingering alcohol.

I laid back down to let my stomach settle a bit longer. I was anxious though, and it showed in my fidgeting fingers. I turned to reach for my journal on the bedside table, but when it wasn't there, I remembered I'd left it out in the stables. I cursed myself and my foolishness.

This was not how I wanted things to go. If things had gone badly, I could have possibly died out there, which was not what I wanted. I didn't want it to be an accident, especially an accident that could be mistaken for intentional. How irresponsible was I, that I almost killed myself with a bottle of alcohol? It would not happen again. No more brushes with Death until it was time.

I managed to get out of bed, wrapping the top quilt over my shoulders to bring with me. I used the railing as I shuffled down the stairs, scared my wobbly legs would give out. He sat in the big arm chair, my grandmother's usual spot, an elbow on the armrest and his cheek propped up in his palm. His eyes were closed, looking like he was on the brink of sleep. I cleared my throat, and he opened them slow, like a tired dog coming back to consciousness.

A smile hit his mouth almost immediately. "Violet. You're alive."

"Barely." I tried to joke, but the word came out a little more serious than I intended it. It didn't feel right to joke about life and death, considering the secret he knew about me.

"You'll feel better soon," he said, standing and allowing me to take his place.

As I settled down, adjusting the quilt, he took the spot next to me, on the end of the matching loveseat. He held a smile the whole time, but he seemed tired. It was obvious that both him and my grandmother had been through an ordeal because of me.

"Thank you. For finding me," I said after a silence between us, fighting off the shame creeping up from under the blanket and onto my face. I thought to tell him I was looking for him, I thought to say that if he had only been there a little bit sooner maybe none of this would have even happened, but I held my tongue.

He nodded in reply, no words necessary.

I wiggled deeper into the cushions of the soft chair and watched him for a long while as he sat there, until he leaned over to curl his arm up on the armrest and lay his head down.

"You look tired," I commented, watching the black circles under his eyes as he glanced back at me.

Laugh lines appeared. "Keeping you alive is proving to be harder than expected." A joke and a toothy grin, then his gaze fell back to exhaustion. It was out of place on his features, I realized. Normally he was so full of life, despite his skeleton physique.

I let the silence sit again, the ticking of the grandfather clock counting the seconds. Eight, nine, ten. "It's so strange that you're here now."

He blinked at me again, curiously.

"I had a dream, while I was out. We were sitting together in the grass and you said something to me."

"What did I say?"

I bit my lip, watching his gray eyes, which were particularly silver with the purple under them. "You said, 'Not tonight, Violet.'"

I waited, but he didn't reply. He just stared at me with innocence, so I continued. "It seemed so real. I felt the rain and the cold after, I think. It was almost like you, the dream you, brought me back to reality."

He hummed, smiling again, but there was something else there. It was that knowing look I had caught before, like he was aware of something I wasn't. "I guess neither of us could stand to see you go yet."

I blushed, wrapping the blanket around me more tightly.

"I found something of yours, by the way." He pointed to the chair I sat in, and I shifted a little to look, catching a glimpse of my journal sticking out of the seat cushions. I snatched it up immediately, hiding it with me under the blanket. I worried it was too late to keep it from his prying eyes though.

"What's the list for?" He confirmed my suspicions, and I cursed to myself under my breath.

"It's nothing." I didn't want to tell him.

He didn't push it, leaning his head back down on his folded arm, but somehow his content silence broke my defenses. It was like he knew I was going to tell him, like he didn't have to fight for it, and somehow he was right.

"It's just, things I want to do. *Before.*"

"A bucket list?"

I shifted in my seat. "Of sorts."

"And these things on your list. Are they mandatory?" Jack asked a lot of questions but this one in particular was far more intentional than usual, and it was noticeable.

I narrowed my eyes. "If you plan on interfering with the listed things in attempt to delay me, then you'll be wasting your time. I already have a date set. I'll do it regardless of whether I finish my list or not."

"OK," he said, barely reacting to my accusatory tone. Just a grin as he stored away the information I gave him. I realized maybe that was all he wanted to know, and I just willingly gave it to him. He was sneaky like that.

❧

When my grandmother was finished with my food, she invited me into the kitchen and Jack took his leave. I wished him a good night sleep, and while he nodded a thank you and returned the sentiment, I caught him concealing a secret look again as he put his jacket on.

I thought about his dark circles and how I hadn't been able to find him, but then somehow, he'd found me. I thought about his innocent words and wondered how many of his questions and answers had really been so innocent. I thought about the way he put the crow to sleep and if he could have made it wake up just as easily.

I was nearly done with my soup when my grandmother sat across the kitchen table from me, dragging me away from the curiosities consuming me.

"Are you going to tell me what all this was about?" She took on a stern, motherly voice that I remembered from when I was a misbehaving child. She wasn't scolding me, but it told me she was serious, that I had to answer some questions.

I didn't object; I owed her an explanation. It took me a moment to gather the courage and admit to the reason though. I didn't know how she would react to me reading her personal documents then confronting my mother over the phone about it. Instead, I played with the spoon in my bowl for a bit.

"I saw the court notice. I called Mom and talked to her. I tried to reason with her, but she just… She doesn't listen to me."

My grandmother looked like something stabbed her in the

chest. She flinched, then put her hand to her mouth. "Oh, Flower." I heard the crack in her voice.

"I'm sorry, Nan."

She reached out, patting my hand as it rested on the table. "Don't apologize over something out of your control." She put her face straight again, concealing her real reaction. She was always the strong one, the rock who didn't show the family her emotions, but I suspected she was losing her grip on them. Just as I had earlier that day.

I turned my palm over and took her hand in between mine, gripping her old fingers firm. She offered a pained smile, before it turned down hard and she covered her eyes as the tears came.

XII

I slept well into the next day, only rising in the afternoon when my stomach finally demanded more food. It was difficult to get up, but I felt guilty and didn't want my grandmother to have to tend to me further, so I willed myself out of bed and into the kitchen.

When she saw me, she insisted on making me a late lunch. I tried to object, wanting to do it without help, but there was no fight in me, so I sat and hydrated while she fried up a grilled cheese sandwich.

"This was what your grandfather loved for his hangover," she said, a tiny smile on her mouth. This was the most entertained I'd seen her in days, and I was at least glad my stupidity had distracted her from the stress for a bit.

Feeling better with food in my system, I continued working on my revival by taking a long, hot shower. The steam helped the last bit of alcohol escape out through my skin, and after my fingertips turned sufficiently wrinkled, I wrapped myself up in a fluffy, dry robe and joined my grandmother in the den.

She had started a fire, the wood stove alight and warming the room, making it dry and toasty, and was now working her way through a few chapters of a book; she always read first, then started her cross-stitch in the evenings, even when I was younger. I sat on the floor with my journal, letting the heat from the flames help dry my hair as I drew tall grass blowing in the wind and Jack's eyes squinting against the sun.

While drawing, the air between my grandmother and I hung slightly heavier than usual. I knew she was concerned about me but didn't want to say anything. I thought about apologizing again, or thanking her for the breakfast, something, anything, but it felt like the silence said more in a way. With my mother, I would have only screamed and argued; in the silence I was able to fully feel the guilt of making someone worry.

My grandmother had always been the one to fret over things, too wrapped up with taking care of everyone else to look after herself. She could seem stern sometimes, closed off, like my mother and myself, but there were real emotions behind her hard exterior. My grandmother was only cold because she had a lot of things to deal with and couldn't let herself get overwhelmed.

I was cold because if I wasn't, everyone would see how close to falling apart I was.

And my mother… I still wasn't sure what made her so stoney, but I hoped it was how she dealt with the guilt and loneliness she put on herself because of her decisions.

Sometimes I wished we could all learn to be a little more warm, like a hangover grilled cheese sandwich, or a hot shower, or wordless company in front of a fire. Instead, we were icey and relentless with each other like the Newport winters.

It was late when there was a knock on the door. Curious, I thought to go answer it, but I didn't want to open the door in just a terry cloth robe, so I glanced at my grandmother, who had now switched to her cross-stitch. She set it aside and rose. After I heard her open the door and greet the person, I unfolded myself and stood with my journal tucked under my arm. I followed into the hall, peeking around the doorframe.

"Good evening, Mrs. Holt." Jack gave my grandmother a warm smile, then glanced over her shoulder. His eyes landed on me as I pried in on their conversation. My face went hot, and I retreated out of sight, only to peek again when he continued speaking. "After yesterday I thought maybe it would be good for Violet to get out of the house with someone for a while. So I thought I'd come by and ask your permission to take your granddaughter out for the night."

My grandmother must have seen his wandering gaze, because she followed it back to me, then returned a smirk to Jack. "It's rather late, Mister De'Morte."

"I had something particular in mind, ma'am. It's not exactly something we can do during daylight hours."

The way he phrased his explanation could have been so suggestive, if he hadn't looked like a naive little boy while saying it. With how innocent he always was, I thought it completely absurd that someone could assume he'd be capable of anything even slightly inappropriate.

My grandmother insisted on being traditional though. "I'm not sure I'm comfortable with Violet being out all night."

"I don't need permission to go out." It was only after I stomped towards them to object that I saw my grandmother's coy expression. She was just trying to get a reaction from me, and it worked. I scowled at her before turning to Jack. "Give me a minute."

My grandmother allowed him in while I went up to my room to put some proper clothes on. As I got to my dresser, I realized my heart was beating a little more wildly than before. I blamed it on how quickly I had taken the stairs, but the fluttering in my stomach suggested otherwise.

I tried to settle my nerves. I'd done things with Jack before, nothing about this situation was different. Yet, I found myself picking an outfit deliberately and playing with my hair a while longer than usual, attempting to get it to sit right.

I grabbed my journal off the end of the bed out of habit, but reconsidered as I held it in my hands. I brought it everywhere; it was my security blanket, often keeping me grounded. Maybe I didn't need it though, not on this occasion at least. Jack would be with me, maybe that was enough.

I threw the journal into my dresser and closed the drawer, leaving my room.

Not wanting to deal with my grandmother's smugness, I hurried past her to get my jacket on as quickly as possible.

"Make sure she doesn't do anything stupid?" She managed a single playful quip before I opened the door to usher Jack out.

"I'll do my best. Goodnight, Mrs. Holt." Jack called back to her as I shoved his back, closing the door before he was completely finished with his goodbye.

We stood on the front step together for a moment, an awkward silence settling between us as I tried to shake off my embarrassment. He didn't seem to mind that I needed a second, and he waited until I zipped my jacket up and finally found his gaze before speaking.

"Hi." He was all innocence and smiles.

I felt the blood rush to my face again, but I hoped the chill of the night made it seem like just a cold flush. "Hey."

After another pause made awkward with his wordless content, he stepped forward, nodding his head to the side to beckon me with him.

"Where are we going?" I asked before I even took a step, realizing I had been eager to know since his mention of having something planned.

He glanced back at me, his lips sliding into a grin that was uncharacteristically mischievous. "I can't tell you, that would ruin it."

"I don't really like surprises, you know," I said, though the words were only a bluff to cover my curiosity.

"I think you'll like this." He stopped to let me catch up, then when I did, he took my hand in his like it was nothing. I wasn't sure if he realized with his perpetual aloofness, but the way he tangled his fingers into mine made the fluttering in my stomach grow far more intense.

I wondered if he'd take me to his car and drive us into town, but I remembered he said he didn't have a car, and that would explain too easily how he got to the property every day. Instead, I had to go on wondering about how he just appeared sometimes, as he led me around the house and out onto the property.

The path he took was the same I led him along days previous, and I figured out where we were going. I kept my mouth shut though, because compared to him, I was beginning to feel I talked too much. As we reached the gate to the garden, Jack stopped and leaned his back against the wrought iron.

"Close your eyes."

I snorted, but when I realized he was being serious, I shook my head.

He frowned. "Don't you trust me?" His expression dropped as though I'd wounded him. If he was acting, he did a convincing job.

The guilt made me groan with playful frustration. It wasn't that I didn't trust him. On the contrary, I knew I trusted him completely. He had figuratively saved me from myself more than once, and quite literally just the day before. That was the problem though. It felt almost like I trusted him too much; I still knew absolutely nothing about him. He was a strange boy with a strange name who answered all my questions with silence.

I couldn't stand his pouting anymore, so I admitted defeat with a sigh and closed my eyes. With the night creeping up on us quickly and engulfing the last bit of evening light, I couldn't see much anyway.

I was pretty sure I sensed him smile again after I complied. He opened the gate, then took my other hand and led me through the garden. I could picture the route he was taking by how he guided me, around the vegetable patch, past the bushes, to the other side of the tall fence full of climbing plants.

"Ok, sit down," he said as he stopped me.

I scoffed. "I'll get my jeans dirty."

He tsked, tongue against teeth. "You're not trusting me."

I rolled my eyes under my closed lids, then did as I was told, letting him hold me steady as I lowered myself down onto my knees. They met something softer than the ground I had expected. I managed to resist the urge to peek, but only a second later, one of my other senses caught something that tested my willpower again.

Violets. I almost didn't believe it when the fragrance wafted past me, but it was so strong I couldn't ignore it and I looked before having permission. It was dark but I could still clearly see them all around us, growing in between the dying roots of fellow flowers, fresh and healthy and fragrant. The impossibility of it had me speechless. The only sound I could manage was a gasp.

"You weren't supposed to look yet," he scolded as he dropped himself down next to me on the laid out blanket. His tone was convincingly serious, but his gaze was gentle and light-hearted.

I twisted my head around, inspecting all the violets that hadn't been there just days before, my mind drawing blanks in shock. I had too many questions, and they all tangled together in my skull. "Why did you...? How did you even...? This doesn't make any sense."

He interrupted my questions with his own. "It was on your list, right?" When I looked at him with confusion, unable to place his meaning past my own bewilderment, he elaborated. "Smell the Newport violets. It was on your list."

I stared. "You did this, because of the list in my journal?"

He shrugged, like it was the simplest thing, like holding the door open or letting someone cut in front of you in line. It wasn't the simplest thing though. It wasn't simple at all. These violets defied logic. Wherever they came from, however he had gotten them there… Nothing about it was simple.

"This doesn't make any sense." I repeated while shaking my head, stuck in my overwhelming disbelief.

"Does it have to make sense, Violet? Can't you just see it as someone doing something for their friend and not question it?"

There was no frustration or annoyance in his voice, but rather, apprehension. A particular tone that told me if I asked again, he wouldn't lie anymore. But it also made me feel like maybe I didn't want to ask again. He knew something I didn't; that had already been established long ago, but he made me feel like being ignorant was easier.

If this curiosity was easier than knowing the truth, then what was the truth?

I sighed, sitting back and drawing my knees up to my chest. I was having trouble ignoring the impossibility of the one violet up in my room, and now he'd presented me with a few dozen more impossibilities. How was I supposed to just be content with his non-answers now?

When I looked at him, his expression was easy and reassuring, and I couldn't help the cautious smile easing onto my lips. If he insisted, I'd let it go, just as I'd let go all of my other questions, but only for now. I stored the curiosities in the back of my head for the day I was finally sure I wanted to know the secret he kept from me.

"This is not something someone does for a friend," I pointed out, after my frustration settled and the silence between us grew a little more comfortable.

I watched out of the corner of my eye as his grin stretched a fraction. He let my comment sit though, aggravatingly open ended, like usual.

XIII

The violets were not the only thing he had planned, as I came to realize. When the last bit of evening light faded away, and the stars came out, he laid back with an arm behind his head and turned his gray eyes to the tiny lights in the sky. *Watch the stars.* I wondered briefly how much of my journal he'd read, and I felt suddenly very aware of the private part of myself he'd gotten a glimpse of through the words on those pages.

His ability to be so comfortable at any given moment was still astounding to me. He could just lay down and gaze up at the sky and not feel vulnerable or scared that I might judge his behavior. Meanwhile, I was always curled up tight, terrified of how people viewed me, always nervous they would see the broken pieces under my skin and scoff at my ugliness. I envied how carefree he was, how easy it was for him to be himself. I wanted it too.

I followed his lead and laid down, trying not to be bothered but feeling embarrassed immediately. I could sense him peeking at me, and I tried to ignore it, until I couldn't anymore. When I turned my head to confront him, his eyes were gentle, and I felt the anxiousness in my chest uncoil slightly.

I looked back to the sky when I couldn't stand his stare any longer, then I spoke to help ignore the shallowness of my breathing. "I was never able to see the stars like this in the city. Too much light pollution."

Out here, with the crisp air and clear sky, with nothing but the bright moon lighting the property, I could see everything. Every tiny little speckle of white on the deep blue canvas above us. It was beautiful in it's overwhelmingness. I imagined the blackness stretching down from the sky and wrapping around me like silk, or sinking under the surface of a motionless, inky lake. How still and quiet it would be.

My thoughts slipped out, my lips loose with him. "It's a little strange, to look up there and see all those stars and realize how insignificant you are. How small and pointless your life is in comparison to the grand things out there."

I heard him sigh sadly, and I turned, seeking an explanation. He closed his eyes for a moment, and when he opened them, I could see the stars shining in the swirling gray.

"You're looking at it all wrong. You can't compare your individual self to the whole of something; you'll always fall short. You're not insignificant. By that logic, each star is insignificant, but take them away, and the sky is just an endless emptiness."

I brought my brows together, considering his point of view as I stared over the twinkling lights in the sky. "But if one of the billions of stars disappeared, I wouldn't even notice," I countered, my words holding a double meaning I was sure he was aware of.

He hummed. "You wouldn't notice if a handful disappeared, or if hundreds or thousands disappeared, but suddenly the constellations are no longer complete, and there are blank spaces, and the masterpiece slowly becomes as dull as a light polluted city sky. Every single star is significant, because it's each one that helps make the sky so overwhelmingly grand."

His words hit me like a hard punch to my chest. The way he spoke tangled me up, like he had a deep, unexplained understanding I could never comprehend. He stared at me with intention, confirming his reply was chosen carefully to have the same double meaning as mine.

I felt something swell in my throat, and I tried to swallow it down but it wouldn't leave. I let out a shaken breath. "But I'm not a star."

I heard him scoff gently, like he couldn't believe what I was saying. "No, Violet. You're so much more than just a star."

I closed my eyes, and the tears I hadn't realized were welling up escaped from my lashes and raced down my temple into my hair. He shifted, reaching out to gently wipe the wetness from my skin with his thumb, like it was nothing.

We both turned back to the vast night sky above us, and I didn't feel the need to fill the silence between us with unnecessary words or questions anymore. I watched the stars as they twinkled against their dark backdrop, never-ending speckles of white against deep navy blue that were only broken by the walls of plants around us. I wasn't sure I would ever know what a perfect moment was, but I imagined the peace I found laying there with him was something close to it.

I didn't know how the night went by so quickly, though I guess it was hard not to lose track of time when there was nothing keeping it besides the moon slowly drifting across the sky. I remembered staring at the stars until my mind drew new constellations, then staring at him until I could see galaxies in his eyes, then closing my own and not seeing anything at all. Instead, I smelt the flowers and imagined a better time when everything didn't hurt and the burning sun and ocean salt fixed all my problems.

I wasn't sure if I actually slept, but it was something so close that it might as well have been, a state of overwhelming calmness and security I hadn't felt in years. I knew it was safe to drift away here. He would call me back to reality when it was time, which he did. I opened my eyes when I heard my name, and the sky had shifted from a deep navy blue to a color slightly more pastel.

"I have one more thing in mind. You aren't too tired, are you?" He'd turned over onto his stomach, and I got the impression that he had switched from watching the sky to watching me. The thought left a blush on my cheeks.

"You've already kept me out all night," I pointed out, although not objecting.

He grinned. "Then a little longer won't make a difference."

We left the garden, and he led us along the edge of the trees, the long way down to the ocean where I had indulged my demons in the days previous. The tall grass we trampled through was wet with dew and it soaked the hem of my jeans. In the distance, birds chirped to welcome the approaching morning, lingering, not ready to fly south just yet. I knew how they felt.

The trees became more sparse as we neared the coast, until they disappeared and all that was left was the sky and sea, meeting in the middle at a straight, endless horizon. We took a rocky path down the side of the cliff to get to the beach, and when I reached the water's edge, I inhaled the salty air, an elixir getting to work on healing my wounded heart. I wondered how different things might have been if I was only allowed to live here instead of trapped in the city. It made me sad to think it might have changed everything.

Of course, if that happened, maybe Grampie wouldn't have had his accident, and I wouldn't have tried to kill myself, and Jack wouldn't need to be here to rake the leaves or mend my soul, and we wouldn't be standing there together watching the horizon.

Stay up all night to see the sun rise.

He'd went for the hat trick.

As the words re-wrote themselves in my mind's eye, a sliver of the sun's fire peeked over the horizon from the east. I could understand why centuries ago people thought the world was flat, and why the sun was a god. When you could stand there and see it emerging from the very end of the ocean, how could someone not think if they travelled long enough and far enough they could find where that fiery face met the sea?

"It's on your list, right?" He quoted himself, breaking me out of my thoughts with his question. I nodded, though I'd already figured out his plan. His intentions, however, still eluded me. I watched him smile as he returned his gaze out over the water. "We won't have very many clear days left now that it's November. I thought you ought to see it before the gray gets in the way."

"Why are you doing this?" The thought blurted out before I could contain it. I wasn't sure I'd get a solid answer, but it was worth asking at the chance I might.

He was feeling chatty it seemed, because he peered down to his feet to consider a reply. "I guess I feel like it would be a shame, for your list to go so unfinished, if you're going to go through with it regardless. If I can't change your mind, I'd at least like to know your last days, however many you have left, are all as beautiful as they deserve to be."

Once again, his words took my breath away, drawing from me more emotion than the beautiful sunrise we stood in front of. I didn't know where he came from or how I stumbled into knowing him, but I found myself glad all my mistakes had somehow brought me to this moment.

Once the sun rose completely up over the sea, Jack suggested we head back. It was with a heavy heart that I agreed. If I had it my way, I would have stayed in that moment with him forever. Unfortunately, time was never on my side; it always kept going even when all I ever wanted was for it to stop.

We took the path through the woods this time, now that there was enough light to see where we stepped. I enjoyed the way the morning sun shone bright orange through the canopy. When the wind blew, it was like the trees were wild tribal dancers, silhouetted by the light of a burning bonfire.

"I've been thinking about the crow," I said, taking the hand he held out for me to help me over a broken tree branch.

He didn't speak, just gave me his curious expression and kept going.

I continued, cautiously. "The way you put your hands over its eyes, and it was like it went to sleep." Perhaps my carefulness was making my curious intention too obvious.

He kept walking, but something about the way he moved showed I had his attention. "What do you think I did?" His tone was much more forward than it had ever been before. It felt almost like he was daring me to voice the questions spinning around in my head.

I opened my mouth, but I felt suddenly hyperaware of the nonsense of my own thoughts. I shook my head, embarrassed. "Nevermind. It's ridiculous."

He stopped beside a large hemlock tree, and when I caught up to him I leaned a shoulder back against the trunk, taking a moment to read him. He wore that same mischievous look as earlier, and I wasn't sure what to make of it.

"I could show you what I did, if you want," he offered, turning to circle the tree, catching my gaze with his soft gray eyes right before disappearing behind the trunk. His next words came behind me, from the other side. "Do you trust me?"

I resisted turning to meet him, biting my tongue to stifle the nervous giggles at his unusual behavior. We'd both been up all night; maybe the exhaustion was making us delirious. "I'm not sure anymore," I replied, teasing, and watched in my peripherals as his lips spread wider.

I wasn't expecting what he would do, so I went rigid when he reached up from behind me and blocked my sight with his palms. His hands were somehow still so warm, despite being out in the cold all night.

He let me sit in the dark for just long enough to confuse me, then innocently asked, "Are you dead yet?"

I resisted another laugh. "No." Although, my heart was suddenly racing.

His hands fell away, and my cheeks were assaulted with the cold again. "That's strange."

I turned to face him, soaking up the playfulness in his eyes. "Maybe it only works with crows?" I suggested.

He grinned that torturous I-know-something-you-don't grin. "Maybe."

I hadn't noticed how close we'd gotten until our banter became silence and I glanced down to see my feet, toe to toe with his combat boots. Heat crept out from my collar and up my neck, my heart pounding an extra beat in my ears. He just continued sweetly smiling, completely unaware of what he was doing to me.

"We should really get you home," he said softly, nodding his head to the side to encourage me to follow him.

When he took that first step away from me, I reached out and snatched his fingers. "Jack," I called him on a shaken breath because it was all I could muster.

He turned back, curiosity in his gray eyes, because he had no idea. Then he tightened his fingers around my own, and my will broke. Before there was time to think about it I peeled away from the tree and found his lips with mine.

Kiss someone, one last time.

I'd been kissed before, but I had never been the one doing the kissing, so I wasn't sure what to expect from my rash actions. I definitely didn't need to be a genius to know what his failure to react meant.

I broke away from him sharply, completely removing myself and throwing my eyes to the ground as a raging fit of embarrassment assaulted me. I didn't even want to see what his rejection looked like. "I'm sorry. That was, that was stupid. I just… It was on my list, is all." It was a pathetic excuse, but I was grateful for any bluff that might make the awkwardness less painful.

When he still didn't speak, I turned to flee in the direction of my grandmother's estate.

"Violet," he said my name, and I stopped. I didn't realized I was shaking until I had to stand there and hold my breath, waiting for him to say something else.

Out of the corner of my eye, I watched him; his brows joined together in a harsh line, a hand coming up to the back of his neck, working out the muscle. I realized I had never seen him so uncertain before.

"Violet."

He said my name again. I turned back this time, seeing his expression clearly for the first time since my kiss. His gaze read torment, and it was a noticeably foreign emotion for him. It made his features hard when they were normally soft and gentle, and I felt suddenly guilty for putting that look there.

The anticipation was torture. It was only after the silence between us became unbearable and I took in a hard, shaky inhale, thinking to fill the void between us with more senseless words, that he finally reacted.

He bridged the gap between us with a couple strides, taking my face in his hands and kissing me back.

I was sure galaxies birthed and died between the moment his

lips met mine and when he pulled away. But when my eyes fluttered open again, I could see the harshness still lingering on him.

"What's wrong?" I asked in a whisper as he rested his forehead against mine.

His frown deepened. "I tried so hard not to hurt you."

I shook my head. "You haven't hurt me."

He sighed, and I saw that look again, the one that said he knew something I didn't.

"I have. You just don't know it yet."

XIV

I wasn't sure what I expected to happen from kissing Jack, but making the silence between us mutually awkward for the first time was definitely not the outcome I wanted. As we walked back to the house, I kept watch over my shoulder, seeing that torn expression stuck to his features. It broke my heart. For a moment, we had something beautiful, and I ruined it as I did everything else.

I should have known I'd scare him away somehow.

We passed the garden again, my time to speak drawing short. It wasn't far to the estate now, and with the way he was behaving, I was terrified that if I left, I would never see him again. He was pretty good at disappearing and reappearing at will, after all.

I slowed down at the wrought iron gate, waiting for the sound of his boots to catch up with me, then turned to confront him without the faintest idea of what to say.

"Listen. I was pretty tired, back there. And, I was kinda just, caught up in everything and I... I acted kinda stupid. And I think maybe there's still some alcohol in my blood from the other night, so really, my judgement isn't to be trusted right now. So, if you...

Didn't like what happened, we could just forget about it. I'd be OK with that. We can just go back, to how it was."

My anxiety did a poor job of filtering my thoughts between my brain and my mouth, leading to rambling that filled the silence.

He stopped to listen, then let the words sit between us like he always did as he took the last few steps towards me and leaned a shoulder on the gate.

His lack of reply provoked me into adding more nervous words to the air. "I just... I feel like it wasn't what you wanted. So if it wasn't what you wanted then that would be fine. It doesn't have to be this way. We can just go back to friends."

"Violet," he interrupted, breaking through my anxious thoughts with a soft tone. "I promise you, if I hadn't wanted to kiss you, I wouldn't have."

I groaned, frustrated with how much I had liked those words. I shifted to stand beside him, grabbing the bars of the gate. I twisted my hands around them to fight the nerves. "If so, then why does it feel so terrible now?"

He sighed, but again offered no explanation or comfort. I wanted to be upset, but I could tell his silence wasn't out of stubbornness. It seemed like he wanted to tell me but wasn't sure how.

I copied his sigh. "You're not really good at explaining yourself."

"If I knew what to say, I'd tell you. It's complicated." He seemed genuine, but those last words were so cliche, I couldn't help but roll my eyes in reply.

I suggested situations that were as ridiculous as his excuse. "Are you like, twenty-five? Do you have a girlfriend?"

He scoffed, but it sounded sad. "If only it was something so simple." His eyes were full of apologies, and I tried to shake off my frustration because I could see he wasn't trying to be infuriating.

Still, I found myself whining. "Why can't you just tell me? You know so much about me, everything. You've read my damn journal, without my permission, might I add. It's not fair, that I know nothing about you."

"You're right. It's not fair. Getting involved with your life, it wasn't fair of me at all."

"Why are you always so cryptic?" I had to hold back an unimpressed glare. "Can't you at least tell me, what you meant back there? About hurting me?"

His face went uncertain again, but I managed a pout and he caved. "I can't stay here, Violet. I don't know when exactly, but I'm going to have to leave, and I've known that from the moment I met you. How cruel am I, for doing what I've done while knowing I can't stay? How selfish? I hurt you, because I kissed you knowing I'd have to disappear eventually." He ended with another sigh, pain finding his eyes. The gray that was a usually tame and level fog looked more like swirling storm clouds in his frustration.

I bit at my lip, choosing my words carefully. "You know, I'm not some delicate little flower that you're going to break." I gathered my nerves and caught his gaze, all rain and thunder, before continuing. "That's what you think, isn't it? Because of… What I did. You think that if something happens, I'm just going to fall apart. Well, you don't have to worry. I've been broken before. Pretty much my whole life. I know what it's like to hurt. You don't have to be scared of hurting me." I paused again, but hated the somber mood I had left it on, so I tried for some nervous sarcasm to finish the words off. "It's not like I'm going to go kill myself over you or something."

He actually breathed a chuckle in reply, and for a moment, I felt the awkwardness lift a little. He covered the slip by clearing his throat and shaking his head. "That wasn't funny." Though his eyes still shined with a bit more brightness than previously.

I shook my head, trying to find the seriousness again. "I'm just saying. If anything, I should be worried about hurting you…" And then I realized how selfish I had been, kissing him back there in the woods. Because I was going to be leaving too, permanently. And I realized how badly I wanted to take back my actions, and how he must be feeling the same way if he thought he was going to hurt me in the way I knew I would hurt him.

There were no more words. I had found the regret he was dwelling in, and now we stood together in the aftermath of our mistake, realizing that the hurt was already inevitable, because as I thought about it, it was beginning to creep up on me. I knew what should happen, but the idea caused an ache in my chest I hadn't felt in a long time. I wished a thousand times over to go back to that moment on the beach, praying for it to be neverending so I wouldn't have to say what I knew was probably the right thing.

Time betrayed me again, and kept ticking, until the seconds grew so long I had to admit defeat to the unavoidable conclusion. I sucked in a shaky breath, holding back the tears that threatened the edges of my eyes. "Maybe it's best we end this here then, before either of us gets hurt more?" I put the question mark on the end because I hoped he'd disagree, refuse, fight it, even though I knew he never would.

That wasn't his way.

Jack's frown chiseled deeper into his features, his only reaction. I felt like he knew what was coming, just as I knew it was the only reasonable conclusion, but it didn't keep it from burrowing deep under our ribs and leaving an emptiness there. I turned away from him, leaning back against the gate like he was. As I tried to catch some air in my shaking lungs, I felt him reach out and take my hand, squeezing my fingers with his.

When he said it was the last time I'd see him, it wasn't one of those magical moments, where he was just saying what needed to be said and we both knew something would bring us back together eventually. The secret part of him, the part that always knew something that was just beyond my understanding, had said it as fact, and I knew there was no changing the outcome, no matter how much I wanted to kick and scream for it to be any other way.

He squeezed my hand a last time, and then he pushed off from the gate and walked away. I closed my eyes to keep myself from watching him go, because I imagined it would be too painful a sight to see. Instead, it was only the sound of his combat boots hitting gravel, until I couldn't hear them anymore, and then I was alone again.

I found myself thankful I had just a few more weeks until my birthday, because even though I knew I'd never actually kill myself over a mysterious boy making me fall in love with him and then leaving me, it was at least comforting to know I wouldn't have to deal with this heartache for too much longer.

When the pain in my chest subsided enough to avoid a break down, I dragged myself the rest of the way to my grandparents' estate.

As I opened the front door, my grandmother was waiting for me. She took a stern expression at first. "You were out all night. I hope there was no funny business."

"No, Nan. I promise," I replied, monotone.

"Did you have a good time, then?"

I forced a smile, hanging my jacket up. "Yeah, it was nice. We watched the stars, then the sunrise."

She sensed something was wrong, as mothers do. "Did something happen, Flower?"

I tried to seem more genuine, but I avoided looking her directly in the eye because I knew she'd see the puffiness left from my almost tears. "No, nothing happened. I'm just tired. I'm going to go sleep for a few hours, if that's alright?"

"Of course dear, I'll be here if you need me." She didn't sound convinced, but as usual, she didn't want to push me, and I was grateful.

As I shuffled for the stairs, she tried to give me a hug, but I avoided it, pretending I didn't see her attempt. I would have broke in her arms if I let her comfort me. Instead, I made it to my room, closing the door as quietly as I could.

I shuffled over to my bed and sat down, the numbness disappearing into an aching hurt, starting in my chest and spreading out into my limbs like poison. I reached out and slid one of the petals of the violet by my bedside between my thumb and index finger, feeling like delicate silk. Then I let myself succumb to the sadness weighing me down.

Tears escaped from my tired eyes. My wrist itched, and I fantasized about ripping open the stitching to satiate something inside me that wouldn't settle. The bed tempted me to slide in and curl up under its blankets, to allow a tormented hibernation to overtake me. It was the only way I knew how to avoid the pain that was waking up inside, for a moment at least.

I'd forgotten to lock the door though, and when I almost gave in, there was a gentle knock as it opened.

"Flower?"

I swiped at my cheeks, getting up and opening one of my drawers to fiddle, pretending to be busy to hide the evidence of my weakness so my grandmother could pretend she didn't notice. Smoothing out my folded clothes, adjusting the items on top of my dresser, anything to keep my hands busy long enough for her to believe the act.

It was easier not to notice. It was easier to hurt alone. I didn't bother anyone else that way.

When she stayed too long, and I felt myself crumbling again, I tried to beckon her away with reassurance. "It's nothing, Nan." But my voice betrayed me, a sob stuck in my throat.

She didn't say anything. She didn't ask questions. She knew that wasn't how the women in this family worked. Instead, she crossed the room and took my shoulders to guide me back to the bed. If I tried even a bit, I would have been able to resist her gentle ushering, but I had nothing left in me to fight. I sat, coiled my knees up to my chest, still trying to keep more tears from escaping, as she collected my brush from the dresser.

She stood at the end of the bed and stroked the brush through my hair gently and deliberately, her pace careful and soothing, and I cried and cried until I had no more tears left to shed.

XV

I woke the next day as one does from a deep dream, unsure of the time or day or year, where I was or who I was, a fragment of my fictional world still lingering in the forefront of my mind. I had slept through the whole day and night, waking in the early morning while it was still dark and quiet, the rest of the world still asleep, making it feel even more like I was still dreaming.

A sliver of cold blue came in from the window, slightly brighter than the darkness around me, illuminating a plate with a sandwich, wrapped in plastic, an offering from my grandmother left some-time during my sleep. My stomach growled violently as I remembered how long it had been since I ate.

I sat up and I reached out a tired arm to unwrap the sandwich, taking a bite and curbing the rolling ache in my stomach, even though I had no appetite whatsoever. My belly growled in relief, but my nausea wasn't so easily dealt with since it sat deep in my throat and was not there because of my hunger. The dull ache in my chest poked at my lungs and made it hard to breathe.

It was cold out from under the blanket, and as my arms prickled with a violent chill I strongly considered rolling over and going back to sleep. The bed was warm, the mattress soft, and it didn't hurt so much to be asleep.

I scolded myself for my weakness. Sleep was a cruel mistress to me, making me forget the pain, just to make it far worse again once I returned to reality. I had been doing such a good job resisting its draw, was I really going to let myself break now?

Involuntarily, I reached for the blanket and slipped it over my shoulders. My hands working on their own, against me, to coerce me back into the bed and banish the pain away again for a few more hours. Because it wasn't just about Jack leaving. It was about my grandmother's money, and my grandfather's state, neither dead nor alive, and my mother's callous actions, both personal and legal. The sleep would take all the worries away.

I shifted to lay back down, but as I did, that sliver of blue light reached past me to the violet on my bedside table, its petals facing me, staring me down. I half expected it to shake its little face in disappointment.

"Don't look at me like that." I'd lost what little sanity I had left, I was sure. Jack took it with each one of the echoing steps of his heavy boots walking away. Nonetheless, the flower's perceived scolding got me to take that last step out of bed.

"Happy?" I asked it, grabbing the glass of water on my night table and taking a drink, then giving a bit to the plant as well.

I tried my best to get myself out of my room and doing something every day, because I didn't want my grandmother to worry about me. Her concern wasn't productive to anyone, and she had her own problems to deal with, which were only being added to now with my mother's insensitivity.

I was familiar with dealing with my problems on my own

anyway. I only had to wait a few weeks, then I wouldn't have to deal with any of this pain ever again. Eighteen years old was just the start for a lot of people, but I felt like I had already dealt with a lifetime of dysfunction. What is someone to do when their body is still very much alive, but their soul is aching to move on?

It was growing harder and harder for me to hide my troublingly emotionless behavior around my grandmother though. At first, I was setting easy goals for myself, like making sure I ate regularly. I spent time in the house, I started fires to warm the den, and I pretended to read or draw so she wouldn't get suspicious.

She sensed something though, probably because it had been almost two weeks since Jack showed his face last, and I hadn't set foot out of the house since. I knew Jack had been a positive influence on me and it hadn't went unnoticed. I noticed it myself after all; the soreness in my cheeks from smiling and the ache in my chest from my wild, lively heart pounding out a reminder of its existence to me.

I decided I needed to commit a little more to my facade. That didn't mean I had to actually find the effort to mend my wounded heart. I'd lost the strength to do that a long time ago, and I wasn't sure it was even possible anymore. I could pretend though, it was simple enough, especially if I got myself out of the house and away from her prying eyes for a few hours, where I could be alone with my dark thoughts.

I dismissed myself after breakfast one morning, taking my journal under my sweater and throwing on my jacket, some gloves, and a scarf. The chill of the approaching winter was setting in quickly, and I had no warm hand to hold onto mine any longer, so I thought it best to bundle up.

I didn't have a location in mind, so I ended up wandering, unintentionally finding my feet leading me to all the places we frequented. I wasn't sure what I expected. Jack had become so ingrained into my life so quickly that his sudden disappearance left me feeling a bit like he had died, and now there was a ghost haunting me. It was as though I expected he would one day emerge from around a corner or appear behind me out of nowhere like he always did.

Once I circled the property, I headed back, passing the garden on the way. I picked up my pace, intending to pass it as quickly as possible because my heart was not ready to face those particularly painful memories.

In the deep, gray, dead silence of the property, a crow's call assaulted my senses and I stopped, searching for the sound. The bird, sitting on the wrought iron gate of the garden a few yards away, ruffled its feathers, almost as if to catch my attention. With my eyes on him, he cawed again, then adjusted his footing and spread his wings, lifting off into the sky.

Something twisted in my gut, dread and curiosity braiding together into an emotion that I wasn't sure I wanted to deal with. Regardless, my feet turned, taking me over to the garden despite the anxiety grabbing hold of my lungs.

I wrapped a hand around the cold metal of the gate and yanked it open, feeling a moment of hopefulness. That feeling didn't last long. Unfortunately, the garden felt as dead as the rest of the property with Jack no longer there. Something about him brought to life the otherwise haunted sleepiness of the area, the garden included.

I wrapped my scarf tighter around myself, defending my ears against a cold wind, and mosied through the garden, feeling a sadness drop in my stomach at how abandoned it felt now. The dead plants around me were foreboding, like this garden was no longer a place of life. Instead, it was a graveyard.

I shuffled myself over to the berry bushes, the sound of my shoes overwhelming against the absolute silence around me, even in the soft dirt. Unconsciously my eyes scoured through the branches and dying leaves, almost giving up until I found a single berry buried deep in the back of the bush.

I dug for it, stuck my fingers with thorns, but the sting was barely noticeable past the sudden palpitations of my heart at the sight of the berry. As I got a hold of it, I tossed it in my mouth before even inspecting it.

The bitter bite of the squishy berry hit my tongue, and I grimaced hard and spit it out. I wasn't sure what I was expecting; there was no logic behind my actions. Just brief, emotional possession that I regretted immediately. What would it have meant anyway, if the berry was still ripe? What would have changed?

I didn't want to return to the spot we had spent the night, knowing the violets would be dried up and dead already from how quickly the cold seeped in. I knew it would hurt to see it, but the pain in my chest was destructive and wanted to drag me down, and I was weak to it. It tugged on my heart strings until I strayed away from the berries and wandered towards the other side of the wall of crawling plants.

I was prepared for pain; I was always prepared for pain. It was happiness I never expected, and it was happiness that hurt the most sometimes. Which was why I found myself unable to catch a breath when I saw the violets, still alive and well, despite the terrible cold making even my bones wither.

It wasn't until later that night, after I'd spent hours in the company of his violets, feeling a brief ghost of what it was like being there with him days before, that I even questioned the impossibility of their survival. Watching my own violet on my bedside table, I laid awake for hours, searching my logic for an explanation which never revealed itself to me.

XVI

A number of strange things began to happen after finding the violets still alive.

No, that was wrong. Strange things were happening since I set foot in Newport and laid eyes on that mysterious, leaf-raking boy in black. Without his gentle smiles and soft gray gaze distracting me though, I was seeing the events clearly for the first time, and really beginning to question what exactly was going on.

It was a bit like having an unassembled puzzle; I knew I had all the pieces, at least to give me a vague idea of what he was keeping from me, but they were just a big pile of incohesive fragments I was having trouble putting together with my stumbling fingers. I didn't know what I was assembling either, so each piece was as much of a mystery as the picture they put together.

I began collecting the pieces though, to the point of becoming obsessive. My lists and doodles in my journal transformed to chicken-scratched notes of my own thoughts, trying to grasp onto every faint idea involving his secret. To prying eyes, my scrawled thoughts would look like the ramblings of a psychopath.

It was unhealthy, I knew it was. I should be moving on. Getting

over him. I was just a love sick girl, hanging on to the last fragments of my obsession desperately. But something turned in my
stomach at the idea of not knowing what it had all meant by my
birthday. Our short time together felt too deliberate to be coincidence, and he always looked at me like there was something more I
wasn't seeing, just under the layers of the reality I was stuck in.

Perhaps mildly psychotic, my devotion was at least continuing
to get me out of the house in my search for clues to the mystery he
left behind in his wake. After breakfast each morning, I assembled a
sandwich and wrapped it up, then threw on my jacket, scarf, and
gloves and set out again to circle all the areas we had inhabited
together, hoping to find… *Something.*

I didn't know what I was looking for. Actually, I wasn't really
looking for anything. More so, I was just hoping to remember a
moment where he had perhaps allowed his guard down and let a
clue slip, something I simply hadn't caught when it happened. I was
trying to relive the memories, to see if my mind's eye recorded
something that would finally string all the clues together.

It was a poor excuse for my self-inflicted torture, but it was all I
needed to justify living in the past.

It took me a few days to find the spot we escaped to together after
my panic attack, since it was just a small alcove where I'd never
been before, and I couldn't remember the path he'd taken while
leading me there. Finding it was both satisfying and disappointing.
Just as the garden, it felt distinctly less full of life without his
presence.

I circled the tree I had previously sat under, then leaned back
against it and took in a deep breath of the cold forest air. It was
just like the day we were there together, and it reminded me of

the fresh, woody smell of his jacket. He had tasted of that smell, along with the salt of the ocean and the sweetness of the blackberries.

I told him I tried to kill myself, and that I was going to do it again. *Why are you so eager to leave when you just got here?* I wrote the words down in my journal as I remembered them, reading them over and over until the sentence, words, letters didn't make sense anymore. I put a question mark next to the quote.

❦

The stables smelt of alcohol the day I visited them, and the scent made my stomach churn as it revived the traumatic aftermath of my terrible decision that night. I found the bottle of whiskey toppled over onto the floor, the last of the drink spilt out onto the old rug, swallowed up by the fabric.

Not tonight, Violet, he said in my dream, a warm breath on my cheek before I was plunged into darkness. Just like the last morning together, his hands over my eyes to block out the burning sunrise, a warm question in my ear. *Are you dead yet?*

When I had tried to kill myself the first time, I had a similar dream. Everything was bright and warm and I felt like my skin was burning, but in the pleasant, comforting way as it felt to sit out on the beach in the sun's rays. Then there was beeping in my ear, so piercing I couldn't ignore it, faster and faster as my heart pounded against my ribs, and it was cold and dark and my limbs ached when I tried to move. I woke to the sterile, suffocating air of a gray hospital room that time.

Maybe the beeping of the heart rate monitor brought me back the first time, so was it Jack's voice that had woken me after unintentionally poisoning myself? It was only a dream though, wasn't it? *Neither of us could stand to see you go yet.* I wrote the words down along with my thoughts, once again finding more questions than answers.

&a.

During my walks, I started noticing a new companion. On occasion I would hear the call of a crow and see him on a branch of a tree or perched on a fence post. I assumed it was the same crow from the garden; I couldn't be certain, but my gut told me it was.

At first he was just there for a moment, and then gone again. I appreciated the sign of life regardless, because it made me feel not so alone in my wandering. Sometimes, I would stop to catch my breath, and I'd hear his cry in the distance or see him circling the property. Was he watching my progress, curious for an answer himself?

He kept showing up more and more, for longer and longer. A ruffle of feathers, and a hop along the branch towards me. I called back to him once, a morning greeting, and he puffed out his neck and squawked at me then took off. His antics were entertaining, pulling me away from the sometimes painful memories I was putting myself through while collecting clues.

I was trying to find the spot in the woods where we had left the bird's corpse for the fox. It was a task I'd spread out over multiple days, because I again had trouble locating the path Jack had led me down. That particular day I was ready to give up, so before going back home, I sat on a stump to eat some of my prepared sandwich. I was joined almost immediately, the crow landing on a branch a few yards from me. He announced himself, and a smirk crossed my features as I swallowed a mouthful of food.

"Do you have nothing better to do than follow me around?" I asked, receiving another caw in reply. I considered what I was doing in the first place, and the fact that I was speaking to a wild animal, and sighed to myself. "I guess I'm not one to talk, am I?"

He disappeared into the air, but within a few short seconds he was back, settling closer, on a lower branch. I watched him, hopping back and forth, turning his head and blinking black eyes in my direction.

I shook my head, amused, and began to pick the crust off my sandwich. "Here, wanna share?" I got up to place the bits on another broken stump nearby and heard him spread his wings and fly over before even settling myself back in my spot. He watched me carefully as he ate the pieces, as if making sure I didn't pull a fast one on him.

I expected him to take off once he finished, but he took the last piece, then ruffled out his wings and settled his feet, clapping his beak at me.

"Greedy. I already gave you some." I replied with a mouth full. I caved though, taking a last bite then breaking the final corner of the sandwich into small bits and tossing them over to him. He hopped onto the ground and happily collected the pieces.

I took out my journal and turned to one of my lists, scratching out the words: *Feed bread to the birds.* Next was to find the fox, and I sighed to myself because I'd been looking for days, and it seemed a futile effort. Even if I could pinpoint the exact spot we had left the bird, that didn't necessarily mean I would find the fox again. She could be anywhere.

What could it even tell me, besides what I already knew? Jack had a secret and I was as far from figuring it out as I was the very first day. I leaned over to rest my chin on my palm, staring at the bird as he finished his last few bites. "It's too bad you can't talk. I could really use a second brain right now."

He twisted his head and blinked those beady eyes at me, then spread his wings and took off. I sighed, finding myself disappointed to be alone again. I took it as a sign to head home instead, so I stood, stretched out my back, and turned to leave.

From behind me I heard the crow call, and I stopped to search, finding him bobbing on a branch further into the forest. I scowled. "I don't have any more food for you, you greedy bastard."

He squawked, then flapped his wings and moved himself to a branch further away, stopping and looking back at me. I didn't believe my own curiosity, and half wanted to shake it off and turn around to go back home. I was tired and I wasn't in the mood to be bothered by a bird.

He ruffled up his feathers and called for me again though, and I growled at myself for my stupidity as I stepped towards him.

It was foolish. It was just a crow, and if I kept following it into the depths of the woods I would surely get myself lost. He kept moving from tree to tree though, stopping to wait until I caught up then moving on again, like he really was leading me somewhere, and I couldn't shake the feeling that he meant to show me something. I kept telling myself how ridiculous that was, how downright *crazy* I sounded.

Then I thought about Jack, and if I told him what I was doing. I imagined him: a ghost taking my hand in his and following the bird along with me to see what mysteries he had to show us. That brought me some comfort, like no matter how crazy I was, at least I knew I was never quite as strange as the boy I was trying to figure out.

After a while of stumbling over rocks and roots, I caught up to the crow a final time, a small stream blocking me from continuing in the direction we were headed together. The bird sat perched in a tree above the stream, so I took a second to settle down, leaning over to play my fingers in the cold, clear water.

I heard the crow take flight, and panic struck me as I stood, following him with my eyes as he took off into the sky. I had no idea where I was and my guide had just disappeared into the sad gray of the sky above the tree canopy. In my frustration, with the bird and my own stupidity for following him, I flicked an obscene gesture towards the sky before plopping down onto the ground with a disgruntled huff.

I didn't have much time to pout about my self-inflicted misfortune. In the quiet forest, it was easy to hear the smallest of noises, like the trickle of the stream over rocks and the rustling of the dried leaves on the ground as something approached me.

I lifted my gaze to find the noise, my heart skipping a beat with painful hope. It was not Jack standing on the other side of the stream though. The disappointment stung, but only briefly, because in the spot I had hoped to see Jack, was the fox instead, frozen in its tracks as it spotted me as well.

I gasped, and it put its ears up towards me, listening, judging. I tried my best to ease my breathing and calm my pounding heart, holding as still as possible to not spook it. When enough time passed, the fox let its limbs unstiffen and skipped over a shallow part of the stream, still watching me cautiously.

I noticed she was walking on her back leg again, and I couldn't help but smile. She stopped when reaching my side of the water, then yipped behind her, and from the brush came two young pups, running clumsily to catch up with her.

She passed by me with her pups, only a few yards away, stopping to point her nose in my direction and sniff the air before carrying on. Once she was out of sight, I let out the breath I was holding, and an overwhelmed sob of happiness shook my chest.

I didn't want to acknowledge the feeling I had, because it was crazy and dangerous and held no grounds in reality. My racing heart whispered suggestions to me though, and I knew he had something to do with this, even if I shouldn't believe it.

Regardless of how it happened, seeing the fox, with her leg fixed and her pups alive, it made me feel infinitely better than I was feeling the past weeks. As I crossed off the words in my journal, I had the brief thought that everything would be alright now. Even if every single other thing went terribly wrong, I could get through it. I was strong enough.

Life tested me immediately upon returning to the estate, and I failed miserably.

Parked outside the entrance was a familiar silver sedan, and the peace my soul found out in the forest dissolved instantly into a full blown panic attack. The driver's door opened, and I felt my lungs collapse.

"Mom…?"

XVII

This was wrong. This was not how it was supposed to happen. She was supposed to stay away so I could have a few more weeks of peace before my birthday. What was she doing here?

"Violet," she called me, and I felt like someone punched me hard in the stomach. I wanted to be sick. This was not happening.

I hurried past her and into the house, clutching at my chest to fend off the pain. "Nan." I cried for her, moving to search in the den, but she emerged before I could take even a second step.

"What is it, Flower?" She reached out to take my hands, trying to calm me.

I couldn't find my voice. My lungs threatened to convulse every time I opened my mouth to speak. Finally, I managed a few words out in a whisper. "Why. Why is she here?"

"Why wouldn't I be here, after you trying again… Alcohol, sweetie? What were you thinking?" My mother came into the house after me, hearing the back end of my sob.

"You told her?"

"Of course I told her, Violet. She's your mother. And you nearly did it again…" My grandmother tried to be gentle and calming, but

I feared it was too late. The panic gripped around my throat, its hands squeezing.

"I wasn't trying to kill myself. Nan…"

"We'll settle it all back in the city. I have a new doctor who really wants to meet you. I think it would be good for you to talk to him."

That's all she ever did. Hand me over to another doctor, like maybe one of them could fix me eventually. My mother walked over to me, her arms outstretched to give me a hug, but I recoiled from her as if she raised a hand to me.

I retreated against the wall, trying to catch hold of a breath that my lungs refused to keep a grasp on, the ache in my throat and chest growing so terrible I felt tears threaten my eyes.

"Come now, Violet. You're being absolutely ridiculous." She went to touch me again, and I blocked her hand with a swat of mine.

"Don't touch me! You can't come back here and act like you know what's good for me. I don't want to go back to the city. I want to stay here. You have no idea what it's been like here!" I don't know how I managed to speak with so little air, but my frustration gave me enough willpower to make anything possible it seemed.

My mother scoffed. "Obviously I know enough. Look at you."

I threw my eyes up to the ceiling. I could feel it again, her bending me, my mind straining, ready to snap. I couldn't stand the pressure. I tried to think of the fox and how strong I had felt moments ago, tried to hold onto that last bit of warmth in my heart, but I couldn't. I couldn't think of anything but the fact that she was here to ruin it all. She was going to take my grandfather's life support away and break my grandmother's heart and then throw me back in a hospital so she didn't have to deal with me any longer. So she could forget. Like she did with her own father. A different kind of life support but a coma nonetheless. I would rot away. Forgotten. Abandoned.

The ripping ache all over my body was too much. I was drowning. I needed air. Running was all I could think to do, so I did.

I dodged my mother's hands and bolted for the door, sprinting so fast my limbs felt like fire. I knew no one would follow, my mother never did and my grandmother wasn't able to, but I ran like it was for my life anyway.

The dark thoughts that wrapped around my neck and coiled up in the corners of my skull were chasing me, biting and slashing at my ankles, so I kept going, kept trying to outrun them, until I knew my body would give out. I ran until my lungs withered in on themselves with every breath; I ran until I collapsed into the tall, frosted grass and they devoured me, the sobs ripped from my chest like violent fissures.

I liked to think that since the last time I tried to kill myself, since coming to Newport, I had tamed the darkness inside of me. It was still there, I was pretty sure it had always been and always would be, but instead of a rabid dog, it was domesticated. I let it off its leash sometimes, I let it consume me, but only in the privacy of my room, late at night, when no one was watching. Then, in the morning, I put it back in its muzzle so it could follow me through my daily routine, like a well-trained pet. When I smiled, people barely noticed the ugly beast at my flank.

I was foolish, thinking maybe I could find a common ground with it. It behaved while I was feeding it, but the moment it got a chance to take over me again, it did. It was wild and ravenous, and in my weakness, I allowed it back into my heart, to tear with teeth and claws at the mended wounds on my soul.

The frost I sat in began to melt, seeping through my jeans and sending a bone-numbing chill through my body. I knew I should get up, but the beast sat on my shoulders, and my legs were barely strong enough to hold up my own weight, let alone its suffocating pressure pushing me down.

I should have known. I should have seen it coming. It was just a matter of time before the thoughts consumed me again. They would tear me apart and leave me with more scars, not just on my soul but on my body, like the one on my wrist. The question was, would they have the decency to finish me off this time?

Somehow I managed to lift myself off the ground, my legs shaking and burning from the strain I put them through. I didn't know where I was. I hadn't picked any place in particular; I just ran as far as my tired limbs would take me. As I walked a little further, I found where my fear had brought me, and something bitter in me laughed.

Jump from the cliff and let the ocean swallow me.

Was the scenery more desaturated, or was I just seeing less color? The gray sky touched the inky ocean at a straight line on the horizon, a black and white photograph. When I stood at the cliff, that line was all I could see for miles and miles, stretching out into my peripherals.

I closed my eyes and took in a deep breath, the first one since leaving the house. The salty air was usually a tonic for my troubled soul, but now it was cold and full of despair. The same bitterness that made me laugh now admired how sadly beautiful it all was, and I agreed. All it needed was a splash of stark color. Red, maybe.

I stepped closer to the edge, leaning over to watch the dark waves crash against the rocks, violent lovers battering each other in their passion, the way my heart always pounded against my ribs until they were both bruised. The wind picked up, a violent gust that blew me back a step. I imagined if it had only been coming from the other direction.

That was a dangerous thought.

I turned away from the horizon, looking at my grandparents' estate in the distance. I knew I should get back, but the idea of returning caused a violent ache to rip through my chest again. I didn't want to go back. I didn't want to hurt anymore. I didn't have it in me. It was much more wonderful here, alone with the wind and the cold, salty air. I sighed, and my breath became fog. Just a little longer here, alone, so I could stop feeling my pulse like a pounding ache all over my body.

I was playing a disturbing game with my dark thoughts, my dangerous lover. They coiled a finger to beckon me closer to the edge and coiled the other hand around my throat like a noose. They whispered terribly sweet nothings in my ear, how wonderful it would be to stay here forever with them. They understood, how it hurt, how I was weak. Just another step closer, and I could take the pain away. Just one more step.

"Violet."

My eyes flew open as the air fled from my lungs. Impossible. It was just the whistling sea wind, playing with my fragile mentality. He was gone. I had heard him say it, and he never lied to me. I looked though. I couldn't resist. Through tears I hadn't known were flooding my vision, I turned back, and I felt my heart pound back to life after stilling.

"Are you—Is this real?" I choked, refusing to blink in case he disappeared again, eyes burning and watering against the cold. It could have been my mind playing tricks on me, my insanity hoping for him to show up, as he always did when I was indulging my dark thoughts. It could just be a last, cruel joke of my psyche. After all, I had spent so much time dwelling on my memories with him, I might as well have been living in a dream.

He nodded though, and a line wrote itself on the spot between his brows, telling me stories of his concern. In direct response, my chest exploded with pain. Crumbling, I held down the sobs that would shatter the remaining fragments of me if I let them out.

"You said I'd never see you again."

"I did."

I sucked in a shaking breath, finally blinking and feeling the salty drops escape down my cheeks. Bitterly warm against my cold skin. "I was trying to remember, trying to figure out..." My rambling words failed me, and I stopped, gathering myself over again. "Why are you always here, when I'm... When I'm... You have to explain this to me. Everything." I demanded on a weak whisper.

I expected him to protest, make an excuse, but he didn't. Instead, he nodded again. "I'll show you. Come with me?" He held out his hand.

I turned away briefly, back out to the ocean, listening to the sea crash on the cliff below. I took a deep breath, and the air was clear again. I was able to step away from the edge of the cliff, towards him. When I could reach his hand, I took it, his fingers warm, squeezing mine together in his. Real.

"Jack." With his name on my lips I finally fell apart, dissolving into his arms. He wrapped me up in warmth, that fresh, woody scent engulfing me. The weight sitting on my shoulders lifted, and the relief threw me around like the waves to the rocks. I shook against him. "I almost..."

He hummed in my ear to stop my thought before I admitted it. With a warm breath against my cheek, Jack whispered, "Not today, Violet."

XVIII

I was ashamed to admit it, but I had been waiting for this moment ever since he disappeared. I knew I was supposed to be moving on, but when I laid down in my bed each night and drifted off to sleep, my mind couldn't help but wander to the fantasy of seeing him again. I pushed the idea away when I was conscious, pretending I didn't wake with fluttering in my stomach and palpitations in my rib cage.

Unfortunately, this reunion was nothing like I dreamt of it being. He held my hand as he led me, just as he used to, but there was a tension in the muscle of his arm that hadn't ever been there before, and an expression on his face I couldn't place. Neither of us spoke, but not because it was comfortable to stay silent; the air was thick with apprehension.

I wanted to tug on his fingers and slow down his purposeful pace, maybe wrap myself around him again until the stiffness between us disappeared, but I could tell that whatever he was leading me to was important. He promised to explain, and it had my gut flopping around and making me feel ill. What if he was keeping this secret from me for a reason? What if, as he had suggested with his omission, I really didn't want to know? What if it would just be easier to go on pretending we were two broken people finding some sanctuary with each other?

I watched him as I followed, with that hard line on his jaw from whatever idea was tormenting him, and the curiosity growled like a beast inside me, despite my apprehension. I needed to know. I was scared though. I was scared it would change everything.

"I've been here, since you left," I said, as I realized we were approaching the garden.

He turned back, his torment fading slightly. "I know." He released his grip on me to pull open the gate.

"How are the violets still alive?" I asked, following him as he entered, eager to fill the silence, to see him speak again and feel the tension lift a little.

"Let me show you."

He turned the corner, but I stopped in my tracks, unable to follow when a bout of panic hit me. He turned back with a question, and I let out a shaky exhale. "I'm scared. That this will change us."

He watched me for a long second, his gray eyes sad, but he didn't say anything. Maybe because he didn't want to admit that it probably would. Instead, he reached out and took my hand again, coaxing me along gently.

When we reached the violets, he kneeled down to the dirt in front of a patch of them. I followed, collapsing hard to my knees, not even concerned about my jeans any longer. He let go of my hand, and I twisted my fingers together in my lap nervously instead.

He turned to me a last time, giving a serious look. "You have to watch, OK? Don't look away. You need to see."

I nodded, my lungs having trouble inhaling with my nerves. He leaned over to the closest little flower, holding himself up with one hand in the cold dirt as the other reached for the plant. He touched the flower with his fingers, his thumb gliding over the soft petal like I had done many times with the violet in my room, but with his touch came a response.

In his hand, the flower began to shrivel, until it withered up and flopped over to resemble the other plants who had succumbed to the winter. In a matter of seconds, I saw it go from very much alive to very much dead, simply from a touch.

My bones went cold.

When I didn't react, he watched me. I could imagine him trying to read past the wide-eyed shock on my face. He called, cautiously. "Violet..."

I tore my gaze away from the now-dead flower and caught his gray eyes, showing me an emotion I hadn't seen on him before. Fear.

I blinked, looking away from him and back to the flower, feeling sinister prickles trickle up my spine. When I stood, he followed, reaching out for my hand, and I reacted before thinking, wrapping my arms close around myself.

"Don't touch me," I said, my voice coming out sharp.

He recoiled immediately, like my words stung at his fingertips. "I'm sorry," he whispered, barely getting his voice out. When I found his gaze again, I saw the wounded expression he tried to hid and felt my stomach twist. He had been unsure, scared of how I would take it, and I think I just delivered the exact reaction he'd been dreading.

How was I supposed to react though, to seeing a flower wither in his touch, die right there before my eyes in a matter of seconds? I didn't even know myself. I stood there, frozen in a state of shock, because I didn't know the emotion I was supposed to display next.

Finally, my lungs drew in a real breath, sharp and short, and I felt the anxiety squeeze at my abdomen, making me ill. I forced words out in place of being sick. "What did you just—? How? This... This doesn't make any sense." My hands shook, the shock wearing off and the panic setting in. I took a step back from him, a nervous laugh escaping. "This is a terrible joke."

The sadness on him was physically painful. "It's not a joke."

The dread hit my stomach so hard I felt like I'd been winded. I shook my head, trying to hold onto that disbelief, but it was gone before I even had a chance to grab onto it. "I watched you just wither a flower. You, you touched it and it died, right there." As the words came out of my mouth, other things fell into place behind them. "And the crow. You just put your hand over its eyes, and then it was dead."

"Violet..."

I gripped onto the sleeves of my jacket to try and settle the trembling of my hands as one thought strung together into another. *Are you dead yet,* his breath on my cheek asked, his palms over my eyes. *I've hurt you, you just don't know it yet.* "And me. You've touched me."

"No, Violet—" He tried to interrupt, but I finished the thought over him.

"Am I dying?" I asked, finding myself surprised by how scared the thought made me.

He managed to finally get through to me with, "That's not how it works."

I looked up at him. "How what works?" The question came out before I was entirely sure I wanted to ask it.

He opened his mouth, but his voice caught somewhere in his throat, and he sighed. He didn't want to say it, I could see the words on his tongue hurt just to think. "How *I* work. It's not... How I work," he answered anyway though, like peeling off his skin and revealing himself in vulnerable flesh and bones, begging me with his cold, gray gaze to not burn him with the salt of my reply.

I closed my eyes to combat my spinning head. "What are you?" I whispered.

He responded with a grimace, swallowing down something hard in his throat and opening his mouth, but he failed to find the explanation he was searching for. When he sighed again, he stared at me, apologies written in the worry on his face.

I felt a shudder up my spine, because never in my life had I thought I would need to ask that question, let alone not get a clear reply. "You're not human?" I asked, under my breath, scared for an answer but unable to keep the words to myself.

Another chill swept over my skin with his confirmation. "No."

My voice shook. "Are you some kind of monster? A demon?" I felt a dreadful panic creep into my veins.

He objected immediately to my roaming considerations. "No. Violet... I'm not—You don't have to be afraid of me."

He took a step closer, instinctively trying to comfort me again, but I retreated and he stopped in his tracks. I could see him falling apart in front of me, but I couldn't stop thinking about the crow in his grasp, its tiny, ragged breaths until he put his hand over its face and then, nothing.

I wasn't trying to hurt him, but when he moved I found myself flinching. He closed his eyes to push down the pain that crept up in him, collected himself, then tried to persuade me again. "You know what I am, I know you do. I've shown you. Everything is there, you just don't want to see it," he begged me again, and then took the smallest step towards me, and I somehow resisted the overwhelming urge to back away. "Please, Violet. What did I do, to the flower, to the bird? What were you doing, whenever I showed up? What were you thinking about?"

Dying. The answer came to me before he even finished his question. The common denominator between all the factors he presented, and as I recalled all the details I had written down and mulled over the past weeks, the bigger picture started revealing itself.

What I brushed off as inopportunity now seemed more than coincidental. All the moments where my dark thoughts overwhelmed me and he was just, *there*: the day out at the ocean, where no one should have known where I was or what I was doing, and he found me; at the stables, when I had drank myself almost into my own coma, and he was there to take me home; today, with my feet at the edge of a cliff, temptation beckoning me to take that last step, and even though he said I'd never see him again, there he was.

Like he was there for a reason, not just accidentally.

I shook my head, because it was impossible, ridiculous, foolish. Surely this was a wonderful dream turned terrible nightmare. I lifted a hand and combed my fingers through the hair behind my ear, tugging at the strands to see if I would wake. If this was a dream, it was the most vivid image I had ever made for myself.

I put a hand to my temple as I turned to wander a few steps away from him, feeling lightheaded. "This doesn't make sense." Only it wasn't true. It made too much sense for what I had seen, what he'd shown me, but it didn't align with what I knew to be true.

He followed cautiously. "It would if you let it."

"This is a joke," I accused, turning to him sharply, seeing him flinch back a fraction.

"I wish I was joking."

"No," I objected, trying to keep my panic from turning to hyperventilation. The air already felt so thin. "You're not. You *can't* be—"

"Why can't I be? What more proof do you need? I've shown you everything."

My franticness was rubbing off, and his shame was turning into frustration. He turned from me and leaned down to snatch a handful of flowers from the ground, vibrant and purple and very alive. When he turned back, he grabbed me before I could pull away, placing the violets in my palm, now wilted and dead.

I threw my hand over my mouth to keep back the panicked yelp, the dried stems and petals falling from between the gaps of my shaking fingers.

A terrible, heavy silence sunk down on us, as we both tried to catch onto a breath. Across from me, he sighed, knowing he had scared me further in his outburst. Approaching more timidly this time, he lowered his words to a gentle murmur. "Why am I here, Violet? You know."

He'd forced the apprehension out of me. I did know. "You're here for me." My voice shook as I whispered on an exhale. "Death."

XIX

My lungs were sore and my head was spinning, so we agreed to leave the garden and take a walk. He let me wander as I wanted, lagging behind a few yards, picking up loud and clear my need for space. He was very good at becoming a shadow, following me so silently that I almost forgot he was there, which seemed fitting now, considering the information I was still coming to terms with.

When the sky started getting darker, a cool blue instead of a frigid gray, my thoughts were more in order so I felt calmer about the situation. Only then did I finally stop walking. I leaned against the crumbly remains of an old stone wall that cut through the field down to the ocean, waiting for him to catch up.

I watched his feet through the long grass as he approached cautiously. I didn't blame his timidness, since the way I handled his honesty had been less than delicate. A look of apprehension was stuck to his face.

"What you said, in the garden. About it not working 'that way.' What did you mean?"

It felt silly asking, because a part of me still felt like this was all a very strange dream. To really come to terms, I'd have to know more, and to know more, I'd have to suspend my disbelief for a brief moment and hear what he had to say.

I watched him shift in his spot, pushing his shoulders up a little, awkward. It was a stark contrast to his usual, carefree, loose-muscled demeanor, and I realized we had found another situation that left him feeling vulnerable.

"I can imagine what it must seem like to you. Watching me touch something and seeing it die. A *Midas Touch*, but with death." He tried to laugh, but it was nervous. His fingers fidgeted until he shoved them into the pockets of his jacket. "It's not that simple though."

I bit at my lip, nodding for him to elaborate.

He inhaled deeply, taking a second to mull over the words in his head, then took a step closer and leaned against the wall also, a few feet away. "I don't just touch things and they die. Imagine how inconvenient that would be. It's more like... I make the process easier."

I hummed with the connected dots. "So unless I'm dying..."

"Touching you will do nothing," he finished, giving a weak smile out of the corner of his mouth.

I didn't comment on the fact that his touch did far from nothing to me. "So the bird. It was ready to die, and you helped it? Like, you took the pain away?"

"Something like that."

"And the flowers?"

He shifted, his shoulders falling, becoming a little more comfortable now that he was confident I wouldn't run from him. "They're a little different," he paused, turning to lean over the wall and dig through the long grass, coming back with the stem of a long since dead wildflower. "Since they're not quite as complicated as people or animals, they're a little easier to manipulate." He held up the dead wildflower, and with the end of his words, it sprung up in his fingers, as if shaking off the death, revived and vibrantly alive again.

I stared, breathless, and when he saw my face he cleared his throat and let his hands fall. "Sorry. Still a little shocking, I guess."

I shook my head, trying to brush it off. "So it's not just a one way thing?" I asked, gesturing to the flower in his grasp, brought back from the dead.

He twisted the stem in his fingers, spinning the petals around. "I said that flowers were different," he countered, pausing to consider his answer before elaborating. "You're partly right though. It's not just one way." He paused, assessing my reaction, then leaned in towards me. When I didn't move, he reached out and gently brushed my hair behind my ear, tucking the flower into the strands.

I felt a red heat bloom on my cheeks, and I averted my gaze to the ground to avoid his gray eyes and run the risk of making it worse. He elaborated in the silence. "If someone is dying, and they're ready, I can make it easier for them to let go. But if someone is dying, and they aren't ready, I can help them back."

I had an instant moment of clarity, remembering my dream that evening at the stables, the hand I imagined, grabbing mine through the darkness. *Not tonight, Violet.* I looked at him, wide-eyed, and he gave me the first easy smile I'd seen on him since he came back.

"The stables. You saved me."

He scoffed out a laugh. "No. Far from it. You made the decision to live. I was just there to lead you where you needed to go."

I hummed again. Maybe he was right. I hadn't wanted to die. Not like that, anyway. Not accidentally, but I wasn't sure I would have been able to make it away from the warm, beautiful place in my head if he hadn't done something. "Well, thanks anyway," I said, offering my first small smile back.

I watched his face lighten a little in reaction, pleased I was warming up. I couldn't stand that look, it made my stomach flutter, so I stared down at my hands again and filled the air once more. "And I thought Death was all about collecting the souls of the damned, or something sinister sounding like that."

I heard him chuckle. "No soul collecting. Sorry to disappoint you. You'll have to hold onto yours."

I fought a grin, shooting off a clever reply. "Darn. You know how eager I am to get rid of it."

"That's not funny," he responded, but I could hear his lips tilting.

"Ok, *Death*." I tested the title, and I watched him grimace. I smirked. "If you're not here for my soul... Then why are you even here at all?"

He pushed off from the wall, rolling his shoulders in a stretch and moving a few steps closer to me. "That's a very good question."

"You don't know?" That surprised me, or at least, surprised me more than anything else he had already explained.

He shrugged. "I never know. I just get a feeling and I go. I go where I'm needed. I don't ever know why until... Well..."

"That must be frustrating."

He shrugged again, thinking of a response and letting out a breath that appeared as fog in the cold air. The temperature was dropping fast with the sun. I was warm though. "It's not so bad," he said, giving me that I-know-something-you-don't look, and my flush deepened.

Just like that, it felt like no time had passed at all since he'd left and now. How easy things had fallen back into place, even though a lingering apprehension stuck at the pit of my stomach, making me painfully aware of the one difference between before and after.

He continued to try and loosen the mood with deprecating humor instead. "I have to admit, I expected a little more... Screaming? Some Hail Marys maybe."

I smirked. "You said you're not a demon though."

"Which is exactly what a demon would say, isn't it?" I watched him attempt his very best sly grin, but it looked so out of place on his soft eyes that I had to hold back a laugh.

"To be honest, at this point, I'm not sure I'd even care if you were a demon, as long as you were the same Jack."

There was still a twisting in my stomach, the uncertainty that went along with the unknown, but I was just so happy to be in his company again that the sheer overwhelming absurdity of everything revealed was little more than a miniscule set back. At that moment, I didn't care who he was or why he was there or that he had death in his fingertips, as long as he stayed this time.

He chuckled, a note of awkwardness escaping with it. I thought I caught him blushing, but maybe I was just seeing things. "I think I can manage being just Jack for a while."

I hummed. "OK."

"On that note…" I watched as he fidgeted with his fingers inside their pockets, then he took another step closer to me, his boots toe to toe with mine again. "Could I kiss you, Violet?"

I felt my heart jump up into my throat. Somehow I managed a word around it. "OK."

His hands finally left his pockets, cupping my face instead as he leaned down and took my lips with his.

❧

I didn't want to go back, but somehow Jack convinced me to. I remembered him saying something about running away from my problems being only a temporary solution. I didn't appreciate how right he was all the time.

I agreed to head back to the estate, but only if he came with me, so we walked together in a silence that was almost as it use to be. I knew it wouldn't happen right away, I had things to think about tonight before I could completely be comfortable around him again, but he seemed alright with waiting. He stayed a few feet away from me, letting me have my space, until I came to him and took his hand when I was ready. It helped to know he wasn't going to force this on me, that my decision to hold onto him was my own.

My mother's car was still out front, and as we got closer to the door, I could hear the two women talking firmly to each other in the kitchen. I gave Jack a last begging look.

He smiled, shaking his head. "You'll be fine, Violet." He squeezed my hand reassuringly, and I groaned under my breath so the women didn't hear us prematurely.

"You don't know what she's like."

"I don't need to. I know you, and you're stronger than you give yourself credit for. I believe in you."

With a blush on my cheeks, I glared at him playfully, unable to stand how sweet he was being. "Your words, while inspiring, aren't going to get me out of trouble for taking off like I did. She wants to take me back to the city."

"Do you want to go back to the city?"

"No. I hate it there. I always have. I feel so much better here."

He hummed. "So tell her that."

"It's not so easy," I sighed, exasperated.

"If I was just able to be honest without you having a heart attack, I think you can manage a conversation with your mother."

"I'm pretty sure I only narrowly avoided a heart attack," I countered, but only out of bitterness, because I hated how right he was.

After the conversation we had just been through, a fight with my mother seemed miniscule. Unfortunately, even though logically I could recognize that the mountain I was about to climb was little more than a molehill, my heart still raced with impossibility.

I wanted to be annoyed, because he wasn't letting me be the

coward I preferred to be, but he was being so sweet about it that I couldn't be angry. Frustrated with his good intentions, I leaned back against the wall by the entrance of the estate and gave him a pointed look. "Couldn't you just be like other boys and use this advantageous situation as excuse to kiss me again, to distract me from my concern?" I tried not to let my cheeks get redder, but I knew they did despite myself.

He choked on a laugh, putting his head down to conceal his reaction, but I saw the smile at the corner of his mouth, and I could tell I'd managed to embarrass him more than I had myself. I took a particular joy in that; it must be difficult to get Death to blush.

"I was trying to be polite, but if you insist…" He shifted closer, and I stood a little taller, feeling my pulse up in my head again. The titillating anticipation fell short though, when the door next to us opened and Jack straightened his back, stepping away from me.

Despite our lips never meeting in the first place, we were caught practically in the act, and my mother's expression was less than impressed.

"It's late, Violet," she said, stone cold.

I gave Jack another pointed look, knowing her tone had proven my previous concerns.

Jack resisted reacting to me, turning his gaze to my mother and throwing on one of his genuinely kind, albeit naive smiles. "Evening, Ms. Holt, I assume. I was just making sure Violet made it home alright."

My mother shot him a glare, then turned back at me. "Get inside."

I watched Jack's face fall, but he brushed off my mother's attitude smoothly, turning to me with a nod. He picked up her hint loud and clear. "Goodnight, Violet."

My mother ushered me in before I could say a proper word

back to him, closing the door and locking it, jumping at me before I even got my jacket off.

"Do you realize we've been sitting here worrying about you all afternoon? You run off in hysterics, we don't know to where, or to do what. We're sitting here assuming the worst has happened, and you've been running around doing god knows what with some boy? Who even is that?"

"His name is Jack. I hired him to take care of the grounds," my grandmother interjected, taking some of the heat off of me. I sent her an appreciative look when my mother wasn't paying attention.

"Do you really have the money for a groundskeeper at the moment, mother? And what do you even know about that boy?"

"My finances are none of your concern, Lillian. And the boy is actually a very positive influence on Violet. It's been good for her, having a friend." My grandmother had a way of brushing off my mother's overbearingness that I was envious of. I guess when raising a child, you learn all their tricks and how to deal with them. It was a little different being the child of that trickster.

I wasn't sure how I felt being talked about like I wasn't there, but so far I preferred it over having to make my own excuses. I always clammed when I tried to talk to my mother, losing my voice and curling in on myself. It was like a mouse trying to fight with a loud-mouthed lion.

My mother gave a sarcastic scoff. "Oh yes, I can see his positive influence. Drinking herself to death and staying out all hours of the night."

I added my first words, timidly. "I didn't try to kill myself."

"And it's barely evening. You're being dramatic." Another expert brush off from my grandmother.

My mother folded her arms across her chest, narrowing her eyes. I could tell she wasn't taking kindly to being ganged up on. "*I'm* being dramatic? Am I? You know what's dramatic? Having a child at seventeen. That's what comes of drinking and staying out all night with boys."

"Lillian!"

I rolled my eyes, the only way to deal with the sting of her constant reminders. "You've made it clear on plenty of other occasions that I was a mistake, mother. No need to bring it up again now." I moved to sit on the steps, feeling as though I might as well make myself comfortable if I was going to take a verbal bashing.

Becoming aware of her sharpness only after speaking, as usual, she didn't apologize, but instead simply lightened her voice with her next words. "I'm just trying to look out for you, Violet. How do you know this boy isn't trying to take advantage of you?"

Both my grandmother and I were so appalled by this suggestion that we both reacted with shocked silence at first. I found my voice first. "Because Jack wouldn't do that? He's a genuinely kind person. But I guess you wouldn't understand that concept, would you?"

My mother was practiced at saying things that sounded pretty and sweet but were actually quite poisonous underneath. The next words to come out of her mouth were a prime example. "I'm just saying. With what's happened, you're... *Vulnerable.* I don't want to see you get hurt."

My grandmother scoffed in disbelief again, amazed with the intention under my mother's pretty words. I forgot that she'd had only an appetizer-sized serving of her manipulation over the years I'd been away. It was a little ridiculous that I didn't react more, but I'd been fed on it for so long it came as no surprise. "It's a real confidence boost when your own mother sees you as damaged goods."

She sighed. "Now you're just twisting my words."

"Enough. I'm not allowing you to speak to each other like this in my house. We are all going to bed to think about what we want to say, and talk about it like adults in the morning." My grandmother putting her foot down was a serious thing, but my mother was always defiant.

"I don't need to say anything else. I'm taking Violet in the morning, and we're going back to the city."

There it was, the first sign of panic, twisting up my gut when her words fell from her mouth. I objected, "I don't want to go back to the city."

My mother tried at a sympathetic look, but it came off judgemental. "Well, you don't really have a say in the matter right now. I don't think your decisions are productive to your recovery."

My grandmother read the anxiety in my voice and pitched in with fire. "She absolutely does have a say. If Violet doesn't want to go back to the city, then she can stay right here with me. And if you have a problem with that, Lillian, then you can go to *court* about it." With her words, she crossed over to me and rubbed my arm to try and calm me down.

It was rare to see my mother speechless. "You know you can't keep my own daughter from me."

My grandmother's resolve was ferocious though. "I can try. I should have years ago, but your father didn't have the heart to start a fight between us. Then you went and took her away again. I've waited years to have her back in this house, in my life, so I'm certainly not going to let you take my granddaughter away from me a second time.

"You're welcome to stay here as long as you'd like as well, but if you plan on leaving in the morning, you're leaving alone."

XX

I would be lying if I said my slumber that night wasn't troubled, but I did get to sleep by some miracle, and when I woke, a cool ice blue was shining through the thin curtains of my room. After rubbing the sleep from my eyes, I got up to investigate the source of the color, since it was noticeably different from the desaturated gray I had been living with for the past few weeks.

Snow. Beautiful, white, untouched snow, covered the ground like a thick blanket and caked around tree branches like frosting, turning what was becoming a sad, dead scenery into a wonderful frozen landscape.

I bundled myself up in a hurry, ecstatic for the excuse to get out of the house and avoid further confrontation with my mother. I wasn't the first to notice the weather though, of course. As I exited my room, an extra pair of socks on to combat the guaranteed chill, I heard the other two women in the house bickering again. I took note to how suddenly the estate had gone from dead quiet to almost too alive simply with the presence of my mother. She wasn't pleasant to be around, but it could certainly be argued that she had a way of livening up a room.

"Where are you going to go, Lillian? The news is reporting another two inches in the next twenty-four hours. You're never getting that little city car out of here in this weather." My grandmother was sitting in the den, her voice calm and collected. I imagined her doing the crossword as she did every morning, her conversation with my mother a mild distraction.

My mother, on the other hand, looked about ready to throw a fit more appropriate for someone my age rather than hers. "I don't really care, I'll call a cab, or a snow plow. I'm not staying here." She had her small bag of luggage with her and was putting her shoes on, ready to leave, as if she thought to just drive out through the thick layer of snow.

I came down the stairs behind her as she threw on her jacket and turned to open the door. In an almost too perfect coincidence, which made me question whether it was a coincidence at all, when my mother opened the door, Jack was out in the driveway with a shovel, standing in snow up to the edge of his combat boots.

He stopped his shovelling and lifted a gloved hand to wave. "Morning, Ms. Holt. Sorry for the inconvenience, but I'm not sure I'm going to be getting you out of here anytime soon." He had a thick, black scarf wrapped up around his face, but I could still see his sheepish grin peeking out from behind the woolen fabric.

I could tell my mother was less than thrilled, which was the cherry on top. She let out a frustrated sigh, shutting the door and spinning around to hang her jacket again. I stole her place at the door, opening it again to call to Jack. "I'll be out in five."

I knew my mother heard me. I knew she was going to follow me into the kitchen. I was done letting her ruin this for me though. I had gotten better since being here, to the point where waking up this morning and seeing the snow made me actually feel *happy* for the first time in a long while. I wasn't going to let her take that from me. Not this time.

My mother stood in the doorway of the kitchen as I finished spooning some yogurt into a bowl. "You don't have time to go out gallivanting with that *punk*. You need to get your things together. I'll call us a service car to pick us up."

"Punk?" I laughed, because of all the words I'd use to describe Jack, punk was an antonym.

She ignored my flippant tone. "If I call now we can be back in the city by dinner."

I replied through a mouthful. "I'm not going back to the city, Mom."

"Yes, you are," she responded without missing a beat.

She knew she intimidated me. It was the only thing she had on me, and it worked momentarily, but when I managed to swallow past the knot in my throat, I straightened my back and tried to hold onto the confidence I had felt before she entered the room. "Nan said I could stay here, so that's what I'm going to do."

She didn't reply as quickly this time, most likely wondering where my backbone came from. "I'm just considering what's best for you, Violet. I'm your mother, and I think we need to go back to the city. Together."

I shook my head, resisting a snarky comment about her not having the right to pull the mother card with how little time she had spent being a mother over the years. I finished off my yogurt and left the bowl in the sink, then turned back to her. "If you think it's so important for us to be together right now, then why don't you stay here?" I'd said it for the shock value. It was a dare that I didn't expect her to take. It rendered her speechless though, which let me slip by her to put my boots on without further argument.

Wrapped up snug in my layers, I left the house to join the willowy boy out in the snow. There was a particular spring in my step, which helped make tracking through the white powder a little easier. Standing up to my mother for the first time in ages made my body feel just a little lighter.

Against the white of everything, Jack's black attire and hair was a stark contrast, and it made him look like an ominous shadow in the distance. The illusion of darkness was broken when he caught sight of me, standing up straight and giving a wave before adjusting his scarf to shield his face from a gust of wind.

I stomped through the snow, bending over as I approached him. I picked up a handful, the wet snow numbing my fingers as I balled it up in my hands.

I saw his gray eyes gleam from under his fringe, his cheeks and nose red with the cold. "Don't you dare," he warned.

Biting at my lip, I threw the ball of snow at him anyway. He blocked with his shovel, the snow bouncing off the scoop with a weak thud. He lifted an eyebrow, then threw the shovel aside and bent down.

"Yield!" I giggled as I turned to run a few steps away, watching him wind up and just narrowly dodging the clump he threw at my knees.

He halted his counter attack and moved to retrieve his shovel again, allowing me to catch my breath after being winded by laughter. When he bridged the space between us once more, he asked, "Have you come to help me?" He gestured to the snow down the long driveway out to the street, hiding a grin on the tilt of his mouth because he knew his question was ridiculous.

I shook my head, reaching forward to grab hold of the shovel's neck and pulling at it to bring him a little closer. "We're playing hookie today."

He gave an exaggerated roll of his shoulders, putting on an unsure expression. "I dunno, Violet, you know I need the money your grandmother is giving—" He couldn't even get through the sentence seriously, a teasing smile spreading across his lips before he finished.

I smirked in reply, giving another tug on the shovel, waiting for him to let go.

"You're a terrible influence, Miss Violet Holt."

I stifled another giggle. "It's funny because my mom thinks *you're* the bad influence."

He stood straight, surprise passing his gaze. "What?"

I sputtered a little at his reaction, clasping a hand to my mouth to hold down the laughter. "She called you a punk."

"A—" His shock slid into a challenging look as his eyes flicked back to the estate momentarily. "I'll show her a punk." With those words, he let go of the shovel, allowing me to toss it aside, then bent down and grabbed me around the waist. I yelped as he stood, taking me with him, my stomach over his shoulder as he carried me away like a sack of potatoes.

I couldn't remember the last time I laughed so hard. I was unable to catch my breath, and my lungs hurt from trying, but it was a good hurt: the type of hurt that left you smiling wide and dizzy in the head. My abdomen burned with pain, and I screamed and kicked my feet and playfully slapped at his back until I couldn't take it anymore and was forced to calm myself down.

"Where are you taking me?" I asked, trying to twist around to keep the blood from rushing to my head. I had no idea how his spindly limbs were strong enough to keep hold of me, but I wrote it off to the whole "not being human" thing.

He didn't answer my question, continuing to carry me until we reached the side of the house where a snow drift had built up against the brick wall. When I settled my laughter, I figured out what he was doing, and began to twist and kick again, but this time I really tried to get out of his grip.

"No, no, no!" I protested, but there was little I could do to keep him from dropping me in the pile of snow. When I managed to dig myself out a little, Jack was standing above me, a smug grin on his features.

"Hilarious," I said, unable to manage as hard of a glare as I wanted to. I allowed him to laugh at my expense, then I held out my hand for help. "I can't get up."

He took pity on me, grabbing my hand to haul me out of the snow. I was not keen on letting him get away with his antics though, so instead of standing after unlodging myself, I pulled at his arm instead and he ended up losing his balance and toppling over into the mound next to me.

I fell into another fit of painful giggles, speaking through tears when I gained control of my lungs again. "I couldn't resist."

He also tried glaring, but it was less effective with the grin he was stifling.

I could feel my heart swell and soar with how much joy it was experiencing at that moment. I hadn't felt this full of life since I was a child, and just like looking up at the stars with him, or watching the sun rise over the ocean, I wished for time to stand still so I could experience it forever.

My laughter wound down again, and I found his gaze. His gray eyes swam with the same aching joy, and I knew the world would stop for us if he had the power to do so. Breathless, I smiled, reaching out to brush some snow from his fringe, but my innocent motion led to less innocent intentions, and before I could stop myself, I leaned over to him and took his lips.

His face was cold but his kiss was warm and he tasted of summer and salt and I knew I could get lost in him if I let myself. It didn't matter that our time together was inevitably temporary, or that he was something other than human and I was just a broken girl with stitches in her wrist, or that we sat in melting snow representing how close the approaching heartbreak of our demise was.

Just another kiss, a little deeper, and I'd be tangled up in this moment forever, just as I wished for it to be.

He shifted and pushed further into my kiss and my heart picked up a hard, fast rhythm in my chest. Then the melting snow that we sat in finally made its way through the fabric of my jeans and time unpaused as I jumped up to my feet when the cold wetness hit my skin.

There was a brief pause before Jack dissolved into laughter at my reaction, with me following shortly after.

XXI

We went to the forest, where there was less snow so it was easier to walk, and the tree trunks shielded us from the biting wind. We unwrapped our damp scarves and took off our wet gloves to allow them to dry as we strolled. As usual, the air was filled with a silence that was comfortable from his side and painful from mine. I averted my eyes away from him when I caught myself staring and tried to keep from holding onto his fingers too tightly when he led me somewhere. I wanted to walk closer to him, but I forced distance because I couldn't trust myself, and the worst part was he seemed completely unaware of what he was doing to me.

He smiled soft and innocent like he always did, gray eyes watching the sky through the sharp, bent branches of the trees, ignorant to the fact that every time he looked at me my face grew hot despite the chilly air.

I had to fill the silence just to distract myself from my own human nature. "I have some more questions for you, *Death*."

"For wanting me to be Jack, you sure do like calling me something else." His words were teasing, but I could sense it made him uncomfortable when I used that word; he was simply too nice to say anything about it.

"Sorry." I grinned with the apology to show I didn't mean anything by it. "I guess I'm just still trying to convince myself that this isn't a dream. It all feels a little surreal." It wasn't just his admission I was talking about either, but also my mother showing up, my brush with actual Death, and him coming back, all in the span of twenty-four hours. Nothing had really settled in yet; I hadn't given myself much time to process any of the emotions I was having, and I wasn't sure if that was a good thing or not.

I knew I was happier than I had been in a long time, but I also knew I was ignoring the things that needed to be addressed, and eventually, the weight of those ignored emotions would come crashing down on me, as they always did. Maybe if I started addressing them now though, it wouldn't be so suffocating later when they engulfed me.

Addressing them meant dealing with some unanswered curiosities though.

"I understand. This is kinda strange for me too. I haven't told anyone before." He climbed onto a tall root as he spoke, casually avoiding my gaze so I wasn't sure how to take those words.

"Really?" I wandered over to him, sitting down on the trunk of a fallen tree nearby. "I'm the only one?"

I caught him smiling as he stepped carefully along a root, balancing himself with little effort even though his feet seemed big and clumsy with his boots. "Feel special yet?" He called me out for my fishing.

I smirked and turned to the ground to hide my blush. "No. I'm sure you say that to everyone."

He jumped down from the root and moved closer to me, climbing up and balancing along the log towards where I sat. "No one else, Violet. Just you."

I had to take a breath to absorb his words and the flutter they brought to my abdomen. I looked up at him briefly, then down at his shoes. "That's impossible." I countered, feeling the heat coming to my face already.

He bent at the knees next to me, a serious expression coming to his face at the accusation. "Have I ever lied to you?"

"No, it's just…" I knew I was already red. I twisted my fingers in my lap awkwardly, glancing away from him while explaining in a murmur. "You're too good at kissing to not have done it before…"

It was silent for a moment, and I peeked out of the corner of my eye to see him hiding an embarrassed grin in the wool of his black scarf. "Oh," he replied after the pause, a laugh in his throat. "Well I can assure you, that's just a fortunate coincidence."

I needed to stop saying things like that; when I made him blush, I drove myself crazy. It was hard not to see him as human when his mannerisms and reactions were so natural. It was probably why I was having so much trouble accepting it. If I could reach out and touch him, wrap myself around him, kiss him, how was he not real? If I could feel his heartbeat and the warmth of his skin, how was he not human?

"Alright. So why haven't you told anyone before, then?"

I filled the silence between us with another question, hoping to move away from the suggestive topic I had brought up. I needed to behave myself, for my own sake. While my mother had been wrong about Jack when she suggested that he could simply be taking advantage of me, she did bring up a very good point. Only it was me who ran the risk of taking advantage, of his kindness and naivety. He was a very good distraction, but he wasn't here to distract me from the things I was too much of a coward to face, and I needed to have the strength to recognize that.

He settled next to me on the tree trunk, letting his gray eyes go up into the sky as he thought. "It's not exactly something that comes up in conversation very much." He grinned, being cheeky with his slight avoidance of the question.

I gave him a pointed look. "Yes but, no one ever noticed? I mean… I didn't know what it was, but I knew something was different about you."

He hummed. "Yes, but I don't usually get close enough for someone to notice."

I blinked, feeling a sadness swell in my chest. "That must be lonely."

"I didn't mind it. I think people naturally just overlook me a little, maybe it's part of the deal. Whatever it is, I spend a lot of time just watching people, keeping my distance until I'm needed." He kept his soft smile the entire time, but something shined in his gaze, a shadow of some long forgotten pain. "It's easier that way anyway. It's easier not to get involved in people's lives too much, since my presence just naturally means something tragic is coming."

"You *didn't* mind?" I asked, after letting the silence between us sit for a while.

He laughed, breathy fog from his lips. "Yeah. Well, I didn't mind until you."

"Stop saying stuff like that. You're proving my mother right about just trying to take advantage of me." I joked to hide the fierce red crawling up my collar.

"Your mother really has it out for me," he commented, letting his smile go a little sly. "It's the truth though. I don't know how to explain it for you to understand…" He paused again, sorting out his thoughts before continuing. "It's all just these feelings in my gut. It's not like I know the future. I don't know what's going to happen or who's going to die, or if they even are going to die for that matter. I'm just there, because I know I have to be there. And I keep my distance until something happens, until I'm needed, then I move on. With you though, when I saw you I just got this feeling, that maybe this time I needed to get involved."

"Was I so charming, that I made you break your rules?" I asked sarcastically, knowing I had been quite the opposite during our first few encounters.

He chuckled again. "Definitely. I particularly liked being called a stalker."

I bit at my lip, holding down a giggle. "You were being a bit of a stalker..." I muttered under my breath, getting a bump on my shoulder from him.

"You're right though... Maybe I was just letting my humanity get the better of me. Maybe I just wanted to know someone for once, to feel connected. I had started feeling more like a ghost than anything else. I missed feeling human. I didn't think or care about possibly getting hurt."

"Strange." I paused, looking at him and catching those gray eyes. "I'd say when I first came here, I felt like a bit of a ghost myself. You helped me feel a little more alive though. Actually, more alive than I've felt in a long time."

His gaze flickered, narrowing a little. "Now you're the one saying things just to try and take advantage."

I thought to protest, because that wasn't my intention, but I couldn't help myself. "Is it working?"

His smile spread a fraction, leaning down to put his forehead to mine. "Yes." His breath touched my lips with the word and I lost mine from my lungs. He sighed, waiting another second, as if trying to find the will to pull away, to be the responsible one. It never happened.

"Can I kiss you, Violet?"

I breathed a tortured laugh, whispering, "I know you're just trying to be polite, but you really don't have to ask every time."

With a grin on his lips from my teasing, he stole mine just as I got the words out.

I would've stayed out there forever with him if I was able to, but after hours, my stomach began to protest painfully in its emptiness, and I was forced to return for dinner. Upon approaching the estate, my mother's car was still in the driveway, and I grew apprehensive about what I would meet on the other side of the door.

I entered the house, and everything was quiet. Too quiet. The type of quiet that was heavy with frustration, where occupants were purposely staying silent to make a passive-aggressive point. I was familiar with this quiet. It was our apartment during the few days between my trip to the hospital and my mother bringing me here to Newport.

"We're in the kitchen, Flower." My Nan called to me, and I discarded my jacket and snow boots to join them, cautiously.

The table was set and my grandmother and mother were sitting with full plates, waiting for me.

"It might be cold. Your mother insisted we not start without you," my grandmother explained as I sat down, annoyance ringing in her tone.

"We waited an hour, Violet," my mother added, finally picking up her untouched utensils as I did.

"I'm sorry. I didn't know I was supposed to be back for dinner," I replied, finding a tension in my jaw.

"Maybe if you hadn't been out in the woods with that boy all day you'd have known."

I couldn't help the stifled laugh that escaped from me, because she was beginning to be downright ridiculous. "Ironic, that you spent my entire childhood jumping from one guys' bed to the next, but I can't even *know* a boy. When did you become so old-fashioned?"

I thought I saw my mother's eye twitch.

"Irrelevant," she said, taking her first bite of her food and grimacing at the lack of warmth. I rolled my eyes and that garnered a further reaction from her. "It's not just about the boy, Violet. Actually, it's not about him at all. It's about you attempting to kill yourself a month ago, and now, you're going off on your own doing god knows what. What are we supposed to think? How are we not supposed to worry, that something has happened, that you've—"

My grandmother interjected with her first words since my arrival. "If you keep treating her like you expect her to hurt herself, she'll eventually live up to the expectation, Lillian." She didn't even lift her eyes from her plate with the words, as if it was just an innocent observation. There was an intention there though, something that said more than I understood.

Across the table from me, I felt my mother's frustration switch away from me to my grandmother. "And you'd know all about that wouldn't you, Mother?" There was poison in her words, and they only confirmed my suspected ignorance.

"You're absolutely right, I would know."

"What?" I couldn't help myself from interrupting, thoroughly confused at how the conversation had gone from scolding me to an argument that now seemed to have little to do with me.

My grandmother put her utensils down to offer an explanation. "When your grandfather and I met, we fell in love fast. Let's just say, we let our infatuation with each other get the better of us, and I ended up pregnant very young and out of wedlock. It was extremely difficult. My mother disowned me, and the only reason we were able to care for Lillian was because your grandfather's family owned this property and had the funds to take me in. We married and had your mother and that was that."

"Then, you spent your life treating me like I was stupid and would make the same mistake as you. You were constantly hovering over my shoulder, never giving me any freedom." My mother chimed in bitterly, her fork also discarded onto her plate now.

My grandmother continued, her words directed at me. "Because I was so scared of her making the same mistake I did, my overprotectiveness ended up just making my fears come true. She got pregnant with you way too young when she wasn't ready as well, only this time the man she made the mistake with was not willing to face the consequences of his actions.

"Because of this, you could say I have first hand experience in the matter and have the right to give advice regarding it." Her last comment was aimed back at my mother, firmness in her tone.

I sat back in my chair, a little dumbfounded. I'd known my mother had me young, and later on, I figured out that it was why my father was never in the picture, but I hadn't heard the story in so much detail before. I didn't know how to react. "You never told me all that."

My mother scoffed. "It doesn't make a difference." But something under her tone implied it was still a sore subject.

I found an emotion with her dismissal. Frustration. "It might have, if I'd known," I said, irritation in my response.

She was always doing that. Keeping things from me like I was still a child who couldn't understand. If I had known the very real struggle my mother went through just to have me, I would have maybe at least understood her perpetual discontentment more thoroughly. It wasn't like it was an excuse for her behavior over the years, but I imagined that it would have been hard, to have a child so young, and alone. Maybe it was why I was with my grandparents so much. My mother hadn't been ready for me. She didn't have the emotional capacity to give a child what it needed.

And she apparently still didn't.

"Yes, well, you understand then, that I did my best with what I had. And how am I repaid? By finding you on the bathroom floor with your wrist slit open."

"Lillian." A scowl from my grandmother, exasperated.

It took me a few extra moments to react as I tried to keep my frustration from bubbling over into an outburst. I put my fork down again, losing the little bit of my appetite that managed to remain after first being scolded. Now I just felt sick to my stomach. The vomit churring in my throat came out as acid words instead.

"I'm sorry I've been a constant inconvenience to you, Mother. Next time you make me feel like offing myself, I'll make sure you don't find me ahead of time."

The tears threatened my eyes, but somehow, I held them down long enough to leave the kitchen and lock myself in my room.

XXII

My mother decided to stay at the estate, much to my dismay. She said it was to prepare for the court case, but when that upset me, my grandmother assured that they were discussing things to try and work them out without going to the law. My mother seemed impartial to the idea, but my grandmother was encouraging so I tried not to let myself dwell on it too much.

It was difficult, considering anxiety had always been a good friend of mine. With the house in a constant state of unrest, I wasn't getting much sleep, and I was getting up early and coming home late just to avoid the suffocating claustrophobia. I was stuck in a limbo state between exhaustion and restlessness. I spent the nights lying awake, lost in my own head, consumed with dangerous, angry thoughts, and spent the days feeling half-awake.

On top of that, my growing infatuation with Jack was hitting the dreamy, delusionally happy stage, to the point where half the time I questioned if whether what was happening was real, or I was just having one of my brief, wonderful dreams that came to me during the short spurts of rest I'd get during my tossing and turning at night.

Jack was noticing. When I wrapped my arms around his waist and rested my head on his collar, I was pretty sure that sometimes I drifted off for a moment or two, lulled by the sound of his heart beating in his chest. He'd whisper warm words in my ear, and I'd haul my heavy eyes open again to come back to reality, his fingers petting the baby hairs at my temple.

I didn't want to be passing out on him all the time, but I couldn't help myself. Being next to him brought me a calmness that was rare in my anxiety-ridden existence. The only other time I remember feeling so serene, so tranquil, was after I had made the cut in my wrist and my consciousness started drifting away. It was a dangerous comparison to make, but I couldn't ignore that the two times I felt most at home were when I was figuratively, and literally, in the arms of Death.

He commented on my exhaustion in his own way. Instead of questioning it, he'd began suggesting that the name Poppy would suit me better than Violet. He asked once if I was seeing another personification during the night, in secret, suggesting that perhaps he was in competition for my attention with the Boogeyman or the Devil. When I asked if they existed, he laughed and shrugged. He even threatened once, teasingly, that he wouldn't come meet me in the mornings until I caught up on my sleep, but whenever I left the house early from being unable to rest in my bed, I'd spend only a few minutes alone before he'd show up.

It was me who finally addressed my tiredness, in the same avoiding approach as he liked to use.

"Do you sleep, Jack?" I asked one day, sitting on a big, cleared off rock that overlooked the beach and ocean.

He was standing, skipping stones on the calm waters, but with my question, he glanced over his shoulder at me and smiled. Obviously, he was encouraged by me finally bringing the issue some attention. "Yes. Sometimes."

"You don't have to though?"

"Not like you have to. Of course, it's an enjoyable way to pass some time."

I dwelled on his answer for a moment, trying to remember a time where I had seen him looking as exhausted as I felt the last while. Even the night we spent out watching the stars, he had been bright-eyed and bushy-tailed the whole time, while I definitely started feeling the heavy lids and sluggish movement of tiredness creeping up on me.

Then there was the evening after he found me in the stables, when he had looked ready to fall asleep on the couch, a set of dark circles rimming his gray eyes, making them vibrant and stormy. "You have to sleep after doing your, death fingers thing, right?"

I heard him sputter out a laugh at my ineloquent, impromptu name for his power. "Death fingers thing?"

I gave him a playful glare. "You know what I mean."

He threw his last stone, then turned to join me on my rock. He sat down so our shoulders touched; I noticed we had naturally drawn closer and closer to each other over the days spent together, to the point where it was hard to pinpoint when my hand was not in his or we weren't orbiting each other in some other way.

"Yes, to your question. Doing my 'death fingers thing' is like, a transfer of energy. And it takes more energy to help someone back to life than leading them on to death," he paused to let me confirm my understanding with a nod, then added an afterthought. "You were particularly stubborn also, that day at the stables. It was like you didn't want to die there, but you also weren't quite ready to come back to life either. It felt like I was trying to convince you."

I chuckled, blushing at his teasing tone. "That sounds like me." I was never really one to listen to others, even if they had my best interest in mind.

"You literally sucked the life out of me. I was exhausted after that." He elaborated further, really driving the point home.

I gave a sheepish grin. "Have I thanked you yet for that?"

"You have. Numerous times." He nodded with the gentle sarcasm on his voice.

"Well, one more time doesn't hurt." I leaned over to bump his shoulder with mine. "Thank you."

"You don't give yourself enough credit, Violet. You chose life. I just helped you get there." Before he finished speaking, I was already shaking my head to brush off his words, so he leaned over to me, taking the side of my head in his hand and pulling me towards him so my temple found his lips. He kissed the skin there, then whispered, "You're always forgetting how strong you are. You chose to live once, you should remember that."

I closed my eyes, his sweetness too much for my pounding heart to take. "Alright," I murmured, knowing there was no sense in arguing with him.

I wanted to ask him why I would choose to keep living when everything hurt so much, all the time. I wanted to ask him why I still felt so comforted by the idea of it all finally ending on my birthday. If I had chosen life, why was everything still drawing me to death? I knew he didn't have answers for me when it came to my emotions. Those were questions I'd have to figure out on my own.

He brought the topic back up after we lingered together in a comfortable silence. "Why did you ask about if I slept though?"

A coy grin crossed my lips. "I have a favor to ask."

ớ

"I don't know about this." We were on the front steps of the estate when his resolve wavered for a third time since walking back from the ocean.

166

I rolled my eyes, turned around to face him, and repeated what I said every other time. "It's not a big deal. It's just sleeping. I'm so tired, Jack. I haven't gotten a good night sleep in days, and I just don't want to be alone." I took his hands and put on a purposeful pout, coaxing him with me towards the door.

He groaned. "This is a terrible idea." He wasn't fighting me as hard as you'd expect for how much fuss he was putting up about it.

"You're thinking about it too much. Like I said, it's just sleeping. Now be quiet so my mom doesn't hear."

He gave another frustrated sound in his throat. "The fact that you have to sneak me in isn't very reassuring."

I glared at him playfully. "It's not sneaking. It's just… Avoidance."

"That's much more encouraging."

I cut off his sass with a finger to my mouth as I opened the door.

We had stayed out particularly late, so the estate was quiet and dark. I assumed my grandmother had already went to bed, and I hoped my mother followed as well, although I didn't put it past her to stay up waiting for me.

We took our jackets and boots off silently, then I laced my fingers with his and led him up the creaky stairs, guiding him on where to step to make the least amount of noise. We got to the top of the stairs, and I was sure we were home free, but as we passed my grandfather's room, Jack slowed his pace behind me, tugging our arms taut.

I stopped, glancing over my shoulder to see him looking at the closed door, something in his eyes that I hadn't seen before. I tugged at his hand and he blinked, his gaze jumping to me, as if breaking from a trance.

I was going to ask him what happened, but as the words formed in my mouth, my mother erupted from her room down the hall, and we both turned to stare, like a pair of deer in headlights.

Busted.

"Violet, what do you think you're doing?"

Jack instantly untangled his fingers from mine and attempted damage control. "I should go."

He tried a smooth escape, but I grabbed his fingers again before he could get away, keeping him there with me. "No. You don't have to go anywhere." With my words, I pulled him along with me, past my mother, towards my room.

It took her a long moment to wipe the shock off her face before she replied. "I don't think I appreciate the idea of you having a boy spending the night." That was her way of trying to make her objection polite and pretty. I wasn't falling for it.

I gave Jack a nudge into my room, then hung back at the door frame to reply. "I don't appreciate having to follow the rules of a woman who hasn't even been around for over a month. Who criticizes me for being out with a boy when all she does is work and drink and mess around with assholes who always leave. Maybe when you start actually acting like a mother, I'll respect your wishes." I entered my room at the end of my words, closing the door and locking it so there was no further argument.

Jack had taken a seat on the bed and was staring at me with a somber expression. I sighed, then gave a little laugh to try and shake off the heaviness in the air around us. "That was awkward." He didn't react, so I bit at my lip, feeling uncomfortable, then sat next to him and asked cautiously, "What is it?"

A sigh. "I don't really like being a pawn to make your mother upset."

I winced. "That wasn't how I meant it..." When I didn't get a reaction, I nudged him with my arm. "I'm sorry," I whispered.

He sent me a hard look, but caved relatively easy. "Just... Don't do it again."

I nodded, then rested my chin on his shoulder. "I won't. I promise. I'm sorry." I apologized again for good measure.

Jack could never hold a grudge. "Let's get this over with then." He nodded to the bed, his eyes softening.

I smirked, commenting on his lack of enthusiasm sarcastically, "Don't be so excited."

"What should I be excited for? I'm just helping you get to sleep, right?" He eyed me, warningly.

I rolled mine. "Yes, just sleep. I promised, remember?"

It had been part of him finally agreeing to come, like he thought if he didn't make me promise, then I'd turn it into something else. He was probably right, but it was frustrating he had to make me so aware of my humanity. It wasn't my fault this his innocent demeanor made me look like a deviant in comparison.

He took his zippered sweater off and I stole it immediately, lacing my arms in the sleeves, the warmth and smell of him surrounding me in a cozy comfort. As I enjoyed the garment, he shifted on the bed, leaning himself up against the headboard, adjusting the pillows to get comfortable.

I snaked under his arm as he settled, resting my head comfortably on his collar bone, trying to ignore my racing heart. I thought about how there was only the thin, black fabric of his shirt left between me and his warm skin now, and I thought about the times I'd imagined this scene in my head, fantasized about it going places that left me furiously red in the face. But I had promised. Just sleep.

I thought it would be hard to settle the violent pulse in my head, but he wrapped his arm around my shoulders and drew me closer to him, then placed a barely there kiss on my forehead that must have been filled with morphine. The moment his lips touched my skin, I felt sweet calmness flood my mind, and I breathed deep the fresh, woody smell of his skin before letting sleep take me.

XXIII

When I woke I was alone, my bed warm from where his body had been. I couldn't say I wasn't disappointed; the idea of waking up in his arms was almost as appealing as falling asleep in them. I knew it was for the best though. Maybe my mother would give me a break if she at least knew he hadn't spent the night.

I blinked the sleep from my eyes and inhaled deep, his scent filling my nose and making me sigh to myself at the comfort. His sweater was cozy and warm, and I thought it strange that it was almost painful to rise every other morning because of the tiredness and the cold deep in my bones, but that morning was so easy. I sat up, looked at the violet on my bedside table, and smiled. It had been a little sad lately, but this morning it was bright with life again. He must have given it a pick-me-up as he left as well.

Before getting up, I searched around my bed, but came up empty-handed. How romantic would it have been, if he left a handwritten note, or something else to show his existence. That wasn't the way he did things though. All that remained in his wake was the ghost of his presence, a haunting feeling within me, leaving me constantly wondering if he was real or just a wonderful delusion.

The calmness he injected into my skull with his kiss the night before still lingered over me, so I thought to continue sleeping; I needed a day of self-care and I didn't want to admit it but perhaps it was best to spend some time on my own to sort out some persisting emotions I had about everything.

Jack's situation I had come to terms with, although there was still that approaching deadline I'd set that would have to be dealt with eventually. It was my mother's presence instead that I was ignoring when I knew I should be facing it. It became very obvious recently that I prefered to be a coward when it came to dealing with the troubling things in my life, but running away wouldn't help me any longer.

So I'd spend some time alone to dwell on it, to sort out a plan of action. I needed to regenerate myself a little, get some emotional strength back, since I had been feeling so drained. I'd need a small snack first; my stomach was uncomfortably empty. So instead of crawling back into bed, I got up and headed for the kitchen.

The house was quiet again, and for a moment, I thought my mother and grandmother had perhaps left. It seemed unlikely that they would go anywhere together right now though, with the tension still taut over everyone. It was only after I stopped and purposely stretched my hearing that I noticed a sign of life.

Beyond the swaying of the house in the winter wind and the beeps of my grandfather's digital heart, I could hear the sniffs and swallows of my mother holding back tears. I tiptoed down the hall to her room, easing her door open a crack.

She was sitting on the edge of the bed, her cellphone in her palm and her eyes casted down. I didn't need to see her face to know she was crying though. I was one of the few people who had ever seen my mother vulnerable like this. It was an easy emotion to identify when it so rarely crossed her.

She heard me and swiped at her eyes as I opened the door a little further. There was no point pretending like I hadn't seen though.

"What happened?" I asked, trying for some compassion while also holding onto a mildly frustrated tone. I didn't want her to get the wrong idea. She had played the victim card with me too many times before. I wouldn't pretend I didn't care, but I also wouldn't let her guilt me either.

She looked up at me, her gaze red. "I called Henry and told him I decided to stay here for a while, and he... He just broke up with me."

Henry was her current boyfriend, who I'd barely had the chance to meet more than a few times, and whose subtle influence was one of the main reasons my mother dumped me in Newport in the first place. I knew his type, because his type was my mother's type: well off and subtly abusive. They were usually just busy enough to justify wanting to keep the relationship "casual" so they weren't forced to give her, or her daughter, any proper attention, and could ditch at the first sign of drama. Which was often, with my mother and I. My mother fell for their tricks every time, feeding her abandonment issues whenever they left, taking her shame and regret out on me by ignoring me altogether.

She had curled up with her admission, like she thought I would have something sharp to say: a rattlesnake coiled in defense, scared but also ready to strike back. Given my history, and what I had spat at her the night before, I didn't blame her. I wasn't about to lecture her though; we were both a mess, I'd realized. Who was I to tell her how she should have done things better, when I didn't even really know myself?

Instead, I ventured into the room, collecting her brush from the nightstand. I couldn't bring myself to offer comforting words, so I just sat next to her and began gently running the brush through her hair, like Nan had done for me. Because despite our differences, despite constantly being at war, despite the neglect and the misunderstandings and the pain we'd put each other through daily, she was still my mother and still a human being who didn't deserve to be hurt by the real life monsters out there.

She cried, and cried, and cried, until the tears wouldn't come anymore and she was left just sniffing and sobbing between the brush strokes. When she'd bundled herself up in a blanket and laid down on the bed, I put her brush back on her nightstand and left her alone, closing the door behind myself. Before I shut it completely, I heard her call after me.

"Thank you, Violet."

I didn't speak. I knew I would ruin it if I did.

As I passed my grandfather's room again, I found myself pausing, remembering the night before. Jack's fingers pulling on mine as he stopped outside the door, a curious expression in his eyes.

When I returned to my room with a bowl of cereal, I took my journal out from its new hiding spot under the mattress. I moved it there the moment my mother had returned, knowing she'd snoop if given the opportunity. I scrawled a quick note to myself: *Find out about that look.* Then, I tucked the journal back and returned to the covers, letting the comforting smell of his sweater banish my concerns.

A single day apart was torturous, so I was relieved when he found me the next morning in the back of the house, my nose in my journal as I drew the shed covered in snow. I had brushed off some of the outdoor furniture, making for a decent place to sit, albeit slightly chilly.

"Feeling rested?" he asked, crawling over the back of the bench to sit next to me. I felt the warmth of his body and I shifted towards him involuntarily, like a flower turning to face the sun's warmth.

"Yes, actually. I feel much better. Thank you for helping, although I was disappointed that you left." I nudged him in the ribs with my elbow, and he smiled.

"I know. I thought it was best I let you have some time to yourself though."

I nodded. "You're right. I needed it. I needed to think about some stuff. And while I'm not complaining, you're too often a terrible distraction." As I said it, I tightened my hand around my pen, trying to resist the urge to drop it in replacement for his hand.

He laughed under his breath. "I can leave again if you prefer?" He teased me by shifting, and I immediately dropped my writing utensil and grabbed his fingers.

"No!" I protested, then hid my eyes in my hand, embarrassed with my own outburst. I hadn't realized how terribly I'd missed him until the idea of him leaving again was presented.

He smiled, pleased that he had successfully toyed with me, and leaned over to kiss the blush he caused to bloomed across my cheeks.

"I'm going crazy."

He shook his head in disagreement, but I continued despite his objection.

"It's scaring me a little, how badly I want to spend every waking moment with you. The fact that this has to end eventually just makes it worse. I've never felt so drawn to someone." I paused, then sighed, further embarrassed. "That sounded less ridiculous in my head."

He hummed, soft and encouraging. "It's not ridiculous." He

stopped there, and I watched him cast his gray eyes downward. I could tell he was keeping words to himself, and I understood. There was so much to say, but we only had a limited time together, and neither of us wanted to use words that could make the inevitable separation worse.

That's what made the silence between us so unbearable sometimes. Knowing I wanted to dive head first into this feeling, but scared of causing a broken heart. It didn't matter if he wasn't quite human or if he knew tragedy like one knows their favorite song, when I leaned against him and heard his heart pound steady in his chest, I couldn't stand the idea of shattering it.

So instead of kissing him, instead of losing myself in him like I wanted to so badly, I leaned my head on his shoulder and tried to be satisfied with just his fingers, playing with mine.

A sharp call in the sky broke through our comfortable silence, and I opened my eyes to watch my friend the crow land on the roof of the shed. With his appearance, I smiled. "Where have you been?" I asked it, then chuckled and offered an explanation to Jack. "That crow and I became good friends when you were away."

"Really? I know that crow as well."

I sat up, turning to Jack to read his expression. He was teasing me with that secret look again, and I glared at him for an explanation.

His smile widened. "He lent me his eyes on occasion."

I let my mouth drop, then shoved him playfully in the arm. "So you have lied to me then! You said I wouldn't see you again but you came back as a damned crow. Stalker!" I tried to be angry, but I failed to muster anything besides mild annoyance, because I couldn't help but feel satisfied to have my hunches proven correct. I had known something was up. Even if it was crazy, I felt him there all along.

His grin turned sheepish. "I couldn't help myself. I was curious, to see if you'd figure it out."

I nodded, my glare softening. "So, it was you that showed me the fox."

He hummed with confirmation. "You needed to see it."

"I did." Even without knowing for sure that Jack had something to do with it, seeing the fox and her pups made me feel better. It was like being shown that even against adversity, it was still possible to come out on the other side, alive. It made me rethink certain things. Until my mother showed up and woke the dark thoughts inside me again.

We dwelled on that secret for a second, my mind swimming with new questions. I had to fill the air again, unable to keep quiet. "I know what you're doing."

He lifted an eyebrow, curious.

"Showing me the fox, taking me out that night to do things on my list. You're trying to change my mind. About killing myself." I wanted to accuse him of it, but the words came out softer than intended.

His gray eyes shined with mischief. "Is it working?"

I narrowed mine. "No comment."

His face lit up as he laughed, and I couldn't help but smile myself, my heart fluttering like a tiny bird in my chest at the sound of it. I pretended to be annoyed, turning my shoulder to give him the silent treatment, so he offered an excuse. "I've spent so much time just standing by, watching the inevitable happen, I dunno, I'm just tired of it. When you told me you were going to kill yourself, I just couldn't help but wonder if there was something someone could do. If there was something *I* could do, to change things."

"A futile effort," I teased, although the words rang with truth. I didn't want him to think there was a chance of changing this. I didn't want him to put his heart into it. The problem was, I could tell he already had.

He smiled soft. "I'll keep trying anyway."

I sighed, rolling my eyes playfully. "You're stubborn."

"Death's like that." He laughed again when I shook my head at his terrible pun.

"I'm stubborn too, you know," I commented.

A nod. "I know."

"And if I don't change my mind?" I needed to ask and he needed to answer, because as much as we could joke about it, make light of it, I had a note hidden in my journal. I knew that while the days were getting better, it didn't mean anything. Better has happened before. Things seem alright for a while, but then they all just get bad again, worse than the times before. I had fallen further and further down that dark hole every time, and it was getting harder and harder to dig myself out. Next time, I wouldn't be able to.

I was positive.

Perhaps it was better, to go off on a high note? When I thought about it, I almost prefered the idea of ending it here, when I was finally happy. Ending it before something could come and ruin everything, as it always did.

He hummed next to me, the shine in his eyes dulling a little. He managed to keep the smile on his face though, for my sake. "If it happens anyway, then at least I had the privilege of knowing you, however short the affair. If all it cost me is a bit of heartache, I think that's a fair enough exchange."

I stared at him for a moment, speechless. Of all the things he could have said, something about his choice of words was exactly what I needed to hear, to plant little seeds of doubt in my own head. While I was trying to lessen the blow of our approaching separation by avoiding getting too deep, Jack was diving in headfirst.

"You're impossible." I turned away from him and shook my head, trying to be upset with his frustratingly charming answer, but I failed miserably. When I turned back to him, I leaned forward and caught his lips, unable to contain myself any longer.

XXIV

The mood in the house had slowly changed after my mother left her boyfriend. I was familiar with the phenomenon, since I remembered it from when I was young. Back in the house she grew up in, with her mother there to care for her, my mother reverted back to the young adult she only pretended not to be day to day.

Just as the many times before, she sulked around the house, looking for sympathy. In the past, my grandmother would shoo me off with my grandfather, and while we were out, she would dolt over my mother, cooing and comforting until she felt better. My mother never learned her lesson and therefore just did it all over again, knowing she'd have a place to go when things soured.

I thought perhaps my mother had grown out of this behavior, since it had been years that she kept me away from my grandparents and this house, but old habits died hard. Unfortunately for her, this time my grandmother was not playing the game.

So instead, my mother wandered around the house, very much like a neglected puppy: sad and begging for attention. My grandmother and I went about our business as if she wasn't there. I felt bad sometimes about doing it to her, but I also felt it was about time she learned she didn't have power over me, whether she tried to force me to bend to her will or coerce me with sympathy.

It worked too. Her snarky attitude was dissolving into a much more somber demeanor. I wondered if all the time she was spending not speaking to us was giving her the opportunity to think about some of the things she had done and said. I hoped some remorse was finding its way into her hard head.

It was in the middle of the night that I realized Newport was perhaps getting to her also.

I had gotten up to go to the bathroom, nothing but a long sleeve shirt and underwear. I barely opened my eyes, but as I exited my room, I saw a shape down the hall. I rubbed the sleep away to be sure I wasn't seeing things, confirming the shadowy figure standing outside my grandfather's room.

My eyes adjusted to the darkness, and as I neared I could see my mother more clearly, standing there with a blanket wrapped around her shoulders, staring at the door that her father laid unconscious behind.

She blinked and looked at me when I was finally by her side, snapping out of a trance much like Jack had. She forced a weak smile, shaking her head to rid herself of the embarrassment of being caught doing… Whatever it was she was doing. She was tired, the dark circles under her eyes resembling my own when I missed out on sleep. Perhaps her thoughts were keeping her up also.

"I've been trying to get the nerve to go in there for days now," she explained, a sigh following the admission.

I nodded, rubbing at my heavy lids again. "I've been trying for weeks."

We stood there for a moment, just a couple of cowards lingering inches away from the fear neither could face. Inside the room, my grandfather's heart monitor beeped, tauntingly.

I offered words to banish the discomfort. "Nan says he can hear you, if you speak to him. She reads to him."

My mom lifted her eyebrows. "Is that true?"

I shrugged, having no way to confirm the theory one way or another. It was a comforting thought, that he could hear, but I felt like it was just the hopes of the conscious. He had been gone for so long now, it didn't make sense for him to hear us, but maybe the idea helped Nan get to sleep at night.

I gave a small smile, wordlessly trying to help her find the strength that I myself had yet to locate, then continued past her to the bathroom.

When I left a while later to return to my room, my mother was no longer in the hall. I assumed she retreated back to her room, as I had done every time I thought I might enter my grandfather's. I was proven wrong though, as I passed his door.

It seemed I was the only coward left in the house.

From behind the door, I could make out my mother's voice, humming the tune she used to sing to me when I was a baby. She had told me once that my grandfather used to sing it to her, and I often liked to imagine him, a beard of brown instead of salt and pepper, singing a small baby to sleep. He was never one for many words, but singing seemed to fit him better. Sometimes I wondered if the image I had in my head was an early memory of him, or just an impression I had implanted in my mind.

All the pretty little horses.

I leaned against the wall and listened as the first words came from my mother's mouth.

When you wake, you shall have, all the pretty little horses.

She never sang anymore, even though I always thought it was her who had the beautiful voice of the two of us. I wondered if it reminded her too much of him. I wondered if this all hurt her far more than she ever let me see.

Birds and butterflies, flutter around her eyes. Poor little baby crying papa.

I could hear the tears on her voice, shaking as she whispered the words, humming the notes in her throat. I hadn't realized my own eyes growing damp. I blinked away my tears and returned to my room quietly.

From under the mattress I retrieved my journal, looking for an old page. *Go to a concert.*

Well, it wasn't a concert, but it was the next best thing. I crossed the words off, tucking the journal back in its hiding spot, and crawled back into bed. I dreamed of horseback riding along the coast with my grandfather and my mother, an experience I wish could have been real.

❧

Jack and I were walking along the same stream he had led me to with the crow to find the fox. We weren't exactly looking for her, rather just wandering, but I wouldn't have minded finding her for a third time. There were fresh footprints in the snow, a sign she'd passed here recently, but other than that, the forest was still and quiet.

I doodled in the untouched snow with a long stick, humming to myself the somber tune my mother sung to my grandfather. It had been the soundtrack to my thoughts the last few days. My humming must have carried through the bare trees to Jack, because when I looked up I caught him watching me, smiling.

"What?" I asked, accusingly, although a smirk played on my lips as well.

He shook his head, but elaborated anyway. "Something is different."

I considered his words, tilting my head to the side a little. "You're very observant."

"It's a good trait in my profession." His grin was too cheeky.

I lifted an eyebrow, offering a joke of my own. "Is that what it is? Just a job to pay the bills?"

He laughed, his eyes lighting up like they always did, unabashed.

I let the silence sit for a second, until my smile died down. "I wasn't really thinking about it too hard, but I guess now that you mention it, things have been improving with my mom."

"I noticed. You're not spitting poison at her as much anymore," he teased, and I glared at him.

"Yeah well, she's always been at the center of everything bad that's happened. You could say that I've come to expect negativity when she's around."

"Bad. Like what?" Jack's curious tone surprised me. It wasn't accusing like when the doctors or therapists would ask the same question. He wasn't asking me to defend myself, but simply wanting to know more about me.

"Well... She left a lot when I was a kid. She would always ditch me here in Newport to do stuff on her own for the whole summer."

"But you like Newport."

I nodded. "I do. I really wish she would have just been around though..."

He hummed, agreeing. "Your mother is still young. It must have been hard for her, having a baby."

I knew what he was doing, gently countering my points with arguments that were so subtle I might not have caught on if I wasn't already aware of his ways. I eyed him but went along with it. "You're right. She was younger than I was now. I can't even imagine having the responsibility over another life when I can't even manage taking care of myself most of the time."

He chuckled. "Well, that struggle probably isn't entirely your fault. If things had been different, perhaps you wouldn't see responsibility as such a burden."

"Maybe." I stuck my stick in the snow, satisfying my itchy fingers when it punctured through the mound. I offered more words. "I didn't want to come to Newport at first, but I ended up liking it more than home. It made it hard to leave, especially when being with my mom back in the city was much worse. My mother was always so irritable with me around. I always felt like I was just a burden."

"Children come with many burdens. Money, time, attention. It can be a difficult thing for mature couples, let alone a young, single mother." Another sly counter.

I gave him a look that told him I was aware of his motives, but he smiled innocently in reply. If he was going to counter me, then I would do so as well. "That's the thing though, she didn't have to struggle. My grandparents had lots of money, they were constantly offering to take me for longer, or take us both in. She was just too stubborn."

"Sounds familiar," he mumbled under his breath, but I heard him and scoffed out a laugh, which garnered a sneaky grin from him.

"She took me away from Newport when I had grown attached to it. To the sea and the garden and my grandparents. I remember crying for days when my mother came to bring me home that summer, because I just knew, for whatever reason, that I wasn't coming back."

As I spoke, I remembered, the dread in my stomach that made me sick and scared when my mother had come to retrieve me and take me home. She had to drag me away and put me in the car; I was reaching out, screaming for my grandparents the whole time. I remembered my grandmother crying.

"That was it. She never took me back to Newport, even though I begged every summer."

He needed a moment to think about this particular bit of information, a line coming between his brows. "Leaving you in Newport was for your mother's benefit, but she would have noticed that you had started enjoying it as well. She wouldn't just take that away from you, from herself, without reason. Have you ever asked her, what was different that occasion?"

I blinked, surprised by the fact that I had never considered his point. "No. I guess I haven't."

He smiled when I proved his suspicion correct. "I'd say that's a good place to start."

I blushed, embarrassed with my own foolishness. "I guess I can let my own stubbornness get the best of me. I remember telling myself a lot that she was simply out to make my life hell." Sometimes I still wondered, but I knew it wasn't really true.

"How else were you supposed to see it from your perspective?" he offered, this time a slightly more comforting sentiment.

I sighed. "I guess there was no avoiding it." I negated the somber tone that thought could have led to by lightening the mood with a teasing look in his direction. "You're very good at playing the devil's advocate. You're supposed to be on my side though, by the way."

He shook his head, eyes gleaming. "Death is supposed to be indiscriminate."

"Maybe, but boyfriends aren't." The words came out of my mouth before I even thought about them. When I realized what I said, I froze, a red heat assaulting my face instantly. I heard him step towards me with those big combat boots, and I turned to conceal my embarrassment.

"Boyfriend?"

How awkward the word was on his lips. I groaned as I continued to hide by facing away from him. "Yeah, I don't know what that was. That was so dumb. Like we're twelve or something. You're Death for god's sake, that word was practically offensive. So juvenile. Sorry, I just—"

He grabbed my elbow and turned me to face him, and when I was, he leaned down and put his forehead to mine, shutting me up instantly. "Stop apologizing," he whispered, the breath hitting my lips. "I liked it."

My heart got stuck in my throat again, as usual. "Yeah?" I managed to croak out past the blockage.

"Yes."

I knew for a fact that I was as red as a damn lobster, but it didn't matter. "OK."

XXV

I liked going out to meet Jack in the early morning, when the sunrise shined off the mounds of snow, making it twinkle like diamonds. The snowflakes would stick to my gloves and my eyelashes and in his hair and it was like we sparkled. Two twinkling stars.

There wasn't much untouched snow anymore; we had trampled through a lot of it during our walks. "Walk" was of course a loose term. It was more like play most of the time. I liked flicking the light powder that sat at the top of the mounds at him, and he liked making snowballs with his bare hands before touching the back of my neck with his frozen fingers. I liked tackling him from behind so we both tumbled into the fluff, and he liked trying to bury me in it before I could get up. I liked kissing him, and kissing him, and kissing him, and I liked that he seemed to enjoy it just as much.

Our antics left us cold and wet most of the time, which had led to taking refuge inside the estate for a number of afternoons. We'd strip out of our jackets and boots, leaving our gloves and scarves to hang by the wood stove as we warmed up in the den. Jack always went to my grandfather's bookshelf, taking a while to choose one, or returning to whatever he read last. I would lay on the carpet with my journal and draw him, recording the way his wet, black fringe air-dried messy and unkempt.

My journal was full of him now. Of the things he said and did, the way he looked saying and doing them. I was addicted to how his eyes squinted as he laughed, and the tilt of his lips when he smiled or asked questions.

"Why are you always drawing me, Violet?"

I turned away immediately, but I knew I'd been caught. A coy grin spread on my face. "I want some sort of record of you. I can't bare the thought of you disappearing and me never having proof you existed. It almost drove me insane the first time."

He hummed, seemingly satisfied with my answer, his focus shifting back to the words on the page. The house was quiet, filled with only the crackling of the fire in the wood stove, the sound of my pencil sketching across the paper, and Jack turning the pages of his book. My mother and grandmother left for a meeting with the lawyers together, meaning Jack and I were alone in the house for the first time. I was painfully aware of this fact, and it was a dangerous thought that circled my head and stained my cheeks crimson.

"You make me terribly aware of myself when I know you're drawing me, and it's a strange feeling. It's not often that I go so noticed," he said, breaking the silence again a few moments later.

I bit my lip. "Sorry." I closed my journal to give him a break, offering conversation instead. "How old are you, Jack?"

He tilted his head, holding his place in his book with a finger as he closed it. "What do you mean?"

I shrugged. "Well, like... When did you, you know? Become like this?"

"Like this?" He teased, amused.

I wiggled my fingers menacingly to make my point.

He laughed, then lifted his gaze to the ceiling to think. "I'm not sure. The years kinda blend together. A long time ago, I guess."

"How long?" I paused, having a thought and letting my eyes widen. I lowered my voice, as if the empty house might overhear. "Like, centuries?"

Another chuckle. "Not nearly that long. More like, a few decades maybe? I can't really tell. Time has become sort of abstract for me..."

"Huh."

It was weird to think of him as decades old, when he seemed so carefree and young. There are people who have wisdom in their eyes, who seem older than they really are, because they've seen the world and know its pain and those things age a person's soul. His gaze was so full of youth though; it seemed impossible for him to have experienced the heartbreak of actually living for so long. It was more like he was stuck in time, suspended, neither old nor young.

I stood, setting my journal down on the armchair then joining him on the sofa. I continued my interrogation, new curiosities surfacing as they always did with new answers. "If you've only been like this for a few decades though, what was there before? The concept of a Death entity isn't exactly a new one."

He was enjoying my questions, and I loved that. I saw a hint of teeth every time he smiled. "I don't really know. I was just like this one day." I dropped my shoulders and he gave me a sympathetic look, as if wishing he could offer me a more concrete answer. Then something came to mind, and he hummed. "I used to wonder... If I was human before. Sometimes I have dreams that seem a lot like memories."

I gasped under my breath. "Do you think you died and became like this? Like a ghost maybe?"

Another tilt of his lips. "I dunno, maybe. I'd like to think so. I like the idea that I was human once."

"It would explain why you're so normal sometimes," I commented teasingly.

Jack leaned towards me, his eyes gleaming with something. "You make me feel normal." His words came out softly this time, meant just for me.

I giggled on my exhale. "You make me feel normal also," I sighed.

On a dime, the air had changed. I felt the flush on my cheeks, a result of laughing and smiling too much, and grew hotter with the intention in his eyes. His gaze dropped to my lips and I swallowed my heart down, out of my throat.

"Violet—"

I interrupted with a frustrated groan and a whisper. "I swear if you're about to ask permission again—"

He interrupted by pushing his lips onto mine.

How wonderful and sweet his kisses always were; I adored them. Soft and careful, like he wasn't just kissing me but kissing the tender stitches of my wounded soul. I had been happy with just these kisses for so long. Never greedy, always satisfied.

This time, something was different. Completely alone, there was no reason to be chaste or quick at the risk of being caught or spied on. No reason not to completely lose ourselves for a moment, or two, or three. The seconds our lips were joined became longer with each separation, our enthusiasm to meet them again made our gentle caresses morph into collisions. A fire caught light inside me, hot and consuming and spreading rapidly.

He raised a hand to my cheek to hold me to him, then the hand was along my jaw, trailing downwards to cradle the nape of my neck. His touch had me burning, like he was brushing away the soot on my skin with his fingers to reveal hot embers underneath. I found myself breathless in the spaces between our lips meeting, my exhales warm like smoke.

I shifted, unable to hold still, trying desperately to get closer to him somehow, but our damned limbs were in the way. He noticed my fidgeting, holding his lips to mine as he reached over and grabbed me behind the knees, hauling my legs over his. I let out a mouse-like squeak at the move, and he grinned against my mouth as he kissed me harder. With our sides now flush, I was able to trail my fingers up along the collar of his shirt, up his neck, and into his still-damp hair, garnering a sound from his throat that could only be described as a purr.

I was almost always on the edge of dangerous with him. I had to consciously keep myself from overdoing things, not wanting to risk moving too fast just because I couldn't stand the flames inside of me. It was no surprise that I was lost before the passion was even lukewarm. Jack was usually much more controlled, always the one to pull away and bring us back down to Earth, as if the human instinct for closeness wasn't quite as strong in him. In this moment though, he was just as lost as I was, just as human as I was, just as completely crazy over me as I was him, and the crazier he got, the crazier it made me.

Watching him through my lashes, I could see the same vicious red on his cheeks that assaulted my own, burning from the inside out. How scandalous that color was, it made my head spin, dizzy with the lack of proper oxygen. I knew already that my dreams would be painted with that color, with the look in his heavy-lidded eyes, with the way he sucked air sharp between his teeth when I dared the tip of my tongue over his lower lip.

I wanted to be under his skin like he was under mine, and the want translated to unconsciously gripping and tugging at his shirt, encouraging him to press on, deeper, harder, until I could feel the rhythm of our obsession mirror that of my raging heart. Hot lava pounded through my veins, and he wrapped an arm around my waist and pulled me against him, and I was sure I would be lost forever in these incredibly long seconds.

I was wrong. It was surprising how quickly the anxiety found me despite being sure I would never be able to find myself. As my heart beat loud and consuming in my ear, it drew attention to the other sound in the house that mimicked it.

Not our breath, or his own pulse, or even the ticking of the tall clock in the hall, but the beeping of my grandfather's heart monitor.

It was so far away, I shouldn't have been able to hear it, but anxiety was good at funny little tricks like that. Making you hear the beep, beep, beeping of something you didn't want to hear and making you think things you didn't want to think, like cold gray and sterile sheets and all the pain, the pain of coming back to life.

My anxiety knew how to kill a mood.

I retreated from him with a gasp that I muted with my palm, holding my other hand to his chest to keep him at a distance. I didn't have the air in my lungs to explain, and it hurt to inhale. Tears came before I could even stop them, overwhelmed and frustrated with my own incapability to shake the panic even during a moment of wonderful bliss.

I managed to glance at him, expecting to see annoyance or confusion, but there was nothing but concern. He reached out for me, but not to take me and kiss me again, or to pull me into him to hold me. He simply took hold of my free hand with his and squeezed firmly.

I couldn't take his kindness. I gasped out some words. "I'm sorry, I don't know—I thought I heard—I'm crazy, I'm sorry."

He shook his head immediately. "There's nothing to be sorry for, Violet. It's OK. Just breathe, I'm here."

I wasn't sure if he knew how effective those words had been.

Even though when I was panicking I always ran, the thing I hated the most was finding myself alone when the anxiety finally let go of me. I held back the sobs in my chest, barely; they threatened to break through with the gentle way he handled my insanity.

He helped me find some air, and when I caught a breath, it was me who bridged the space between us again as I collapsed into him and he wrapped himself around me. I pressed my ear to his collarbone and listened to the hard pound of his heart, letting it soothe me. Before I could stop them, my thoughts slipped from my lips in a whisper. "I think I'm falling for you."

I heard the air from his lungs leave in a sharp exhale, and then the pace of his heart quickened just a little. "It feels like I've been falling for you since I first saw you," he answered, his words in my hair.

I held my tongue with my next thought. I was terrified of how hard I would hit the ground once I finished falling.

XXVI

After settling down in a long, comfortable silence, I realized the irony in the rhythm of Jack's heart being what ultimately calmed me down. Eventually, I was able to find some words through the fog of my thoughts to help explain my outburst.

"When I tried to kill myself... The first time... It didn't feel like dying. It felt like finally waking up. Like everything was backwards, like I'd been dead the whole time and I was just a ghost, lingering. It felt wrong. Like I didn't belong. But while I was dying, I felt relieved. It was like the world straightened itself out. Dying was so warm and welcoming. It was what I wanted living to be.

"And coming back was... The worst thing I've ever experienced. It was like how dying should have been. All the pain I'd put off, I was feeling all at once. Every time my heart pounded it ached so bad that I just wanted to end it all over again. I had to sit there in the hospital with nothing but the sound of my own body reminding me that I was still... *Here*.

"When things get really quiet in this house, it's like my grandfather's heart monitor gets louder. It's all I can hear sometimes. And it reminds me of the hospital, and that this is living, that I'm alive, that I'm still on the side of sleep that aches. And that's such a terri-fying realization sometimes that I'd rather go on pretending to be a ghost."

They were the best words I could find, but I could tell they weren't good enough. There would never be words to explain, but at least I was trying for once. Maybe I understood better now why seeing my grandfather like that, in a physical representation of my fictional limbo between life and death, overwhelmed me so much. My grandfather personified my trauma in one convenient trigger. Like me, he was also stuck between worlds, not exactly living but never quite dead either, and it was a nightmare.

While I was reaching out to death though, he was still clinging desperately to life.

I tried to brush off my dark admission with an attempted laugh. "You must think I'm crazy."

Jack shook his head. "I thought we went over this? You're not crazy." He leaned over to me to kiss my temple, the soft smile on his lips tapering down to a more thoughtful look as he added, "I know better than you think, what it feels like to try being alive when you've spent so long as a ghost. Sometimes it can seem easier to stay an apparition."

I hummed, considering for the first time what Jack and I had in common rather than noting the things that separated us. If he was some sort of spirit, maybe we were existing in the same life and death limbo together. Did it hurt his cheeks to smile like it did mine? Did his heart also swell with aching pain when we kissed?

I wasn't sure I could handle the answer. Instead, I teased, "Well you at least must be annoyed that I ruined the mood."

"Don't say ridiculous things," he scoffed, but his tone was gentle.

"It's not ridiculous. I'm annoyed." I smirked sheepishly when I got him to chuckle.

"There's no need to be in such a rush, Violet." Now he was teasing me, and in return, I glared at him.

Admitting defeat, I added a sigh. "OK. Well if *those* plans are put aside for now, then maybe there's something else you can help me with."

He tilted his head, giving me his attention.

I took a deep breath, unsure of myself. I knew if I let myself though, I'd keep putting it off, keep running away, until it was too late, and the thought of that caused me even more pain.

Sometimes it can seem easier to stay an apparition.

"Come with me, to see my grandfather?"

He blinked, surprise fluctuating to hesitancy. "I… I don't think I'd be much help."

I squeezed my fingers together around his. "You'd help by just being there. You just calmed me down from a panic attack. I can't even do that myself. I'm not trying to use you as a crutch or anything…"

He shook his head. "That's not what I think. It's just…" His eyes flitted away from mine briefly, up to the direction of my grandfather's room. "Wouldn't you want to be alone?"

"I can't. I can't go in there alone. I'm not strong enough. Maybe I could be, one day, but I'm scared I won't have time to get strong enough. You make me stronger, though. You make me feel like I can do anything." I leaned into him, accepting his arm around me when he reached.

"You *can* do anything. You just don't believe it yourself." His words were scolding, but the tone was gentle. "But if you want me to… I'll come."

I hummed, smiling and whispering my appreciation as I nuzzled into his neck. I took a long, slow breath, taking in that amazing smell I was addicted to, letting his warmth and the pulse of his heart smother the struggle of before.

Maybe he was right. Maybe there was something in me that could do it by myself. I stood up to my mother after all, something I hadn't done in years. My strength felt so fleeting though. I had trouble getting my weak fingers around it, holding onto it. It disappeared as fast as it hit me. It wasn't reliable enough yet.

Jack, on the other hand, was nothing but reliable. When I needed him, he was there. His presence saved me from myself more than once, so maybe it could give me the strength to get past the pain and finally find the nerve to fight.

I stood and took him with me by the hand, leading him out of the den and up the stairs. As we approached my grandfather's room, I was tempted to pass it and lock us in mine to instead continue where we had left off in the den. I scolded myself though, rooting my feet to the floor so I didn't run away as usual.

I glanced at Jack and caught him staring at the door again, like the night I had snuck him into the room. I tugged at his fingers, and he blinked, turning to me.

"What is it?" I asked, curious just as last time.

He smiled, but he was hiding something. "Nothing. Whenever you're ready." He nodded his head towards the door, encouraging me.

I felt put off by his behavior, but I trusted Jack. He kept secrets from me in the past, but only ever for my own good, and when I needed to know, he told me. Some things were better left unsaid sometimes. There were things that were painful to know, so I didn't ask. Not right now, at least.

I stepped forward instead, taking a breath to settle my nervous fingers before reaching out to open the door a sliver. That terrible beeping was inside my head, but Jack squeezed my fingers tight and it helped me stay grounded. When the anxiety gripped me, I felt so out of control, but with my hand in his, there was something keeping me solid and whole, keeping my feet planted firmly in reality.

I got the door completely open this time, a feat I hadn't managed to accomplish on the occasions I tried to enter the room by myself. I felt my lungs tighten in my chest, my breath becoming short and quick, but I somehow kept from falling apart.

I turned to Jack, who was watching my grandfather with a unfamiliar expression. "He's not even that old. Like your grandmother."

I nodded. "My family has a history of having children young. No one had the will to keep it in their pants, I guess."

His eyes flickered, and I caught it. "That explains a lot." I knew his quip referred to me, and I nudged him and put a finger to my lips. I tried not to acknowledge the fact that Jack had me joking, in the room with my grandfather, something I never thought would happen in a million years.

"My Nan says he can hear you," I whispered, and Jack mimicked zipping his mouth shut. I turned back to my grandfather, laying in his bed, looking already gone. "I've been wanting to talk, but I don't know what to say."

Jack's gaze softened, then he tugged on my hand, taking us towards the bed. I followed, carefully, still feeling sick to my stomach from the nerves. Jack stopped at the foot of the bed, squaring his skinny shoulders and clearing his throat. "Good afternoon, Mister Holt. My name's Jack. De'Morte."

I managed a smile. "What are you doing?"

He glared, playfully scolding me for interrupting. "I'm introducing myself. That's what men do. They introduce themselves to the men in the lives of the girl they like."

I rolled my eyes. "Are we in the fifties?"

"It's a sign of respect. He would have done the same to your grandmother's father."

"Before or after he got her pregnant?" I snickered to myself.

Jack pretended to ignore me, but he was smiling too, and he had to shake the grin from his face before speaking again. "I've been seeing a lot of your granddaughter recently. I'd be lying if I said I wasn't taken with her immediately." He started by looking at my grandfather, but with his words he turned to me, squeezing my fingers. "She's special, and I feel privileged that she gives me the time of day. I know that Violet doesn't have a father around, and that you've been the closest thing to that for her, so I hope you can forgive me for not asking your permission to see her before now."

My face was red with his compliments and my own embarrassment, even though my grandfather was not awake to actually take part in the conversation. I imagined him trying to hold a somber expression, trying to play the daunting father figure, but failing miserably. He was never a man of such formalities. I imagined he'd be as charmed by Jack's naivety and politeness as I was.

I nudged his shoulder. "You should shake his hand. He'd like that, if he was awake. He always said you can read a person with their handshake."

Jack smiled and nodded, releasing my fingers and moving over to the side of the bed. Jack's lack of timidness gave me courage, and somewhere between the time we had entered the room and then, I felt calmer. I was able to look at the man, lying lifeless in the bed, and think about beautiful days napping in the summer sun with him instead of horrible, never ending gray. I remembered his boisterous laugh, and the way he hummed to himself while reading, and the sound of his pencil on paper as he drew long, straight lines.

I watched as Jack leaned down a little, reaching for my grandfather's hand that sat motionless by his side. He took it in his, gentle but firm, and I waited for the curt shake that men give each other, but it never came.

I searched for an explanation on Jack's features, and I saw him staring, stunned. His gray eyes glazed over, glued on my grandfather's face but not really looking at him. He was holding my grandfather's hand and standing as still as a statue, but he was somewhere else entirely in his head.

I felt a cold chill take over me, and I took a step closer, reaching out to touch Jack's arm, but before I could reach him, he shifted.

I watched him lift his free hand.

"I hear you. I can help," he whispered words, barely an exhale, and not for me. Then, with the hand he'd moved, he reached for my grandfather's face.

I all but tackled him. Grabbing Jack by the elbow, I yanked him away so hard that he stumbled and ended up on the floor. Shaken, he blinked, the glaze in his eyes dissolving as he came back to reality. He looked as if he wasn't entirely sure what happened, but as he glanced around, seeing me standing above him, my shoulders rising and falling with angry, ragged breath, I was sure he figured things out.

"What are you doing?" I asked, under my breath, because I couldn't manage to be any more forceful.

I watched Jack's expression fall. "Violet…"

"Answer me."

He swallowed. "He's suffering."

"How do you know that?" I took a forceful step forward, and Jack scrambled to his feet to retreat from me.

"They show me, Violet. The dying souls, they show me their pain. The crow, you. When I touched him, your grandfather, he showed me."

"So you try to kill him?" My eyes were watering, and I was used to tears, but this anger took me by surprise, like a piece of hot metal inside of me. I balled my fingers up into fists until my nails bit at the soft flesh of my palms.

Jack shook his head, trying to reason with me. "I was trying to help. He wants to let go."

"He doesn't. He's still alive, and he's still fighting!"

"He's not. He's trapped. The machines are keeping him here. He wants to go but he can't."

I bit my lip to hold back a scream. I couldn't think straight. All that was running through my mind was how he had just tried to take my grandfather from me. Just like my mother was doing. Just like she already did so many years ago by not letting me come here.

I wouldn't let anyone take him from me again. Not like this. I wasn't ready.

Jack reached out, as if making an attempt to comfort me, but I withdrew from him like the coward I was.

I said one solid, heavy word. "Leave."

His face dropped. "Violet…"

"Leave!"

He flinched, stepping back, like the word had slashed at him. His gray gaze fell to the floor in surrender. "Please… Don't do this. I'm sorry, Violet…"

His begging made me feel guilty and that made me even more frustrated. More tears sprouted in my vision, and I couldn't tell what the pain in my chest was for anymore. Everything just hurt so bad, and my anxiety, wrapped like a snake around my lungs, hissed and lunged in Jack's direction, so he had to be the reason, right?

"I don't want you here anymore."

He shut his eyes tight as I stabbed at him. When he opened them again, they were glossy with pain.

I wanted blood. My darkness snapped at my flank, egging me on. "Leave. Please," I said, softer this time. A warning, because I knew I couldn't keep the panic from consuming me any longer.

"Vi—"

"Leave!"

This time it was me who shut my eyes, yelling the word as I collapsed to my knees, unable to keep myself on my feet through my convulsing sobs. I curled up into myself, the dark thoughts coming down on me like a predator on a wounded animal, tearing and ripping at my flesh and making me ache with pain.

Was I screaming at Jack, or the demons in my own head?

When I realized what I had done, it was too late. I opened my eyes, and Jack was gone, and something terrible stabbed me in my chest, through my ribs, twisting until I was screaming and sobbing so hard I thought my throat would bleed.

XXVII

I made a mistake. I knew I had, but I was too stubborn to right it. I twisted my logic, defended my ridiculous pride, and reminded myself why I was angry in the first place. He had tried to take my grandfather from me. I was right to banish him from the house. I was right to never see him again. It's not like it mattered; it would all be ending soon for me anyway. It was for the better. If I broke his heart now, I wouldn't have to later.

My chest ached though, and I knew why, even if I tried to distract myself with spite and frustration. I wasn't as alive without him. I wasn't as human without him. I could already feel myself curling up, reverting back to the girl I was after awakening in the hospital. The girl that hadn't wanted to be alive and had been so close to death. The girl still obsessed with the idea of leaving. The girl that was so finished with life she might as well already be a ghost.

When my mother and grandmother came home, I was wrapped up under my covers in the dark of my room. They must have noticed something was wrong, because my mother came to my room almost immediately. She knocked, which was unlike her. When I didn't speak, she entered cautiously.

"Violet?" She peeked around the door, and I expected a certain expression to pass her face when she saw me. The annoyance that always branded across her features when she caught me sleeping all day or skipping meals or doing my other destructive behaviors. The look didn't come this time though. Instead, she seemed legitimately concerned.

"Why are you in here? Did something happen?"

I shook my head, brushing it off as I avoided her gaze, just as I did whenever someone asked me about my problems. She could wear sympathy on her but that didn't mean she actually wanted to know. No one actually wanted to know, except maybe Jack.

"It's nothing. I was just tired, so I sent Jack away and was trying to sleep some."

She watched me for a moment, uncertainty between her brows. "Are you sure?" she asked again.

That was the first time she hadn't settled for my excuses, and I recognized what she was doing. She was actually trying to reach out to me. The look in her eyes was encouraging, as if to say to me that it was OK to tell her, if I wanted.

This was not a time when I was willing to attempt a mending of our relationship though. I was still too much of a coward, and more than that, far too sharp after my fragile bits had been broken.

"I'm fine," I insisted, holding my rickety walls up, wanting her to leave before my weak arms gave out and let the protection around my heart fall.

It's not that I wanted to be alone, but she was not who I wanted around. Even if she did want to help, even if she really was concerned, I was scared: that something would unintentionally come out of her mouth, something that made me feel terrible, as it always did. Something that would slash at my vulnerabilities. I didn't have the strength. Not now.

She turned her eyes down, but withheld any further reaction to her rejection. "OK. Well, we'll be downstairs, if you need us." Again, an offer unlike her.

Before Newport, my mother was always busy. She worked late and stayed out even later, and when I began showing warning signs, she ignored them and occupied herself even more to have an excuse for not seeing them. To be honest, I was still surprised she had found me in the first place, that day in the bathroom, sitting in my own blood.

My wrist pulsed with a phantom pain, and I clutched it to my chest along with the blanket, curling up tighter. I nodded to my mother to dismiss her, and she gave a weak smile before closing the door again.

The loneliness fell down on me like a suffocating, heavy pressure. Tears flooded my eyes again, but I held my breath until they passed. On my bedside table, the violet watched me with what my insanity read as a somber expression. I scowled to myself and turned away to face the window instead, feeling the guilt in my gut again.

I closed my eyes and tried to calm my breathing, but I couldn't muster a deep inhale, so my chest continued to protest in pain every time my heart slammed against my ribs, in time with my grandfather's heart monitor. Reminded of him, lying lifeless in the next room, I finally dwelled on what Jack had said.

He's suffering.

I imagined my grandfather, stuck in that painful, dark dream I had been in before Jack's hand reached out and brought me back to life. The darkness didn't suit him. He was always a sunshine and blue skies kind of person. It hurt to even think for a second that he was trapped somewhere so empty, let alone for years. What had my grandmother's heartbreak, my own heartbreak, done in the long run? What had our selfishness forced my grandfather to go through?

Desperate for an escape from my guilty thoughts and the overwhelming anxiety, I pinched at the soft skin on the underside of my upper arm, hard, until I was sure it would bruise. It helped for a sweet half-second, as my lungs were made to suck in a hard breath and my ears were filled with my own gasp at the pain. I did it again. Then I caught myself and stopped, and the beeping and beating came back.

I heard something else past the sounds in my own head though. Tapping. A light rap on the window, like heavy rain, only I knew the sky was clear today. I twisted and peeked over the bulk of my pillow with one eye to see the source.

The crow, sitting outside my window, tapped on the glass with his beak and watched me with beady black eyes.

He lent me his eyes on occasion, Jack had said. I remembered.

"Go away," I muttered, glaring at the animal. The bird stopped making noise and tilted its head, blinking. If I was crazy, I would say maybe he was pleading.

I growled under my breath. "I said go away." Though my frustration was growing, my words were weaker; I had trouble sounding genuine, because a part of me wasn't.

The bird turned on its feet, looking as if it might finally fly and leave me alone, and my heart shot with pain. He didn't leave though, to my surprise. He settled instead, sitting himself on the sill and nuzzling his head down into his feathers to rest.

I glared, but this time I held my tongue. Instead, I burrowed myself into the blankets and settled as well, pulling the covers over my head so I didn't have to see the damned animal that Jack was using to spy on me.

As annoying as his insistence was, the suffocating loneliness was a little less heavy on my chest as I closed my eyes again to try and rest. Knowing he was watching me just outside the window made me feel a little stronger. I wasn't ready to forgive, because I was terribly stubborn and cowardly, and it would take time for me to walk back after always running away from my problems. He was always willing to wait though.

❧

The crow was not at my window sill when I woke up the next morning, but I found myself wrapped up in Jack's sweater, not remembering putting it on during the night but thankful I had done myself the favor. His smell surrounding me as I came back to reality gave me the strength I needed to take a deep breath and will myself out from under the covers.

I felt a bit like I'd been hit by a car the day before. My body was sore with an after-ache left behind in my chest from the crying and gasping. I could tell my eyes were still puffy; I would have to put a cold cloth on them before going downstairs. I imagined I was probably sporting a nice pair of dark circles along with the puffiness, since my sleep had been riddled with terrible dreams of darkness and pain.

I realized in the night, while my dark thoughts took a familiar spindly shape in my psyche, curling fingers around my wrist and promising to lead me away from the pain forever, that I had simply replaced one love affair with another. Death was courting me long before Jack, and it was a relationship I had almost committed to permanently. I knew it was unhealthy, and yet my addiction was unmanageable. I was weak for the sweet nothingness it offered me. It was my security, my safety, and it was the thing that helped me get through the day. Knowing I had an escape, knowing there was always a way out if I chose… I could always stop trying to live and just give into it.

Coming to Newport, meeting Jack, gave me the chance to recover, to not need the sweet abuse that my dark thoughts offered. Instead though, I was just replacing the strength I got from my unhealthy indulgences with strength I got from Jack's attention. As proven by his absence, my happiness was a superficial emotion, and that darkness still lingered under the surface, just waiting for the moment Jack was no longer around to kiss away my weakness.

Last time Jack was gone though, when I was sure I would never seen him again, I was so close to something positive. I found distractions that, while slightly questionable, made me feel productive and sometimes even hopeful. Seeing the fox, I had felt a strength inside me all my own: perseverance. For a while, I breathed easier than I had in years, my heart lighter in my chest. I almost found something good, and I did that mostly on my own.

I needed to find a way to support myself, to encourage myself; I needed to find the strength inside me that Jack always talked about. My own courage. While I hated to torture Jack with sending him away, perhaps it was for the best. I needed this time to be alone, I needed to start facing my fears, to stop running away like a coward, and I needed to do it by myself.

What better way to start, than getting out of bed on time and going down for breakfast?

I got dressed in cozy clothes and two pairs of socks for extra comfort. I pulled Jack's sweater tighter around me as I left my room. While passing my grandfather, I paused, putting my palm to the door. I peeked in, the anxiety threatening my lungs briefly. I didn't enter the room, but I stood there for a while, just watching my grandfather, lying peaceful.

They show me their pain. He's trapped.

I leaned my forehead against the wood of the door frame, then retreated and let the door close again.

The smell from the kitchen hit me before my family's chatter did. Something was burnt, or burning. I hurried my pace, worried there was a fire, but once I got to the bottom of the stairs, I heard my mother and grandmother laughing.

I entered cautiously, off-put by the unusually pleasant atmosphere in the room. When I showed my face, both women turned and smiled at me.

"Morning, Flower," my grandmother said from over her crossword.

I offered my own smile, but I tried to avoid looking at my mother, save she noticed the bags under my tired eyes and said something unintentionally hurtful.

"Did you sleep alright?" My mother asked, and the question was so simple and innocent that I stared for a moment in surprise.

I took the second to consider my answer. Maybe I could be a little more honest this time, since it was obvious she was making an effort to be less callous. "I was having terrible dreams."

My mother's thin brows came together in concern. "Something bothering you?"

"Yeah. I think it'll be alright now though." I caught her gaze, suddenly not so concerned about her seeing my worn appearance.

She nodded, wordless understanding. "Good to hear."

I took a revitalizing inhale and got the stench of burning again. "So, why does it smell like there's been a bonfire in here?"

My mother and grandmother exchanged glances, then my mother let her head drop in embarrassment.

"Lillian attempted a peace offering breakfast, much like you did your first morning here. She wasn't quite as successful with it as you were." My grandmother's voice was unimpressed, but there was a hint of humor hidden in her tone.

"I tried to make scones, but put the heat too high and burnt them." My mother added, covering a blush on her cheeks.

"The coffee is good though." My grandmother reached out for her mug and brought it to her lips afterwards.

I smirked as I crossed the kitchen towards the pot. "Coffee it is then."

My mother let her head fall into her palms. "I tried…"

To my surprise, a small chuckle escaped me. It was sort of pleasing to see my mother so self-deprecating. "It's alright, Mom. It's the thought that counts."

She offered a smile and a silent thank you with my words. I nodded once over the brim of my mug as I took a sip. It was warm and smooth, and as I felt it defrost the chill in my bones, I couldn't help but think that this cup of coffee and conversation was a promising start to something positive.

XXVIII

I decided to keep my schedule relatively similar to how it had been the last time Jack was away; I got myself up at a decent time, ate breakfast, and left the house bundled up in winter clothes, his sweater underneath. I knew keeping myself busy worked to combat my anxiety last time, so I expected it would help now as well.

While a part of me was hyperaware of the loneliness, I forced myself through it, knowing it was probably best to clear my head for a while. Jack was a wonderful distraction, but distractions were something I had too many of. It was strength I needed, to face the things I was ignoring. Real strength, my own strength, and I would never find that in myself if I was constantly focusing on other, more *appealing* activities.

Jack, completely unaware of my reasoning for keeping him away, most likely still thought I was angry. I guess I was, somewhere in my core, but if I could make room for the idea of forgiving my mother for her mistakes and misdeeds, forgiving Jack would be incredibly easy when it was time.

I could tell he was desperate to make amends though. I often caught that damned crow, perched on tree branches and circling the sky, keeping an eye on me. He tried to be sneaky about his stalking, but I was sure he was oblivious to just how aware I was of his presence. He was waiting to hear the words, waiting for my permission to return, but he would stay away as long as I gave no sign of wanting him back.

That was easier said than done, because even though I knew it was for the best at the moment, I found myself missing him terribly. Every time that crow settled nearby, ruffling his feathers all humble and charming, I had to resist giving in and whispering his name to call him back. I told myself that this wordless companionship was all I got to enjoy for now, at least until I learned how to not fall apart without him holding me together.

I went to the garden, always drawn there for all the memories involved. I was curious recently, about the flowers that were there weeks before. They were under the snow now, and I was pretty sure even Jack's power could not keep the flowers alive when they were smothered, but I couldn't help but check it out.

The crow was there before I was, cawing at me as I approached the gate. I gave him a pointed look, but besides that, I ignored his presence. Even though having him there, knowing those black beady eyes could be showing Jack what they were seeing, was far more comforting than I was willing to admit to myself.

I confirmed my own suspicion once inside the garden. Digging up the snow showed a bunch of very dead violets buried underneath. While I wasn't necessarily disappointed, I did feel sad that the magic of that night was confirmed as just a memory now. As I sighed, I heard the crow take off into the sky, with intention it seemed, although as quickly as the thought crossed my mind, I was distracted.

The gate opened, and I'd be lying if my heart hadn't stopped for a moment in anticipation, only to continue at a hard beat when it was my mother who entered.

"There you are. I was hoping I'd catch you in here one of these days. You always did love your grandmother's garden."

I offered a smile, though it was weak. I was still slightly wary of her attempts at making nice with me. Even though she seemed to have humbled a lot in the past days, my heart had trouble trusting.

"I was just checking to see if it was spring yet," I joked instead to cover my discomfort, and she accepted the sentiment with a little laugh.

"Not quite. Newport winters are pretty persistent. Although, you haven't really seemed to be minding all that much recently. You've been spending a lot of time out with that boy. Jake?"

I cringed at her mistake. "Jack. And I've decided to take some time to myself."

She frowned. "Did you two break up?"

Those words were strange coming out of her mouth. To know she even considered us "going out" was very awkward, and I found myself blushing. "Not exactly. I guess I just thought that I needed some time to think some things through."

My mother hummed, nodding. "I can relate with that sentiment. Even though my recent 'time alone' hasn't exactly been voluntary. Self-reflection is healthy, even if it's not always wanted."

I was surprised with how comforting hearing her say that was. Acknowledging the fact that she was purposely making the changes I was noticing. It bloomed a tiny bit of hope in my heart.

We sat together in silence, both of us unsure of what to say, and yet it was slightly less awkward than previous occasions. Finally, my mother offered words. "I used to come here all the time when I was your age too."

I blinked. "Really?"

She nodded. "I loved the flowers. I named you after my favorite."

A smile hit my lips without my permission. "I didn't know that's why you named me Violet."

She nodded again, this time her expression going a little somber. "That's probably my fault. There are a lot of things you don't know, because I wasn't around to tell you." Another admission that surprised me. I found no signs of victimhood or fishing for sympathy in her voice either. Just sincere regret.

I remembered one of my last conversations with Jack, about my mother, about the secrets she had never bothered to tell me, and I never bothered to ask about. This seemed like as good a time as any.

"Mom?" When she turned to me, her eyes were curious. I paused to muster the courage. "That last summer I was in Newport, before you wouldn't let me back. What happened? I know you couldn't possibly have wanted to hurt me…" I hoped, at least.

She frowned, the question paining her, or perhaps the answer did. She paused as well, also needing to find some bravery, maybe. "Your grandfather didn't want you to know about it…" she started, as if perhaps she could get me to change my mind about wanting to know, but she continued when I gave no objection. "That summer, your grandmother and I had a pretty bad falling out. I was with someone who wasn't good for me. Your grandmother was just trying to help, but I didn't want it. So when we failed at coming to a compromise, your grandmother threatened to go to court to get custody of you."

I stared, stunned by this information. I tried at words, but they never really came.

My mother added to hers, to ease my shock a little. "It never happened. Your grandfather talked her out of it, which was most likely one of the reasons why you never heard about it. But not before I got wind of her idea. I got angry. Spiteful. Old feelings surfaced, and I lashed out and hurt her the way I knew would be most effective: I took you away."

To hear my mother admit so regretfully to her self-serving behavior was the only comfort offered from her words. The rest was all troubling. I reminded myself, that we were both guilty of making terrible mistakes, and that forgiveness took strength and courage, two things I was trying desperately to find at the moment, but I just wanted to be a coward and be spiteful like she had chosen to be. I wanted to lash out, to hurt her in some way, like she had chosen to hurt my grandmother, and me.

I realized though, that I was not helping myself by copying my mother's way of dealing with problems. Her sitting in front of me, with tears in her eyes and a broken heart, was the example of exactly why I shouldn't lose myself to my own petty emotions. So instead of saying something nasty, I didn't say anything at all.

She sighed, dropping her head a little. "I'm sorry, Violet. I'm coming to realize that a lot of my choices have been terrible ones. I'm coming to realize that I might be to blame, for a lot of things. A lot of terrible things that have happened, to both of us. I'm beginning to regret a lot."

I swallowed down the knot that rose in my throat, closing my eyes to keep my breathing level. I wanted to be angry, to be the weak me, but I wouldn't let myself cave to my negativity this time. I was better than that. I recognized that my mother was trying here, she was laying herself bare, and that this was a chance at positivity in our mostly toxic relationship. I wouldn't be the one to ruin it.

I kept my mouth shut again.

She surrendered. "I understand if you have nothing to say. You've said more than enough before, when I refused to listen. I'll let you alone. Don't stay out too long, you'll catch a cold."

I watched her stand, nodding when she gave a last glance at me.

It was for the best, to let me have a moment to clear my head of the growling frustration inside me. I couldn't think straight about any of it with her there.

Before she left, she turned back to call to me for an additional thought. "I found your book in the den last night. The leather one."

Panic. "Did you read it?" I tried to keep myself calm, but I could tell my back straightened in reaction to her mention of my journal.

She shook her head though. "I put it up in your room. That's all. I just wanted you to know, in case you were looking for it." She smiled, then closed the gate and left me alone.

I breathed a sigh of relief when she was out of earshot. It took me a second to realize that not reading my journal was the first sign of respect she'd given me in ages. It caused a pain in my chest; she was giving me privacy, even when she shouldn't be.

Tears; they escaped my eyes without permission as the guilt stung and stabbed at my heart. How weak was I, falling apart the moment some ghosts from the past showed themselves? My anxiety poked hard at my ribs, trying to get me to cave, to run, to scream, to break. It ridiculed me, my idea that I would find some inner strength and get over this. I was too broken to fix myself now. I should just accept it. It was so much easier to give up.

Above, I heard the crow again, landing on top of the gate. I swiped hard at my tears and glared at the animal. "Why can't you just leave me alone?" My words were barely a whisper though, because I wanted the opposite really. I wanted the person behind those beady eyes to save me from this pain.

He would. I knew it. All I'd have to do is say the words, and he'd be there to make this ache in my chest go away. In a heartbeat. That was the thing though. I'd never get over any of this if I kept running and hiding from it. No matter how badly he would try, no one could truly save me from myself. I would have to do that on my own.

I bit my lip to keep myself from calling his name, watching the black bird as he hopped a step closer to me and then dropped something he held in his beak. As quickly as the item fell into the snow, he'd opened his wings again and flown away.

I mopped up my tears again and rose to my feet to get a closer look. I didn't believe my own perception at first, and had to cross the garden and pick up the object before I acknowledged what it was. A violet, vibrant and purple and full of life.

I sighed, a smile reaching my lips through the tears as I twirled the small flower it in my fingers.

"You're impossible," I whispered, to myself, or someone else maybe.

XXIX

The days became more difficult. My mother and grandmother were beginning to mend their relationship, and it started to feel like I was the one left behind in terms of emotional healing. A lot of forgiving was happening, but for some reason, I was still holding onto resentments I couldn't shake.

What I really wanted was simply to talk to someone, but I had isolated myself, and now I didn't know how to reach out again. Those dark thoughts had their claws in deep, tearing through my soul when I tried to pull myself away, so I stopped trying. My mother wanted desperately for me to open up to her but I just wasn't ready to be so vulnerable, and I had grown prickly with my grandmother since finding out that she was the one to threaten court intervention first. While the two women were finding the strength to set aside all their mistakes, I was holding onto more and more reasons to be upset.

Of course, there was one person I wanted to talk to, but he was off limits for now, a decision that I was determined to stick with even though I was proving weaker than I thought myself to be.

Without Jack's gentle encouragement, my darkness crept up on me. Late at night, when all I could focus on was the beeping, I fell victim to the darkness' terrible suggestions. The anger was better anyway. Holding onto grudges would make it hurt less when the time came.

Every now and then the emotions became too much. They scared me sometimes, and I considered falling apart to whichever woman I saw next. I would go out walking all day, until my feet were sore and calloused, to combat the weakness in my resolve. Or perhaps it was strength to fight my negativity.

That was the biggest problem, things were beginning to get fuzzy again. My walks became a bit like I was escaping, running away, but there was nothing triggering me beside the chance that I might have to actually face all the painful emotions I was smothering with anger and resentment. There was something dark and heavy in my gut, and I was scared of it coming up. I wasn't sure I could handle it, especially on my own. Not yet.

The problem was, nothing I was doing was helping me find my strength. My proactivity was waning, and instead of adding more things to my plate to keep myself busy, I was just shying away from the world. I should have been trying to speak to my mother more, trying to empathize with her like I'd started to do. I should have been speaking to my grandmother about what my mother had recently told me, to understand her side of the story.

I should have been trying to speak to my grandfather; it was going unmentioned, but I knew the day he would be taken off life support was approaching. I was pretending I didn't know though. I couldn't handle the idea of him being taken from me when I wasn't ready. Not again.

I was feeling like a ghost once more. I was floating around this world, full of living, breathing people, but I couldn't quite reach their vibrancy. It felt like I was at the other end of a very long tunnel, distant, unable to reach out and interact, no matter how badly I tried.

What was a ghost to do when she was surrounded by life?

It was this question that brought me to my grandfather's door. If I was not quite alive but also not quite dead, then perhaps he and I had the most in common out of everyone.

I opened the door, quickly this time, ripping off the bandaid. I thought maybe it would dull the pain, but it didn't work. The sight of his corpse-like body froze the air in my lungs. I turned and closed the door again.

"Coward," I scolded under my breath. I took a moment to compose myself, then looked around, hoping for a solution to present itself. It did, as I glanced to the wall and found a picture hung there, a slightly fuzzy shot of my grandfather's laughing face.

I remembered the photo. It was one I took, of many, when I had been playing with my grandmother's film camera a long time ago. I burned through three rolls, and most of them were pictures of nothing at all. My grandmother had gotten angry, because the film was expensive, but my grandfather told her to let me have my fun.

I took the picture off the wall and brought it with me. This time, when I opened the door and saw him there lying motionless in the bed, I held up the photograph in his place. Something deep in my chest uncoiled, allowing me enough air to keep from drowning in my anxiety.

I pulled down the sleeve of Jack's sweater over my palm and stuck the fabric to my lips, smelling it to get a hit of his wonderfully calming scent, becoming a tiny bit more relaxed. My limbs thawed just enough that I could take a step into the room.

My grandfather couldn't give me any answers, but I wasn't sure I was even looking for them. I was just looking for ears to listen to the emotions I was too scared to share with anyone else. So I kept my eyes glued on the photograph of his smiling face as I crossed the room to sit in the chair next to the bed.

I sat there silently for a very long while. So long, time disappeared, and I got an idea of what life was like for Jack. The world and its seconds and minutes and hours didn't exist, just me and the trapped soul I sat beside.

Somewhere in my disappearing sense of time, I found words. They started flowing from my mouth like they had been waiting to escape my lips for ages.

"I've been gone for a really long time, Grampie. Most of the time wasn't my fault, but these last few days have definitely been my own choice. I should have come in here a long time ago, but something kept scaring me off. I guess maybe I thought, that if I just refused for long enough, then I could keep you here forever and it would all be ok, but I'm realizing that time doesn't stop just because you want it to."

I swallowed down something hard in my throat, blinking back tears as I continued.

"You should see what's happening right now. I bet you, after all the bad blood... You thought you'd never see your daughter and wife getting along again. They are almost there though. I guess I imagine that's why you talked Nan out of taking Mom to court over custody of me. If she had went through with that, it probably would have killed any chance for them to make amends. You were always looking out for the family, even though we were never really looking out for each other."

I paused again, to catch my breath, lowering my words to a whisper to get them past my breaking voice. "I know Jack said you're suffering... And I've been thinking about that a lot lately. Actually, it kind of keeps me up at night. I hope it's not like how I imagine it, because I keep dreaming of you in pain... I don't even know if you can really hear me right now, but if you can, I'm sorry it's taken so long for us to let you go. But I think you'd appreciate the fact that you've actually managed to bring us all back together even while in a coma. You would have liked that. I hope you can forgive us for keeping you around a little longer, while we sort out the last few things. I think it's mostly me that needs more time.

"You see... I never really wanted to leave Newport that day. I never got to say goodbye to you, and then the accident happened and... The aftermath kinda almost killed me. There were some other things there too, but I always felt like I never got to say goodbye to you. Because of that, I've also been too scared to actually say goodbye now that I have the chance."

It was these words that finally set me off for good. Feeling and knowing it was one thing, but once the thought slipped from my lips, I felt the emotion flood out of my heart like a heavy wave, crashing rough against my ribs and lungs. I leaned down and rested my forehead on the bed, keeping my eyes on my grandfather's picture but reaching out to take his lifeless hand.

"I wish I wasn't so weak, Grampie. All I want is to feel better, but sometimes it's like it would be so much easier to just give up. Actually, that's a thought I have a lot. All the time. And it was kind of comforting at first, but now it's starting to scare me. I don't want to give up, especially not now, when I know you've suffered all this time for us. I don't know if I have it in me to fight anymore though. You can probably understand that, after being trapped here all this time. I'm suffering, little by little, and the pain doesn't seem to want to go away. Sometimes I can barely feel anything, but other times, all the hurt just consumes me. I don't know what to do..."

The sheets soaked up my tears as they escaped down my cheeks. My chest hurt so badly, it felt like I would burst. It was so quiet. Just

the beeps of his electronic heart, counting away the seconds passing. The worst part was, I knew he'd have the perfect response, if
he could answer. That was the problem with being a ghost though:
we couldn't reach out, even to each other.

Despite the fact that the weight of absolutely everything was
pushing me down, so hard I felt like I would fall right through the
floor into oblivion, I held onto the one thing that gave me a little bit
of hope.

I talked to him. I talked to my grandfather, after all this time.

I'd fallen asleep with my hand gripped around my grandfather's,
and I woke hours later, slow and drowsy and not entirely sure
where I was. The confusion lingered just long enough to be
pleasant for a moment, lost in the unknown of time and space and
who I even was. The stale air and the bitter fragrance of my grandfather's sterile sheet assaulted my senses soon enough though, and
the anxiety had me on my feet and out of the room in seconds.

My heart ached, because it felt wonderful to not know who or
where I was, even just briefly. A blissful forgetfulness. I wondered
if dying would be similar, like a vivid dream that faded away as
your consciousness returned, only it was the images of your life
that faded as you woke to the consciousness of whatever came
after. Would I forget all the pain as I died? Would everything stop
hurting so much? It had before, after all, out there in the golden
fields of my subconscious, with Jack brushing my hair behind
my ear.

My mother and grandmother walked in through the front door
after I exited my grandfather's room. There was a somber mood to
the air around them, and I wondered if they had gotten into an
argument. They'd been making nice with each other over the last

few days, so I couldn't tell if bad blood was overdue, or if the trivialness of an argument was in the past now.

"Violet. You're here." My mother offered a smile, but there was something underneath, an emotion I couldn't place. She had done such a good job at hiding her emotions under a frigid exterior over the years that I found myself having a hard time reading these new expressions.

I offered a nod and forced something resembling my own smile, then turned with the intention to retreat to my room, as per usual every time the two women were in the house with me. I just couldn't stand trying to connect with them. It took so much energy when I was always exhausted, and I still felt like I was just pulling further and further away.

"Wait, Flower."

It was my grandmother who called me this time, and I stopped my retreat to meet their gazes again. A part of me silently begged them to let me go, so I could be alone with my dark thoughts, because at least its abuse was familiar. Another part of me hoped they would finally force me to take part in a dialogue; I had been too quiet lately, and they must have noticed.

"Come to the den with us? We'd like to discuss some things with you." Coming from my mother, those were scary words.

I remembered her sitting me down after being released from the hospital. How she told me that my behavior was really putting a burden on her, that she was going to bring me to Newport, leave me there so she could tend to herself when I needed her to care for me the most. Sometimes I wondered why it was so difficult for me to forgive her, when she was obviously trying to make up for her behavior. Every now and then though, I was reminded of the moments I tried so hard to forget, the pain she had caused with the smallest of inactions.

Since my mother had shown up, and since I banished Jack, I was thinking a lot about that first attempt at taking my life. How I was too cowardly to cut the other wrist and make it go faster. How I hadn't even locked the bathroom door. I wondered if I was even serious at all about dying, or if maybe I just wanted to prove to myself I was still alive, prove there was blood in my veins and air in my lungs and things could still hurt this body I often felt disconnected from. It was only after brushing shoulders with Death and waking to return to my painful existence, only after being abandoned again, that I became addicted to the idea of finding that sweet nothingness I almost embraced during my dream in the hospital.

I didn't hold my mother responsible for the series of events that led to my obsession, but the part she played in the tragedy made it difficult for me to forget the scars I was left with.

Let alone forgive.

Apprehensively, I followed the women into the den and sat myself down in my grandmother's comfy armchair. Something heavy lingered in the air, and I pulled the sleeve of Jack's sweater to my palm to take another hit of his scent, hoping it would loosen the knots tied in my stomach.

The women sat together on the couch by me, exchanging a couple of glances with each other, both of them unsure how to start. My grandmother offered words first. "Your mother told me about your talk in the garden the other day."

I didn't speak, giving only a blink to acknowledge that I followed.

My grandmother nodded, then looked down at her hands. "I understand it's why you've been distant with me the past week, and I don't blame you. I just wanted to offer a few details about how I had come to the idea, so maybe you can more clearly see where I had been coming from, and forgive me like your mother has."

I blinked again, waiting.

She stopped, but kept talking when she realized I wasn't offering anything further.

"Your mother dropped you off to me earlier than she usually did that particular summer. Obviously, for a while, the two of us have not been on great terms, but I always took you in when she needed me to. This summer something seemed different though. I was beginning to grow concerned about the situation. It was obvious that motherhood was difficult for Lillian, and it was taking its toll on her, and you were beginning to get to the age where it was harder to explain away your mother's absence. It was becoming obvious that the situation was not healthy for either of you. When I tried to contact your mother that summer, to try to talk to her about these issues I had, she was never available to speak. Her flippant disregard of my concerns made me even more worried, and in a moment of frustration, I threatened to file for custody.

"Your grandfather talked me down and convinced me of why I didn't want this for the family. I loved your mother, so I didn't want to take you from her, and ruin our relationship. That spitefulness was not productive. Unfortunately, I had already made the threat, your mother took it seriously, and she came to get you without discussion. And as you know, since then our communication has been limited… So there has never really been time to hash out our emotions."

My mother added some words when I offered no reply again. "These past few weeks, your grandmother and I have had some time to talk things over and come to a bit more of an understanding. Regarding the things that have happened, things that were said, and our feelings regarding your grandfather."

I had to say something this time. I couldn't keep holding my tongue without seeming difficult now. "I know you guys have been getting along better. It means a lot to me. I'm also not angry at either of you for what's happened, but I think I need some time to come to terms with everything."

I tried to be as diplomatic as possible, without diving too deeply into my actual emotions. I wasn't angry, and I did understand, but I still couldn't allow myself to let go of the pain left in my heart in the wake of their actions.

They both smiled, looking very much like mother and daughter for a moment. Relief rose in each of their faces, but concern still lingered. It was my mother who spoke again.

"We didn't want to force you to talk to us, considering the circumstances. Since we're so centrally involved in whatever emotions you're feeling, we were worried about forcing you into a conversation you weren't ready to have yet. So we've been trying to give you some space, but these last few days we've been concerned."

"Your mother told me that Jack and you have broken up." My grandmother interjected with a pained expression in her gaze.

I resisted rolling my eyes. "We didn't break up... I just needed some time to think, and I felt like he was just distracting me..."

My mother nodded. "Well, whatever is happening... We just don't like to see you isolating yourself like this. This boy, whatever he was to you, he was obviously at least a friend. And we both feel like perhaps you need a friend right now."

I scowled. "I don't need anyone. I can handle things on my own. I'm not a baby." Maybe if I said it aloud, it would be true.

My grandmother frowned. "There's nothing wrong with having someone around, to help you, to talk to. Sometimes you can get lost in your own thoughts and need someone else to help walk you through them. We feel like maybe it's important that you have someone, someone else besides us, to talk to. Especially right now."

I kept my mouth shut, not wanting to admit how scarily accurate my grandmother's sentiment likely was. Jack had a particular talent for leading people to places they were scared to go. When I didn't say anything, the two women exchanged a glance, disappointed but obviously not willing to start an argument.

My mother inhaled, letting out a sigh but admitting defeat to my stubbornness. "Alright. Violet, your grandmother and I have come to a decision regarding your grandfather. It wasn't just a decision we made lightly. We had a lot of conversations that we had been avoiding for a long time, and we worked out a lot of feelings that we both had about the situation. We also spoke to a lawyer about it and came to an agreement, which brought me to dropping the idea of going to court over it. We decided it was unnecessary when we were both in agreement." She stopped, reading my face, and I tried to keep it blank even though I could feel my throat tightening up as she spoke.

I knew what was coming. It took everything to stay seated in the chair and not run out into the snow in my bare feet and disappear.

"We simply don't have the means to keep your grandfather on life support anymore, and your grandmother has agreed that it feels unfair to your grandfather to hold onto him like this. He was not the type of person to want to be kept in a bed like this... We both feel like it's important and necessary for us to finally let him go. It's the best time, we think, when the three of us can be here for each other."

I didn't breathe, didn't move my face, didn't react at all. If I allowed myself, it would all be over. My composure would crack. I bit my tongue and kept a death grip on the numbness. Just for a little longer.

"Do you understand what this means, Violet?" my mother asked cautiously, clearly put off by my lack of emotion.

I gave a curt nod, but nothing more.

My mother and grandmother exchanged looks again. I imagined they expected a more dramatic reaction from me. I couldn't let them see that though. I couldn't let them see me fall apart. They didn't know how to pick up the pieces. They would bloody their hands trying to put me back together, and I couldn't stand the idea of being the painful thorn in their otherwise flourishing reunion.

"Do you have any questions, Flower?"

My grandmother was concerned, urging me with her eyes to let go of whatever it was I was holding back. They wanted to help, but I didn't want it. No, I couldn't take it. It would hurt too much. It was so much easier to disappear and let the dark thoughts consume me.

I shook my head, offering the first words in a while. "I just want to go for a walk. If that's OK?" I managed a level, even tone.

They looked unsure of how to react to that question. It didn't matter, because I was already up and leaving.

I left calmly, taking slow, careful steps away from the estate. My breath was shallow and barely there, but I didn't want to let go of my facade just yet, not when the women could be watching me leave through a window. I walked all the way out to the treeline, then weaved myself through a maze of trunks and roots, until I couldn't see the house anymore, until the forest and silence were the only things surrounding me. So quiet, the only sound was the increasing heavy pound of my heart, reminding me.

A-live. A-live. A-live.

There were tears in my eyes before I realized, dripping down and chilling my cheeks as the cold air got to them. In the haunting silence around me, my heart pumped louder and louder in my skull and the little air I sucked into my lungs sounded like a hurricane inside. So loud, my existence in this space. How could a ghost be so disruptive? So solid and real?

How painful it was, to be alive.

I screamed into the endless nothing, because there were no words for the tearing fissure in my heart, no expression for how it felt to shatter inside while my body kept its shape. I stopped only when my lungs gave out and forced me to inhale a deep, cold breath. My head spun. My voice echoed off the spindly fingers of the naked trees around me, disappearing into the deep, consuming gray of the sky above.

I looked at my feet, feeling the throbbing pain in my chest, my heart pounding violently, protesting, wanting to escape this painful prison it was trapped inside. What had it even done, to deserve this torturous fate? Nothing but a good, faithful heart that kept pounding no matter how badly I beat and bruised it.

Then I realized, that no matter what happened, no matter how far down in the blackness of my own thoughts I fell, my heart would be faithful to me. It kept drumming out the beat of my existence, kept reminding me of my solidness. As weak as I was, the strength I had was right there, in the always surviving muscle in my chest. I could get through it, as long as I followed its lead. Even if I curled up into myself and cried until I couldn't anymore, and the pain made me want to scream out into the world for no one to hear, my heart would keep slamming against my ribs and pushing me forward through time, one beat at a time.

I could do it. I could survive this, if I wanted. My heart would fight for me, even if I wouldn't.

With the thought, it was like suddenly the mysterious language of my own pulse unveiled itself and I knew exactly what the beat was saying. I could do this alone, but I didn't want to. I closed my eyes and whispered on a sigh what my heart had been screaming for.

"Jack."

My body was a burden and my legs were too weak to hold up everything resting on my shoulders. My heavy head was too full of darkness to stay upright. As my knees gave, I was caught around the waist, and instead of collapsing, I found myself engulfed in an unmistakable warmth.

I didn't need to open my eyes. My face buried in his collar instinctively, that smell, like the woods and the sea and everything my heart yearned for, filled my lungs and rid me of the infectious blackness in my skull. His lips caressed my temple, banishing the breathlessness.

"I'm here, Violet."

XXX

As the sun was beginning to set, Jack took my hand and slowly led me home. I was drained of energy, my head pounding from the sobs, but I had no strength left to cry over the physical or emotional pain anymore. My body reduced itself to minimal functions, all to keep my heart beating through the torture.

So I followed without fuss as he pulled me along, my hand in his grip, his eyes watching behind him every so often to make sure I wasn't falling apart. He didn't have to worry though. As much as it all hurt, I knew my heart was stronger than ever, with his fingers tangled in mine.

I opened the front door to the estate and my grandmother and mother erupted from the kitchen within a second. I didn't blame them for waiting on me, with my track record of disappearing.

I wanted to smile, to banish the concern on their faces, but my body wouldn't allow such effort for a simple facade. I was broken and running on fumes and I couldn't hide it any longer. Their worry managed to fade a little when I brought Jack into the house behind me. They must have known that at least with his return, I had someone watching out for me.

No one said anything as we took our shoes and jackets off, and I turned to take Jack's hand again to lead him up to my room with very little acknowledgement to the women watching us. I wasn't even thinking about what they thought or if they had objections. I needed to curl up in his arms and regenerate myself. I needed his morphine kisses on my forehead to stitch up the tears my self-abuse had left on my soul. There would be no argument about it.

"Violet." My mother called after me when I was halfway up the stairs, Jack in tow. He put his eyes to the floor, but I turned to look at her over my shoulder, trying to muster a look that dared her to object to him being there.

She read my gaze and shook her head. "There's dinner, in the fridge, if you get hungry. Let me know, if you'd like some water or, anything."

I blinked, as much of a thank you as I could offer, then turned and continued to my room.

The night had already begun to creep into my room, full of shadows and cool blue, with a hint of summer my bedside violet gave off. I closed the door behind us, and the muscles that kept me walking all the way back to the estate finally gave. I leaned back against the threshold, the idea of making it to the bed unbearable.

Jack gave my hand a gentle tug, but I resisted, bringing him to me instead. As he neared, I closed my eyes, and his hands were around my face, his forehead finding mine.

"Why did you keep me away for so long?" he whispered, his breath touching my lips.

I sighed, guilty. "I was scared."

"Of me?"

"No." I shook my head, my nose nudging his. "I was scared I was just using you, to distract myself from a pain I refused to face. I was scared that if I lost you, I'd just fall apart again." Which is exactly what happened.

"Violet…"

"I'm weak without you," I whispered, reaching out to grip around his sweater, a strain coming to my voice with my frustration.

It was his turn to shake his head, a sigh escaping. "That's not true. When I first met you, you had already given up. I could tell. I saw that same look on your face that I felt all the time. That disconnection, feeling like a ghost. And you weren't looking for help, you had accepted it.

"Now though, with everything that happened, you still tried to fight, and when it started hurting too much, you reached out for help. You're strong, Violet. You're just wounded. A flower smothered by the winter snow seems defeated as well, but it always blooms again, bigger and stronger than before."

I let out a breath, as close to a scoff as I could manage. "I'm not a flower, Jack."

"No, you're not just a flower. Or a star. Or a ghost. You're a soul. A living and breathing and hurting soul and yet still the most beautiful one I've ever come across."

He caused a knot in my throat as my eyes found a few extra tears that they hadn't shed earlier. My chest ached. "I want to believe I'm strong, that I can come back from this, but I don't know how. I don't know how to let him go. I don't know how to let myself live. I don't know how to be OK with this. I can't think straight anymore. Everything is dark…"

His thumbs swiped at the wetness as it escaped down my cheek. "Let me help… I want to help…"

In a clear, immediate reply, my heart threw itself at my ribs towards him, pushing me forward that last fraction of an inch, my lips finding his for a brief moment. It was easier to kiss him than face the inevitable words that should follow his offer. He wanted to help, while he still could, before it was too late and our affair would come to the tragic end it was destined for.

I should have continued my isolation. I knew it would hurt less in the long run, when my birthday came and I chose to take the painless escape that I had been planning since arriving. It was easier if I started severing my ties early. I was too wounded to fight off his barrage on my defenses though. If this would end in ruins eventually, what was the harm in letting him try to make it better? Even if he couldn't, even if he really was just a sweet distraction to the pain that would eventually consume me again, at least my last few weeks could be a wonderful delusion with him, and then I could leave it all.

Jack would keep the pain at bay, and Death would take the pain away.

I hated how truly comforting that was.

He let me drag him to the bed, where I buried myself under the covers and into his arms, wrapping my limbs around him so tight that I wondered where my newfound strength came from. It was resolve, to never let myself banish him away again. If it was possible, I'd etch into my memory his smell and the beat of his heart. This moment, in his arms where nothing could touch me, not even my own darkness.

Secrets came out in between the steady rhythm of our own inhales and exhales, my face in his sweater and his lips in my hair.

"I was scared too." His voice carried through the still air.

I held my breath, to hear his next whisper.

"I was scared that the next time I'd see you would be to help you let go."

Instinctively, I wrapped myself further around him, showing him I was still solid, still very much alive despite myself, despite often feeling like I was fading between existence and abstraction.

He shifted, moved his hands to guide my face up, and leaned in to me. I felt the concern written between his brows as he put his forehead to mine again. "I'm the most selfish Death there is."

"Why?" I asked to his lips.

He sighed. "I want so badly for you to change your mind… I want so badly to see you choose to live. It's a forever consuming thought for me. I've been around to help so many people move on, to take the pain and the fear of dying away, but I can't bear that thought with you. How terrible it would be, to have to help you disappear.

"So I've gone out of my way to show you the precious things about life, hoping I could make you see past whatever evil has its grip on you and realize the beautiful things you would be giving up, the things about life that I couldn't quite touch anymore, that I longed for.

"I fear that, while my intention was to keep my distance, my selfishness got the better of me. And when trying to show you what there was to live for, I became tangled up in life as well. I tried not to get too close, but I was weak for you. You make me feel this shadow of what it's like to be alive again. I know you have trouble feeling it, but you are so full of life, and you have no idea how addictive it is. I would be foolish, not to fight to help you keep that.

"But for you to accept life again would mean choosing to live without me. To force you to make that decision… After everything I've done, after I've stolen your heart from you. I'm cruel to you."

I shook my head. "You couldn't be cruel even if you tried." I felt his smile against my own lips from his closeness, a grin that stretched across his face despite himself. I kissed it, garnering a sigh when we parted. I offered an afterthought. "And don't give yourself so much credit. You didn't steal my heart. I handed it over willingly. You take better care of it than I do."

He gave a breathy laugh. "Maybe I can teach you how to handle it with a little more care."

I hummed. That sounded nice. "Maybe."

❧

I woke to that familiar feeling of being in a train wreck, my body exhausted, aching with the agony I had put it through the night before. It wasn't so terrible though, because instead of having to force myself out from under the warm covers, alone with a chill in my bones and darkness gripping my heart, I was able to pull myself closer to the lanky boy in my bed, wrap up in his tree-branch limbs, and let his smell thaw out my frozen soul.

When I snuggled closer to his body, I heard him sigh through his sleep, his arms instinctively tightening around my waist as he buried his face into my neck. I actually felt a smile tug at the corner of my lips, tangling a hand in his hair to hold him to me.

As I stroked my fingers through his fringe, he woke as well, his eyelashes sweeping over the skin just under my ear, giving me barely there kisses on my collarbone. He spoke between each one. "The things I would give, to stop time right here, even just for a second. I feel so alive right now. To know how fleeting this moment is, it hurts in the most beautiful way."

"You're saying that pain is beautiful?"

I felt him smile on my skin. "Life is beautiful, and life is full of terrible lows and amazing highs. Pain, and pleasure." With the last word he lifted his head a little and trailed his lips up along my neck to kiss a tender spot on my throat, and he grinned wider when goosebumps jumped up over my arm.

I couldn't quite shake the lingering sadness, despite how badly I wanted to. "I wish I could see it like you do. When I think about life, when I think about waking up to all this hurt all the time, it feels more like any pleasure I have is just a distraction from the pain."

Jack frowned a little, and I felt the downturn against my skin. "But how would you know it's painful if you hadn't first experienced something pleasant?"

His contradictions made me smirk. He was always good at making me see the things my darkness blinded me to. "I guess I hadn't thought of it like that. After so long, it becomes hard to remember when the happiness faded to sadness. It becomes even harder to remember the moments of happiness within the sadness."

He hummed in understanding, the sound vibrating in my collarbone, then he lifted himself from my neck to catch my gaze. His eyes were bright and silver today, shining in the morning lowlights. "Are you happy right now, at least?" he asked, nudging his nose against mine to encourage an answer.

I let out a tiny laugh, then hummed, delaying my reply. I took a second to tease his mouth with mine, close, but never actually kissing, and when I retreated, laying back onto the mattress, he lifted himself over me to follow the taunt I'd made.

He playfully glared at my stalling, and I giggled again, giving in. "Maybe I'm a little happy right now."

He leaned a little closer. "Good," he said against my lips as he took them finally in a slow, deliberate kiss that left me warm and foggy in the head.

Despite having more than enough time to enjoy the kiss, it still felt like too soon when he pulled away, and I had to hold back a frustrated growl.

His eyes roamed to the violet on my bedside. "You keep forgetting to take care of it," he scolded, although his tone was closer to playful as he reached over me and slid the soft petals of the flower between his thumb and index finger. With his touch, the flower's sad appearance brightened a little, its drooping petals perking up.

"I shouldn't be in charge of taking care of another living thing. I can barely manage my own needs most of the time," I commented, a self-deprecating laugh escaping. It was obvious I didn't find much humor in the statement though, and the chuckle was out of nervous habit.

He shook his head, returning to me, resting his forehead to mine so I got full view of his eyes and the sincerity in them. "You're doing fine." After his reassurance, his gaze moved down, and he lifted the hand he'd touched the flower with, grazing his thumb gently over my lower lip. "I wish your pain was as simple to fix. Just a touch."

I exhaled a shallow breath, closing my eyes, unable to stand his torturously sweet attention. "You'd be surprised how effective your touch is sometimes," I whispered.

I hadn't said the words with the intention of them being suggestive, but he seemed OK interpreting them that way. "Really?" His thumb glided across my cheek. "In that case…"

Just as he was about to kiss me again, a knock sounded from the door, and I let out a groan under my breath that made him fall into fit of silent laughter. In retaliation for enjoying my annoyance, I crawled over him on my way to open the door, straddling his torso for an extended moment before standing. He went red, a bit from the laughing and a bit from my teasing, and grabbed a pillow to hide under.

It was my grandmother at the door, and the first thing she did, before even looking at me, was try to peer into the room. I opened the door a little further, so she could confirm that we were both still fully dressed and nothing funny was happening, then raised an eyebrow to ask if she was satisfied.

She grinned and said, "There's pancakes." Then nodded her head towards the stairs.

"I think we're fi—"

"Would you like some pancakes, Jack?" My grandmother ignored me and peeked into the room.

I was about to protest again, when Jack bounded up behind me with excitement. "Sure, Mrs. Holt, I'd love some pancakes."

I glared over my shoulder at him, and his smile went cheeky.

My grandmother clapped her hands together with pleasure, turning to head back downstairs. As Jack moved to follow her, I grabbed his arm and pulled him back, the playful irritation still stuck in my eyes.

"I was trying save you, but if you don't want help, then it's your funeral," I commented.

He laughed. "I hardly think breakfast with your family will be a death sentence."

I raised an eyebrow, but chose to hold my tongue, knowing the situation would speak for itself.

XXXI

There was an awkward air in the kitchen when we entered. As usual though, Jack was completely unaware of the mood of the room, instantly going to my grandmother's side to grab a pancake for himself. I wandered over to my mother instead, preparing myself a cup of tea.

I could feel her watching me over the brim of her coffee, and after a moment, I sighed and begged under my breath to her, "Don't be mean to him, please?"

I remembered the things she spewed before, taking her past personal frustrations and placing them on him so she had an excuse to be suspicious. Jack was so sweet; I didn't know how he would handle her sharpness if she wanted to pull it out on him.

Next to me, my mother raised an eyebrow and smiled teasingly. "Me? I'd never."

I hadn't thought this through far enough. I brought a boy into my room, twice, without permission. The old version of my mother would have punished me with verbal abuse and emotional manipulation, but this woman might just torture me with excruciating humiliation instead. This wasn't going to be a tense interrogation, but rather simply, what could she do to embarrass her daughter the most? I was sure the color dropped from my face at this realization.

Jack sat down with his pancakes, blissfully ignorant to what was about to happen. I, on the other hand, shifted from pale to red.

"So, *Jack.*"

Here we go.

He lifted his gray eyes to my mother as he took a bite into his mouth, all smiles and naivety as he awaited her question.

"Have you and Violet had sex?"

I covered my face. "Oh my god."

Across the room, Jack choked on his food. When he managed to swallow, he answered through a cough, "No, ma'am."

"You're aware of her grandmother's and my own situation when it came to our parental status?" My mother took a seat across from him, placing her coffee down.

Jack watched her, dumbfounded and needing a second to find his voice. "Violet has mentioned only the bare minimum. You both had children young."

My mother lifted an eyebrow. "So you understand then, why it's important to us that she's being *careful.*"

"Oh my god..." I turned to lay my head on the countertop in my arms, unable to fight the embarrassment assaulting my face.

Jack seemed to have gathered his composure though. "Of course, I understand. I would never take advantage of Violet though, if that's what you think."

I heard a pause, peeking up to see my mother at a momentary loss for words. She gathered herself quickly. "Given Violet's situation, it's hard not to be worried that someone coming so quickly into her life doesn't have ulterior motives."

"Because she tried to kill herself?" Jack shot the question off immediately, his voice polite and gentle. His quick reply caught my mother off guard again. Perhaps she hadn't expected me to share those details with him. She underestimated how close we actually were.

"Well, yes," she said, finding herself stumbling now.

He nodded. "I understand why you'd be worried about it. It must have been really hard for you, not knowing how to help her."

I stared from across the room, in awe at how Jack managed to turn the interrogation around so easily. Just like when he played the devil's advocate against my own dark thoughts, he picked all the right words to make my mother realize that her concerns were unnecessary.

She looked down at her coffee, clearing her throat of something before replying, "Yes, it was. It is."

Jack smiled, warm and genuine. "I think it's amazing that Violet has people in her life that care about her as obviously as you and her grandmother do. I feel like sometimes Violet has trouble seeing the good in people, even in herself perhaps, but I'm glad to see that her family is looking out for her, even if she's stubborn about accepting your help."

A stunned silence sit in the room, until my grandmother chuckled over at the stove. "Good answers, kid."

I sighed, relieved as I watched my mother smirk in surrender. Even she couldn't argue that Jack hadn't passed her test with flying colors.

He took another bite of his pancake, then added as an afterthought through a mouthful, "You're right to be suspicious of me though. I do have an ulterior motive."

The two women paused, and I gave him a questioning glance when he caught my gaze.

He held back a smug look, knowing he had their attention, and hammered the last nail into his saintly coffin with his finishing words. "I'm trying to get Violet to appreciate life again."

&

Jack was pleased with himself, a self-satisfied grin playing on the corner of his mouth as we escaped the house yet again. He didn't have to brag about it for me to know that he was silently gloating about his victory over my mother's spontaneous attack on his character.

Despite wanting terribly to get wrapped up in this positive emotion surrounding us, there was a discomfort lingering deep in my chest. There were so many things left unspoken since I had banished Jack last. I knew I should talk about them, talk about anything, just to get a little pressure off of my lungs, but I had trouble finding the words.

Normally Jack was fine with silence, but it was as if he could tell I needed to speak and couldn't get a grasp on my voice. He tried to coax some words from me, gently. "Your mother sure has changed. It's good to see her looking out for you."

I hummed, circling a tree trunk, watching my feet as I stepped over the roots, one by one. "I wish she wouldn't. It would make it easier if she didn't care." I had meant for the words to come out light, joking, but something about them turned too serious.

Jack's expression shifted ever so slightly. "Are you still planning on killing yourself?" While he didn't sound surprised, I couldn't help but hear the disappointment.

I hung onto my answer, because I wasn't sure of my own feelings anymore. I had proven to myself that there was something in me, something that hadn't been there weeks before, that wanted to fight for the life Jack introduced me to, but there was still another part that was too tired of trying.

"I dunno. I guess obviously I am, since you wouldn't be here anymore if I wasn't, right?"

He nodded. "I guess so." After his words, he waited patiently for further explanation from me.

His silence was always persuasive. I sighed, leaning back against the tree. "I see how my mother has changed, and I see this potential of forgiveness sometimes inside me. I know that despite everything, I love her, and I like the idea of giving this a chance, of seeing if any healing can be done. Especially since I know it's what my grandfather would have wanted. But I'm having so much trouble reaching out to her... And some days I still feel like a ghost. Some days maybe I even prefer being a ghost, because it hurts less."

"After running away from everything for so long, it can be scary to finally turn around and face the emotions you've been hiding from. But you talked to your grandfather when you thought you'd never be able to, and you called me back for help when you knew you needed it. Don't you think you can open yourself up to her as well, when you're ready?" Encouragement in his most gentle, subtle way.

"I'm sure I could." I paused, kicking my feet through the snow, having trouble expressing the darkness in my head. It always sounded so foolish vocalized. I knew it was wrong, I knew this urge to leave was not really logical or justified, but it was there. I couldn't shake it. "I think I'm scared to though. If I still want to die, even if it's just this little part of me, I can't think about actually mending our relationship. It would be easier, for everyone, to just let it stay broken." I failed at expressing myself clearly, and I wasn't sure if it was accidental or not. Perhaps I hadn't wanted him to know the darkness of my actual thoughts.

He interpreted it anyway. "You don't want to forgive your mother, your grandmother, because you're scared of hurting them when you kill yourself?"

Said from someone else's mouth, I realized the truth in the words. "Yeah. I guess I am."

He nodded, understanding, although there was a line between his brows. "If you disappeared right now, what makes you think they wouldn't be hurt?"

"They would be." I wasn't stupid. I had always known my actions would be selfish and painful for anyone left in my wake. I always found excuses though. "But maybe it wouldn't come as a surprise at least. And maybe they could turn my death into something positive. They are already mending their relationship, so I'm really the only thing causing strain around here. They would be better off without me."

"I'm sure they don't see it that way." Jack tried to keep his tone even, but a hint of frustration snuck in when he objected. My own logic mirrored his annoyance. I knew I was being ridiculous, but I was infected. I couldn't think straight, I couldn't feel right, and how was I supposed to promise to get better, to stop my self-destruction, when I couldn't even admit to myself what was best for me?

"If I died, they would just have more reason to support each other. You're the one who said it, sometimes death is just a small part of a bigger picture."

Jack almost growled, heat in his eyes. "That's not how I meant that, Violet." He didn't appreciate his words being used against him.

"But it makes sense," my darkness insisted.

He denied it, firmly. "No, it doesn't."

I swallowed down my own frustration at his argumentative behavior. "You're still here. That means there's still a part of me that is thinking about killing myself. As long as I'm thinking it, as long as it's still an option…"

Jack interrupted my thought, trying to banish it. "And what if connecting with your family is the only thing that will take that thought away from you?"

This was a point I stumbled on. The darkness didn't have an answer, and my anxiety caught in my throat as I searched for the retort, but it never came.

I sighed, suddenly exhausted. I wanted to spit fire at him but I held it back, knowing the words coming out of me were no longer myself speaking.

He read my surrender, dropping his straight shoulders to let go of the tension between us. He approached me instead, leaning close to put his forehead to mine. "You don't have to decide right now. But please, Violet, at least consider what I'm saying. I told you I want to help, so I'm only telling you what I know will make a difference."

He was right, as always. I should just listen to him. He knew what was best for me. Even if I didn't agree right now, even if I didn't think what he was saying was possible, I should still listen, because when it came to my own thoughts, some of them were not to be trusted.

"Alright." I nodded, and in reply to my concede, he pet his thumb across my cheek, banishing my stress. I closed my eyes, his attention too sweet. I would miss this. My throat knotted up. "Just promise me something, Jack."

I felt his forehead wrinkle against mine with curiosity. "Of course, anything."

My breath shook across my lips, because a fear I had been trying to ignore just wormed its way into my skull. I wasn't only scared of hurting my family, although that was a huge thought riddling my mind. Part of me knew the healing I needed started with them. If I was able to heal though, if I was able to let go of the comfort that came with my decided death-day, then Jack wouldn't need to stay here any longer. "You'll let me know, if I do change my mind one of these days. You won't just disappear. You'll say good-bye, right?"

It was as if I'd stabbed him with those words, like the thought hadn't occurred to him until that moment. He inhaled sharp, closing his eyes tight. "Of course, Violet."

"Promise…"

"I promise. No more disappearing."

XXXII

December had crept up sometime between when I banished Jack and when I called him back. With my mother and grandmother busy taking care of things concerning my grandfather and the plan to remove him from life support, the estate did not feel warm and cozy like expected during the Christmas season.

Despite being very far off from the fuzzy joy that came with the holidays, I recognized the warming of the house, and with it, I felt my bones thawing. I gave the credit to Jack, who not only helped me open up and become a little more vulnerable around my family, but he seemed to make my mother and grandmother relax also.

After he had stayed the night three days in a row, I expected my family to object, but they seemed to enjoy having him around as much as I did. I imagined they appreciated that someone was there for me, especially when they had been spending so much time away from the estate, resolving last minute things in preparation.

Jack brought a particular warmth to the air around him, which contradicted what he represented. Then again, his power wasn't one way, like it often seemed. He led people to where they needed to go, so maybe he was doing that now, with all of us. Leading the three of us back to a life where our egos were no longer wounded and we could forgive each other.

Unlike a few days before, I was able to find some positivity when I woke in the mornings. There was something about waking up next to someone, in the wee hours of dawn, when time was almost still, hearing their heartbeat along with yours, that made a strong case for living. I was scared to put it into words, even in my own head, but I knew this swelling in my chest when I curled up against him and he pulled me closer, tight and safe, was something worth staying alive for. Even if I only got to feel a ghost of this after we parted ways, it was still something worth holding on for. The dark thoughts would creep in once the sleep faded away, but there was that moment, before completely waking, where I found myself glad to be able to see another day.

That morning was different. I woke twisted in the blankets, cold and hyperaware of the empty place in my bed where my not-quite-human was supposed to be. I got up to search, taking the blankets with me, feeling a tightness in my chest as a hint of anxiety set in.

"Jack...?" I searched the hall for a sign of life, finding myself with a dreadful twist in my gut, having to remind myself that he promised to not disappear.

"Morning, Violet."

I jumped from my skin as his voice came right behind me, turning to scowl at him.

He grinned coyly, reaching out to take my face in his hands. "I'm sorry, I didn't mean to scare you." He put his forehead to mine, kissing me soft and slow in apology when I grumbled.

"You'd think I'd be used to it by now," I whispered to his lips. He had a tendency to disappear and reappear at will, and intentional or not, he seemed to enjoy startling me regardless.

"Old habits," he replied, a little too mischievous.

When he pulled away, I reached out for him, objecting. I wasn't sure I'd ever get enough of his kiss, his closeness, but right now I at least wanted a little more. He conceded to my silent plea, allowing me to lure him close as I pressed my back against the threshold of my room, kissing again.

It felt as if he was trying to keep things tame, but his slow, gentle tending to my lips drove me to the edge too quickly, and my eagerness encouraged him to follow. When I had let a pleasant noise accidently slip from my throat, he retreated, turning my sound into frustration. I tugged at his shirt and brushed my nose against him to will him to continue, and he breathed a laugh onto my lips, a fervorless scolding in his gaze and a telling flush on his cheeks. He didn't cave though.

I thought he was going to discreetly suggest that I behave myself, but his words contradicted his behavior. "When is your family getting home?"

My breath caught in my throat, unable to articulate an answer to his question and the suggestion behind it. He teased a kiss over my mouth to coax an answer out.

"I… I don't know. They've been gone for most of the day lately," I replied finally, under my breath.

He hummed, a grin on his face that I could feel. "That gives us lots of time." He kissed me one more time, slow and careful, before pulling away from me completely, save for my hand that he took in his. "Come with me."

I followed with my fuzzy head that he'd kissed into submission, not objecting until he had me climbing the narrow staircase into the attic.

"What are we doing?"

If he thought I'd enjoy tumbling around with him in a dusty storage scaffolding, he was wrong.

Jack didn't reply. Instead, he just nodded for me to continue, and I screwed up my face in annoyance at him. While his silence was charming and mysterious most of the time, every now and then it was downright frustrating.

When we neared the top of the stairs, Jack slipped by me to arrive first, leaving my sight for just a moment as I took the last few steps to meet him. I found him with a pile of boxes, their outside marked "XMAS."

I raised an eyebrow. "Don't tell me you're one of those people who gets really excited over the holidays." I didn't mention the fact that I used to be one of those people.

He smiled wider. "I thought we could set stuff up while your mother and grandmother are out, having it all decorated by the time they get back." With his words, he dusted off one of the boxes.

So that was his intention. A flush bloomed on my cheeks with my embarrassment at what I had mistakenly thought. Despite myself, his excitement was infectious, and it made me follow his good mood into one of my own. Feeling playful, I told him, "It's a good idea, but I'm lazy and that seems like a lot of work. I would much rather…" I reached out for him again with my words, teasing my lips over his.

He chuckled, apparently never growing tired of my unmanageable hormones, bringing a kiss to my lips. When I wouldn't allow him to part from me, he muttered into the kisses I pushed on him, "I can't remember what a proper Christmas feels like…"

I groaned with his words, feeling the guilt he'd purposely induced. "Ok, fine, let's do this."

He grinned, satisfied with his win, giving me one more kiss before diving into the boxes.

§

It took too long to put all of my grandmother's decorations up. After taking the boxes down from the attic, unloading them into the den and entryway, and sorting through each one to see what we wanted to use, it was already the middle of the day.

I offered to make us something to eat to get out of a little bit of work, and Jack seemed to be satisfied with this exchange. He sat at the table and worked at untangling a knotted mass of different colored garlands, strings of lights, and thick, rich velvet ribbons trimmed with gold as I prepared some food.

Something about the very normal motions of housework distracted me from the usual lingering emotions that had been revolving around me lately. I wouldn't admit it, but I was looking forward to the women's reactions when they returned to a decorated house that evening. Like me, they had probably also forgotten what time of year it was and were also due for a reminder. It wasn't difficult to get lost in something, and forget the little, but often important things, like family and tradition.

I was quickly just as wrapped up in the excitement as Jack was, so much so that I suddenly wanted everything to be wonderful. No, perfect. This would be my opening up. This would be my reaching out. If I couldn't connect with my family with words, I would do it with actions, with Jack's help.

We realized quickly that the artificial tree my grandmother owned simply wasn't going to cut it. The corner of the den had a high enough ceiling that the seven-foot plastic pine looked more like a shrub, and I was caught up enough to be convinced by Jack rather easily when he suggested going out to get our own tree.

It took too long to find any decent trees; most were far too tall, and the others were still young and sparsely branched. I objected to everything we found, until it began to get late and I was forced to pick the best one, even though it was nowhere near as perfect as I wanted it. Jack didn't seem to mind, reassuring me that it would be fine as we chopped it down and carried it to the house.

We shook it free of snow and brought it inside with not too

much difficulty, setting it up in the old, rusting tree-stand my grandmother had buried deep in one of the boxes. I complained the whole time about its bare branches, but Jack continued to insist it was fine. It wasn't until we stood back together, his arm locked around my neck to nuzzle into my hair, that he gave a curious noise into my ear and said, "Huh, I guess it does look a little sad."

When I glared at him, he returned a coy grin, tightening his arm around my neck and placing his lips on my temple when I tried to squirm out of his grip. He was teasing me as I would come to realize, when he released me and approached the tree, reaching out and taking one of its bristly twigs between his fingers, petting it through his grip.

His touch encouraged the plant, and before my eyes, it sprouted additional green needles all over, filling out the gaps and making it look healthy and fresh. Jack turned back to me and raised an eyebrow with his self-satisfaction.

I glared again, but it was softer this time. "Show off." I combatted my sour tone by moving forward for an appreciative kiss.

It took us the rest of the evening to decorate the tree, which we did to the crackling sound of the wood stove burning and the rolling growls of our stomachs as we became hungry for dinner. There was no time for snacking though, Jack insisted, wanting to have everything finished before my family joined us. Even though I had put cookies in the oven and the sweet smell was becoming unbearable.

Jack was climbing on top of furniture to put the star on top of the tree, the final touch, when my mother and grandmother came in the door. The first thing they saw must have been quite the sight: a lanky skeleton boy all dressed in black, his shallow features lighting up as the star glowed warm yellow.

"What is all this?" It was my mother who asked first, reaching out to touch a hand over the garland and lights we'd twisted around the railing of the staircase. "This place looks just like when I was a kid."

"Where on Earth did you find the decorations? I haven't put them up in years," my grandmother commented, and I thought I caught some tears in her eyes, past her wide smile.

"Ask Jack," I answered, pointing to the boy as he scurried down to get his feet back on the floor.

Standing on solid ground again, he grinned sheepishly. "I might have snooped a little. I hope I didn't impose. I felt like this place needed a little bit of warmth."

It still surprised me, how good he was at bringing things and people to life, even when it contradicted his purpose.

"Well this calls for dinner, I'm sure you two are starving," my grandmother said, lifting up a large paper bag. "We bought Chinese! It doesn't really go with the Christmas theme though."

I objected, feeling my stomach turning in hunger pains. "No, Chinese is great!" I stole the bag from her, plopping down on the couch to unload the goodies onto the coffee table. Jack disappeared for a moment and came back with plates and utensils, and we all hunkered down for a cozy dinner by the light of the newly decorated Christmas tree and the heat of the wood stove.

When we finished, my grandmother collected the dishes to clean them and Jack stood to offer help, leaving me alone with my mother in the den. It was the first time we were alone together since speaking about why she had taken me away from Newport, and once the others left, I could feel the discomfort settle in slowly. I tried not to let it take over me, but I couldn't help feeling its grip tightening.

"We haven't had a proper Christmas in a while." It was my mother who broke our awkward silence.

My first reaction was to send salt her way, but I held my tongue and tried to reword my reply. "You never wanted to put decorations up at the apartment. You said it was just work, putting them up and taking them down."

She smiled, but it was far from a happy expression. Closer to wounded and shameful. "That was mostly just an excuse. It was hard celebrating Christmas. It was your grandfather's favorite time of the year. He loved all the decoration and lights. Ever since moving away from Newport, I've had trouble during the holidays."

"I assumed it was something like that. You used to come home even less during the end of the year." I fiddled with my fingers to fend off the frustration that itched at the back of my skull.

Silence, and then a huff of air. "I've been a terrible mother."

I didn't speak, because I couldn't find the strength to disagree. I again tried to reword my thoughts into something a little more productive. "I would be lying if I said I thought it wasn't too late… But you could always try to prove me wrong."

I peeked out of the corner of my eye to catch her lips turn up a little, swiping at the tears that threatened her eyes before turning to me. "I'm glad to see that you've found someone so good to you… My biggest fear, from the moment I found out I was having a little girl, was that you'd turn out like me. Always settling for less than you deserve. Obviously that hasn't happened though."

Something about the way she talked about us had me embarrassed, and I tried to stop her with a moan under my breath, but she continued.

"You should see the way he looks at you. Like you inspire him. You should think about that, Violet. You should remember that, every single day. I wish I knew what that was like, to be able to bring someone to life like you two do with each other."

"Mom…" I warned, begging her not to say the words on the tip of her tongue.

"He lov—"

Jack interrupted before she could finish, and I exhaled the breath I had been holding.

"Violet, your cookies have been compromised." A smirk played on his face as my grandmother approached behind him, crumbs at the corners of her full mouth.

I was thankful for the excuse to leave the room. Not because I wasn't legitimately happy to be having a heart to heart with my mother, but because as she put those words in my head, I realized I didn't want to hear them. I was too terrified, even coming from a third party. Because if I heard them, my brain would realize just how much pain I would be in store for when Jack finally left.

When he left... That's how I thought those words. Another thing I tried to ignore, even though my heart understood what it meant. *Not when I left.*

XXXIII

The next morning came with a certain bittersweetness; the dreamy joy of the night before became a fading memory, and the beeping of my grandfather's heart rate machine reminded me of the seconds ticking away, counting down the time I had left in this current reality. Limited was my moment here, with my head nuzzled into Jack's collar, my nerves almost settled for the first time in years. A race, to see if I could get strong enough to survive when the time finally came for everything to change.

It was early, the house still asleep from the previous night. I crept out of bed and through the house like the ghost I had grown accustomed to being. The lingering warmth from the night before had me feeling more alive than ever though, even in the stillness of the house's slumber.

Despite my own personal realizations, the night before had been perfect. I felt my heart thawing itself, letting my family in, allowing actual happiness. There was only one thing wrong, something that left a guilt in my stomach similar to the morning-after hangover I'd experienced after drinking myself almost to death out in the stables.

My grandfather hadn't been there, and something about that felt wrong.

It hurt, to know he wasn't able to see the mending he was helping us to get through. I told myself that he knew, or at least, would know, but I worried. Would the knowledge get lost somewhere between life and death? Would he die only remembering the broken pieces he'd left behind? I couldn't bare the thought. If he could still hear me, I wanted him to know everything.

I gathered a plate of cookies from my batch the night before and made my way silently up the stairs to my grandfather's room. He always loved when me and my grandmother baked. He usually ate more of our sweets than the both of us combined. Before we even realized it, the batch was completely gone just from him stealing the treats. I knew he couldn't eat them, but maybe somewhere inside him, he could at least appreciate the smell.

I opened the door into my grandfather's room, and I braced myself for the anxiety that would take hold of my lungs, but when my eyes laid on my grandfather, the panic never quite set in. Something was different this time. I wasn't scared; I was sad. Sad that I'd wasted so much time already. I wouldn't waste anymore.

I wasn't sure how long I was in there. It must have been a while because the sun added a little more light to the room, and the smell of the cookies wafted away the sterile scent I hated so much. I spent a lot of time talking at first, a gentle whisper that was still far too loud for the silent house. Eventually I stopped and just sat there, holding his hand, trying to find something in me to reassure myself that I could handle all the things approaching. I found tears in my eyes, and I wished briefly that my grandfather could squeeze my fingers back in encouragement.

A knock came to the door, and I expected Jack, but it was my mother who peeked in.

"I thought I heard a voice."

I swiped at my tears, nodding. "I was just telling him about last night."

My mother smiled. "He would have enjoyed it. Although I imagine he would have been the one with the idea of doing everything all in one day as a surprise."

I mirrored her small grin. "That sounds like him."

"When I was a kid, the estate was usually decorated from the first of December all the way into late January. He loved the Christmas season. No amount of cold to keep the warmth out of his bones."

She put pictures in my head, of my grandfather up on a ladder, nailing strings of lights along the roof edges, tacking a wreath on every entrance and mistletoe over every threshold. It was easy to imagine him getting caught up in the holiday spirit.

"He would have been glad to see someone upholding the tradition finally." My mother added, when I wasn't able to find words.

"It wasn't my idea. It was Jack." I didn't want to take the credit. If it had been up to me, I would have stayed wrapped up in bed all day.

"I know, but you helped, and your grandmother and I are thankful. We hadn't realized it, but we really needed last night. All this preparing for… Well, I don't think we realized how difficult it was becoming." A somber tone fell over my mother's low voice, her eyes turning to my grandfather for the first time, something glossy in them.

I nodded, turning away, my gaze unfocusing as well. "I understand. I've been struggling myself, to prepare. I'm trying to find it in me somewhere to be ready." That was the first time in a very long time I had admitted a genuine emotion to my mother. Without even thinking about it, I allowed her to see my cracks, get a glimpse of my darkness, of the pain that riddled me.

She noticed, rendered speechless. I purposely avoided looking back at her, something caught in my throat. I saw her watching out of my peripherals, the frown line coming between her brows, and then she cautiously stepped towards me. My shoulders tensed, subconsciously defensive as she neared me, but she continued to approach, slow and careful, until she was able to reach her hand out and place it on my shoulder.

The weight of my thoughts was replaced by the weight of her palm, and to my surprise, a sigh shook from my lips as I closed my eyes. I squeezed my grandfather's hand once again, and then removed my grip from his skin and wrapped my fingers around my mother's instead.

Something hurt in my chest, but not in the usual way. It wasn't the pain of a new wound, or an old one being forced open again. It was the strain of an underworked muscle coming back to life. It was my heart swelling, stretching to make room for the love my mother badly wanted to offer me.

I returned to my room and slipped back into Jack's arms, and he wrapped himself tight around me like he always did, like he would banish the darkness from me if he had to. When he stirred from sleep finally, feeling the heaviness of my thoughts as if they were there in the room with us, occupying space, he offered that we go somewhere else. With the sound of my grandfather's machines still lingering in the distance of our silence, I agreed to his offer gratefully, knowing I probably needed the air. My head was foggy, and I felt numb as a result.

Subconsciously I led us out through the snow, past the garden, to the stables. It was the first time we were there together, while both of us were conscious at least. I knew why I was there, but I was scared to face the idea of speaking about it. If I let my thoughts out, would that make them real? I couldn't commit to those wavering emotions yet.

He still wasn't entirely aware, although I imagined he had an idea. When we entered the stables, he watched me as I wandered around, before coming over to take my hand to squeeze my fingers in his. How effective the gesture was, at ridding me of the smallest bit of stress.

I pulled him with me as I continued around the tack room again. Like last time, I touched my free hand over my grandfather's drawers and his drafting table, dust coating my fingers. What I wouldn't have given for one last day in this room with him. A day of drawing to old swing music, with the sound of horses tapping their shoes on the hay in the next room.

I leaned back on my grandfather's desk and led Jack close, trying to gather some words, anything to express the emotions that swelled in my gut over my memories and missed opportunities. I couldn't catch a breath though, and no words could summarize the wound in my heart. It was all coming on so strong; I just wanted to not feel it for a moment longer.

"I'm here, Violet," Jack whispered, as he leaned over to kiss my temple, and it was comforting, but then something terrible twisted in my gut.

Not for much longer.

How many seconds would be cheated from us, because of the inevitable end approaching this relationship as well? Whether I chose to follow my darkness or follow my forever beating heart, one of us would have to disappear. The thought itself hurt almost as much as everything else.

I reached up for Jack's scarf, untangling it from around his neck and using it to pull him down to my lips. He obliged, kissing me soft and sweet, intending to banish the anxiety and coax the words out of my mouth. It wasn't working though. The lump in my throat swelled and the pain in my chest throbbed harder and I was desperate to smother it with *something*.

I kissed him again, slightly rougher, deliberate, trying to stop thinking, trying to lose myself in him for a moment, because maybe we wouldn't get another chance. My desperateness was easily misinterpreted as a fast growing passion. I willed him even closer to me, discarding the scarf and replacing it with my hands on the back of his neck. He stumbled trying to comply.

Jack attempted to keep some control, trying to resist the draw to my lips to let us catch a breath, but I wasn't allowing it. I brought him back under with me every time he tried to surface, insisting we drown together. He broke. That insanity inducing flush found his cheeks as his retreating shifted to advancing.

It still wasn't enough though. Like the last time we had lost ourselves together, the anxiety easily found me, chasing right at my heels. No matter how quickly I dove into him, it was faster; it would catch me if I didn't do something. Without even thinking, my hands snaked under his jacket, sitting on his thin hips briefly before my fingers went for the waist of his jeans.

He reacted. Immediately he had his hands around my wrists, pulling them away from him. He lingered close though, lacking the strength to separate the magnetic draw of our lips.

"What are you doing?" he asked in a whisper as he loosened his grip around my wrists.

I fought the panic that crept up on me. "I want you," I said with another kiss, willing him to let me go crazy so I didn't have to face the pain, sitting and waiting for me.

He had trouble stopping us, but he did. "No, you don't. Not here." He tangled his fingers with mine, pinning them back against the desk, away from him.

I leaned forward for another kiss but he managed to keep me away from his lips this time. I felt the familiar sting in my nose from erupting tears, panicking. The hurt was right there, just under the surface.

"I need you," I begged on a breath.

"Not like this, Violet," he sighed against my lips. He had found his resolve somewhere. "I could never forgive myself."

I yanked my hand free from his grasp and used it to shove him away weakly, frustrated and angry, although those emotions dissolved immediately into the helplessness that had been waiting there to pounce on me. When I tried to let out an angry huff, it came out a sob, and as quickly as I'd pushed him away he was back, wrapped around me.

"How then? When?" I whispered when I was finally able to catch onto a breath, because all I could think of was my grandfather's beeping heart monitor, our time together slipping through my fingers like melting snow.

He kissed my temple. "There's time."

"Is there?" I didn't believe him, because I could only fight my erupting emotions for so long. The darkness in me was getting smaller and smaller, because of him, because of my family, because of my own heavy beating heart. The smaller it got, the harder it was for me to hold onto my plan. How long, before he was able to tell that my mind was mending, that death was no longer such a beautiful option to me?

He shifted, putting his forehead to mine to catch my gaze. "I promised I would tell you, Violet. No disappearing, remember?"

I sniffed back tears, nodding small. "I remember."

"Then trust me. There's time."

I sighed, and he let me bend my head down and bury my face in his chest. *There's time.* I tried to repeat the words in my head, a comforting mantra, but I couldn't help attaching a terrible addition. *But how much?*

XXXIV

Jack was reading in my bed, and I was next to him on my stomach, drawing in my journal once more. I tried not to, but I found it difficult to keep myself from replicating the line of his neck and shoulders as he stretched out, his gray eyes fixed to the letters on the page.

It was Jack who broke our silence first, obviously aware of my staring but not wanting to comment on it. Instead, his gaze went to the journal, then he sat up and twisted himself around to lay on his stomach next to me. "I haven't seen you with that much lately." An innocent observation that had intention.

I nodded, giving a smile. "I know. I guess I haven't needed it much. To be honest, I'm only using it now because I don't have much else to draw in."

"There's a lot of negativity in that book. Maybe it's best that you're distancing yourself from it." Encouragement.

I scoffed a little to banish his praise. He gave me too much credit. "I sleep with it under my mattress. I don't think I've given it up quite yet."

He hummed. "Even so. Out of sight, out of mind." I opened my mouth again to argue, but he didn't allow it, shifting closer, crawling overtop my back and nuzzling ticklish kisses into the nape of my neck as he pried over my shoulder. "You know, you're a wonderful artist, Violet."

I huffed again, but the sound was with little fervor thanks to his lips on my skin and in my hair. "My grandfather was an architect. I guess I learned a few tricks."

"You should do something with it. Not many people are able to make beautiful things like you can."

"It's not so simple."

"It would be for you." His argumentativeness was gentle, and I didn't have the energy to fight it. I let his warm words soak into my skin and loosen my bones a little. He was so good at making a picture of this future I could have, that I almost believed it. I almost wanted it.

He reached over me and started flipping through the pages, and I let him with barely a thought. I hid this part of myself away from the rest of the world, this darkness that still lingered around me, in the form of dangerous thoughts and little notes on how to kill myself scrawled on parchment. With him though, it was easy to let him see it. There was no shame, no need to hide. He never judged. He accepted every part of me, even the dark corners.

He stopped on my lists, a few things crossed off, a number of them because of him. I watched him smile, and I remembered the beautiful night we had spent together, almost suspended in time. Instinctively, he moved closer to me, another kiss into my hair. "There are still things left undone here."

I followed his gaze to the page, humming in agreement as I read over the list, miniscule points that meant nothing now in the grand scheme of things. All except for a few. I took my pen and started scratching off some things.

Find out of the fox survived. I had forgotten to write this off my list thanks to the unexpected appearance of my mother. I slid the pen across the words, striking them out.

Talk to Grampie with three strong underlines to show myself how important this was. I'd done that now. Twice, actually. That was something to be proud of. I went to strike these words out too, but Jack stopped me.

"You should talk to him as much as you can, before you have to let him go. Don't cross it off yet. Keep the reminder." He gave me a soft kiss on the temple with the suggestion, and I nodded, agreeing. I left the words as they were.

Find out about that look. I had forgotten this note, but reading it, I recalled what had triggered it. Jack, staring strangely at my grandfather's room as we passed it. Jack read the words too as I lingered on them, then he gave me a questioning look, begging for an explanation.

"Could you feel my grandfather's pain, his struggling, even before you touched him?"

With my question, he understood what I had seen, and let his eyes fall a little, somber. "Sort of. The first time we passed that room I just felt… Drawn to it. Like I was needed."

"Is that how you felt with me?"

He tilted his head to the side, timid to agree with those words completely. "It's how I feel with everyone that needs me, but usually it only happens right at the end, when they are dying already. It's just a tiny pull, that I have to follow. With you it was different. I don't know how to explain it. I felt compelled to go to you ahead of time, and it was like I was being dragged towards you, even when I tried to separate myself."

I smiled, but there was a bitterness to it. "But your desire to be with me, it could just be the same as any other person you've helped."

He flopped down onto his stomach next to me with a sigh, and I watched him shake his head. I opened my mouth to argue, but he stopped me. "It's not the same. I know it isn't. I chose this. I wanted to know you." He looked at me with sincerity, but underneath was a glimmer of something I was familiar with. That gaze that said he knew something, something I didn't. It had been a long time since that look had crossed his face.

When he caught my smile shifting into a curious frown, he leaned into me and kissed my cheek, wrapping himself around me until I was drowning in his attention and couldn't be bothered thinking about silly looks anymore.

Jack noticed the other things not scratched out in my journal while we snuggled. After a while of hugs and nuzzles that turned into kisses, he peeled himself away from me, despite my protests, and left the room, demanding I stay there and wait. Through the crack of my bedroom door I saw him shuffling about, and I wanted badly to ask what he was doing, but every time I called for him, he would politely tell me to be patient, and I would groan in teasing frustration.

Finally, what seemed like hours later, he called for me to follow him. I got up and he took my hand, leading me out of my room. As we walked, we passed my grandfather's room, and I paused outside, caught up in my curiosity. Jack allowed me to stand there for a moment, taking a step back towards me to offer his comfort.

It felt so wrong, to tell that my heart was mending while he was still stuck in that room, being kept alive by our selfishness. The least we could do would be to *let him go*. Was this what my mother had been speaking of this whole time? That we needed to say good-bye, properly, so we could move on? Has she also been so broken, as broken as I was, all this time? That would explain a lot.

"That day, that I let you in there, you said he was in pain," I whispered, frowning.

Jack nodded. "I did."

"Is he still? Do you know?"

He looked down. "Most likely."

"Well… Do you think he at least knows… Can he hear us? Does he understand that we're letting him go soon?" I wanted comfort, to know we weren't knowingly dragging out his torture.

Jack sighed. "It's hard to say. His consciousness was barely there anymore. His thought processes were hysterical. It was the only reason I got so caught up… I never apologized for that by the way."

I shook my head. "Don't apologize. You were only trying to help him."

"I had no right though… It wasn't my decision."

I didn't speak. Perhaps he was right, but I had forgiven him. I knew that if my grandmother and mother knew what I knew, knew that the man lying unconscious in his bed, kept alive by machines, was screaming for release, they would want to let him go just as badly as me. Just as badly as Jack had wanted to. I couldn't steal the goodbye away from them though, even if I knew I was doing it for my grandfather.

I would have to carry the burden of his suffering a little longer, until my family was ready to release him and move on like I wanted to do. Until then, I had to try and continue to make him understand by speaking to him.

"When the time comes, will you help him move on? Will you make it easy for him?" I turned to Jack, a plea in my eyes.

He frowned, then led me into his collar, so he could whisper to me. "Of course I will, Violet. Whatever you want."

I nodded, wrapping myself around him to accept his comfort, hiding my eyes away in his skin so I didn't have to see the door to my grandfather's room anymore.

After I let out a heavy sigh, Jack kissed my forehead and took my hand to continue to whatever he was working on previously.

Like earlier that week, he once again had me climbing the attic steps towards a mystery.

When we arrived, I saw what he had been diligently working on right away. In a cleared out spot in the middle of the floor, he'd set up a mountain of blankets and pillows that were clearly scavenged from around the house. Across from the nest of textiles, also on the floor, was an old television which had long since seen its days.

As I grinned a little in surprise, he stepped away momentarily and hauled a box towards me, opening it up to reveal a pile of VHS tapes. "It's not the movie theater, but maybe it's acceptable?"

I sighed and smiled, reaching forward for his shirt. "It's perfect." I savored his pleased hum as I brought our lips together again. He kissed me back long enough to lead me over to the blankets and sit me down, then he turned away to turn the television on.

"I'm not sure if that thing even works anymore. My grandparents probably haven't used it since I was a kid," I commented, as he checked that the cables were all in place and plugged in.

He flicked the switch on the screen and it came to life with an electronic buzz. With the success he looked over his shoulder and lifted a cocky eyebrow.

I laughed. "I didn't say it wouldn't work, I just said I wasn't sure. And anyway, the VCR could be broken also."

As I spoke, he fished out a tape and popped it into the machine, which accepted it and came to life as well. I got another look from Jack, and I rolled my eyes playfully.

I'd like to say we were content to simply sit there and enjoy the movie, wrapped up in blankets and each others company. I was never content to simply waste time with Jack though, especially since our seconds together ticked away quickly. I'd also like to say that something more happened. It would have been perfectly beautiful, to finally share with him that moment of humanity I craved, of feeling whole and alive again, on the floor in a tangle of pillows and blankets and limbs.

Unfortunately, before the movie was even over, and while I had just found the nerve during our kissing to timidly sweep my fingertips along the bare skin up under the back of his shirt, we were interrupted by my grandmother calling for me to come down. When I groaned into his lips, Jack grinned wide, kissing me again, deep and long until I forgot that I'd been called in the first place and the woman had to yell for me again. Reluctantly I pushed him away, sending him a scowl for his antics, although there wasn't much behind the look.

XXXV

I walked in on a familiar scene. My grandmother and mother sat together on the sofa, waiting for me to sit next to them in the airchair. There was something different this time though. Despite the room being filled with warm, colorful lights from the Christmas tree, and the comforting heat from the wood stove, there was a heavy discomfort in the air.

My mother greeted me, putting on a strained smile. I'd gotten used to the surreal happiness we had all been feeling the last few days, so coming back to reality was a little strange. Seeing the stress on my mother's face as she invited me into the room reminded me of the things we were all dealing with, the things that even love and family and wonderful memories couldn't quite erase.

As I neared, with Jack following behind me, I saw my grandmother hide behind her hand. Something fell into my stomach, making my body feel heavy. I stopped, but Jack's hand found mine and he nudged me forward, encouraging.

My mother assessed us, unsure, then cleared her throat before I sat down. "Perhaps you want Jack to wait upstairs?" Her words could have been one of her demands hidden under a suggestion, but her tone was actually sincere this time. A legitimate question.

I considered, then sat down anyway. "I think I'd like him to stay. Is that alright?" I offered my own respectful tone, since she had omitted from talking down to me.

My mother looked at Jack one more time, knowing there was no sense fighting it. "If that's what you'd prefer, it's fine."

I nodded a thank you, tugging Jack's fingers to get him to sit. He was uncomfortable, I could tell, but he stayed regardless, perched on the edge of the armchair I sat in. When I tightened my hand to show him my silent appreciation, he squeezed back.

My mother turned to my grandmother briefly to ask if she should start, and as my grandmother peeked up from her hands to wave at my mother, I saw that the old woman was hiding red, tear-filled eyes. The thing that dropped in my stomach previously fell even further. The dread made me feel ill.

Across from me, my mother sighed and sat straighter, folding her hands in her lap, fidgeting as she tried to figure out where to start. I subconsciously took a deep breath and held it. Perhaps I knew what was coming, but I still didn't know myself well enough to tell how I would react. Was I strong enough yet, for what she was going to say?

"These last few days have been exceptional. I don't think any of us expected to get along so well, considering the things we all have had to come to terms with the last few weeks. There's been a lot of bad blood with the women in this family. Obviously, I am well aware of that. I'd like to think that things have improved between the three of us though. Would you agree, Violet?"

With her question, she gave me a hopeful look, like she really wasn't sure what my answer would be. It surprised me, that I was still such a mystery to her. That she still seemed to want my forgiveness so badly. I half expected her to get tired of grovelling, but she hadn't given it up yet.

I gazed down at my knees, swallowing something hard in my throat. "Yes. Things have improved." It was all I could muster, because how could I put into words that I was still hurt, but was trying to allow her to make things right? Was there a turn of phrase, to describe finally coming out of an emotional shell?

"Your grandmother and I think so too. And it's had us thinking a lot. About the family, and Christmas, about the past and the future. About what your grandfather would have wanted, for us, for the women in his life."

I knew where she was going. I could feel it in the air. It was getting harder to breathe. "I've been thinking about that a lot too." Particularly about the future. The future that I hadn't decided if I wanted or not.

My mother smiled, as if she understood. She had no idea though. "I assumed as much. So we decided, it was only fair to let you in on one last decision, regarding your grandfather." She paused, to let me speak perhaps, but I had no voice so she continued. "This decorating you kids did… It reminded your grandmother and me a lot of the past, when I was still living here and we would decorate the house. It was one of your grandfather's favorite things. Christmas was always his favorite time of year."

My grandmother interrupted, with a teary, wavering voice. "One year, shortly before the accident, he grew out his beard for the whole year so it would be long, salt and pepper, and then he took the carriage out with one of the horses. He gave the children in town carriage rides around the countryside. He loved how happy everyone always was during the Christmas season." She smiled while recounting the memory, and then let her face fall back into her hands, concealing another bout of pain.

Without even thinking about it, I let go of Jack's hand and

reached out to my grandmother to comfort her. I took myself by surprise as I realized what I had done. Was this what it was like, to connect for once with someone else? It hurt. It hurt a lot actually, but my heart raced against the pain, reminding me I had been through worse and I was alive.

My mother blinked away tears that threatened her eyes as well. "We talked a lot about it the last few days, since you two set this whole thing up, and we came to an idea that we think we're happy with, but we want to know that you are in agreement."

A frown creased my brows, and I nodded for my mother to continue. I wasn't sure I wanted to, but I knew I needed to hear it.

She sighed and nodded back, taking a deep breath also. "We want to let your grandfather go on Christmas. We could have family and friends over for a Christmas dinner. Everyone could say their goodbyes… Your grandmother and I agreed that he would have liked having everyone together."

Christmas was only a few days away. They wanted to let go of him then? How could I handle having his death day be on Christmas? How could I handle having to let him go so soon?

I exhaled as I leaned back into the chair again, not even knowing I had been holding onto another breath. I expected the pain to hit me, but as I sat there, my brain working around the words she just offered me, nothing overwhelming took over. My heart hurt, of course it did, because it always did for my grandfather now that I knew he was suffering, but the anxiety that normally took hold of my throat was surprisingly absent. There was just a lingering sadness.

I swallowed it down some so I could reply. "I think that's a wonderful idea. He would have wanted everyone together. He would have wanted us all here to support each other." I was able to fight back the tears that stung at my nose, as I mentally added *the sooner the better.*

Reading my mind, Jack leaned over and put his lips to my hair.

Both women were surprised with my actions, but next to me, Jack simply squeezed my hand again, encouraging, as if he knew all along that I could handle whatever life threw at me. I wished I had the confidence in myself that he had in me. I wished I wasn't always second guessing myself. This moment just proved to me that I was stronger than I thought.

With the realization, I sniffed back the swelling emotion to add one more thing. "I just, have a request, if it's OK?"

My grandmother and mother both watched me, nodding to show they were listening.

I closed my eyes, giving a slow exhale, calming down. Was I ready for this? Perhaps I was. Perhaps I had been underestimating myself. "Can I be the one, to let him go?"

Both women gave me a blank expression, and as the silence stretched, I panicked and backpedaled. "I mean, I don't have to be. He was only my grandfather. Obviously if one of you wanted to do it, then it would be more important to you. I just felt… I just felt like maybe, if I could, I should." I looked down at my hand in Jack's, unsure of myself, but with his reassurance, I let out a bit of my heart to the women across from me. "Mom was talking a lot about closure before, and I was just thinking, that maybe I need some of that, that maybe doing this would help me find some…"

It was my grandmother who finally replied. "If you think you need to be the one to do it, then of course you can."

We talked a little while longer, before Jack and I returned to my room. Once behind a closed door, I let out a heavy sigh. Reading my mind, Jack wrapped himself around me, and I melted.

He didn't have to say anything, just being there was enough.

What would I do, when he wasn't there to keep me on my feet when I was ready to collapse? Was I ready to hold myself up on my own two feet, or was I diving headfirst into murky waters? Jack had faith in me, I could tell he thought I made the right decision, but I still wasn't sure.

I didn't know how he did it. Just kissed away my dark thoughts with his lips to my forehead. I hummed, sighing again, the weight on my shoulders lifting briefly with the exhale.

"You'll be there, to make sure he goes safely?" I looked up at him, pleading.

He nodded at my silent begging, banishing my doubts. There was no need for them. "I'll be there."

I nodded back, closing my eyes as he pulled my head into his collar, holding me together. We stayed like that for a long time, until the anxiety creeped up on me and I had to voice my thoughts so he could help banish them.

"Am I ready for this?"

The words were about letting my grandfather go, but perhaps they applied to something more. A secret still in my head. Was I ready to let go of him, of Death, of the comfort I had gripped onto so tightly for so long? Was I ready to live instead?

His breath kissed my cheek as he scoffed. My heart missed one of its hard, pounding beats. "Of course you are, Violet." His words answered both my questions too accurately. As if he had heard my secret, as if my heart had told him in morse code.

Jack fell asleep while wrapped around me, but my brain was wild with activity and I couldn't rest. Instead, I sat awake, staring at him so I could remember every detail of this beautiful moment.

For when he left.

That sneaky little thought that had been creeping its way into my brain for days now. My heart constantly raced with its liveliness. The darkness in me was almost all gone now thanks to that little seed of doubt and Jack's wonderful comfort, which I sometimes wondered whether it was magic itself. Perhaps he was unwilting me, with his touch, like he did with the violet on my bedside, one kiss at a time. Perhaps that was why he slept so much. I heard Jack's scolding voice in my head.

You don't give yourself enough credit.

He had told me once, that perhaps the only way to live was to let go of the idea of dying. That perhaps the only way of letting go of the idea of death was by accepting the people who were filled to the brim with life all around me. I started letting them in, and I could feel the warmth filling up my cracks. My darkness didn't seem so inviting anymore. In fact, the shadowy fingers that had once gripped so tightly around my lungs seemed like barely smoke now.

I refused to accept those tiny little thoughts though, because accepting them meant Jack would have to leave, and I still needed him. I told myself it was for my grandfather, but I knew a part of me was just being selfish. I wanted him to stay with me, for as long as possible. I would hold onto that last bit of darkness with all my strength, just to keep him with me a little longer.

I slipped out of Jack's thin arms quietly, scared he would hear the whispers of my racing heart. Once on my feet, I fished out my journal from under the mattress and left the room. I had to tell someone. My heart had to speak, or else it would explode. Who could I speak to though, that wouldn't make the secret real?

My grandfather greeted me in the only way he could: mechanical beeps. The sound of them still put me on edge, but I managed to enter the room and sit down next to him without too much of a problem this time. I sat there for a long while, mulling in my own thoughts. Jack had said that he wasn't sure if my grandfather could hear me, but I hoped he could. I hoped that he could understand everything. I hoped that if he could talk, he'd smile and say everything was going to be alright.

I felt like if he knew right now, that his death had the meaning it did, it would make him happy. That in death, he brought us all together. I also felt like, if he knew what was hidden in the back of the journal I held firm in my grip, he would be disappointed.

No more. Even if the decision had to be kept secret for now, someone needed to know to make it final. I would make the promise to him, whatever consciousness he had left.

"I won't waste this sacrifice, Grampie. I'm sorry I was weak, but I'm stronger now."

As I spoke, I realized there were already tears in my eyes, making it hard to see as I opened my journal. I scratched off the words underlined three times: *Talk to Grampie.* Then, I flipped through the pages, lingering on the doodles of the fox and the crow, of the violets, of Jack, reaching the back cover where my note was tucked into the bindings.

I took it out, the paper folded twice and dated for my birthday. I didn't even look at it; I just held it briefly as I watched my grandfather, then began to tear the paper into bits.

It hurt. It was like saying goodbye to a lover. The comfort I had once known, I was letting go of. I knew it was for the best though. I put the torn pieces back into the journal, then buried the book under my grandfather's mattress. I used his sheets to wipe up my tears, holding his hand for a moment.

"I'll live. I promise. For you, for Nan, for Mom, and for myself."

After gathering my breath, I returned to my room and crawled back into Jack's arms carefully. He pulled me close, as he always did, but something felt different this time. It wasn't as warm as his hug usually was.

He sighed soft into my hair, calm and pleasant as usual,

although I was almost positive I heard a hint of something else there. Something that tugged at my pounding heart and made my throat tight.

I couldn't keep the words back. My heart spoke before I could stop it. Into the skin of his neck, I whispered, "I love you, Jack."

I heard the rhythm in his chest miss a beat. Mine followed its lead.

"I love you too, Violet."

I bit on my lip to keep it from shaking. "Forever?"

He hummed sleepily and kissed my hair. "Forever."

I should have been happy, but tears found my eyes. If it was forever, why had it felt like goodbye?

XXXVI

It was short notice to say the least, but in a group effort between myself, my mother, and my grandmother, we contacted extended family and friends to invite them to a Christmas dinner in honor of my grandfather. Some people were surprised to hear from us, particularly my mother, and others offered congratulation for "burying the hatchet." It seemed that, like many families, the drama of our own had leaked out to the aunts and uncles and cousins over the years. Nevertheless, my mother took the comments with grace, and I somehow followed her lead.

Some people couldn't make it of course. We had Holt's all the way out to the West Coast; they offered their condolences and best wishes. A surprising number of people said they would attend though, even cancelling plans to show up, which was heartwarming. It seemed my grandfather was a popular man, unlike the women in his life.

With the guest list decided for the "going away" party, planning for it started. To be exact, what would be part of the large dinner that we decided to prepare.

"He always liked Christmas dinner," my grandmother reminisced.

"You used to say that his deadly sin would be gluttony," my mother added.

The older woman chuckled. "And he'd tap his belly and say he was just getting ready for hibernation, and then sleep away the afternoon to get out of helping me with the dishes."

I wish I would have been able to be around for more Christmas holidays. The way the two women talked about it, I longed to be included. It was like nostalgia, for a time I never lived or experienced. All I remembered of Christmas were long ago memories of setting up the store bought tree and putting on the one box of ornaments that my mother allowed us to have. After a while, we stopped setting up the tree all together.

I reminded myself to not be bitter, pushing away that toxic thought of frustration and jealousy, and instead tried to make the best of this last Christmas I would have with my grandfather. Even if he wouldn't be conscious to enjoy it with me.

We decided on some of his favorite dishes, a traditional meal, with a turkey and a ham because my grandmother said that Grampie could never decide. With a list of items made, Jack and I went into town to collect the massive amount of food.

I drove, because Jack said he didn't know how.

"How is that possible?"

He grinned. "I dunno. I might have known at some point but, I don't remember now."

"In your previous life, right?"

"Maybe I was a racecar driver?"

I grimaced. "No, you don't have a southern accent. All racecar drivers are from the South."

"Are they now?" A laugh escaped him when I nodded matter-of-factly. "Where do you think I was from then?"

I took a moment to think, glancing at him before turning my eyes back to the road. "Washington. Somewhere on the coast."

"Really? How come?"

I smiled soft, taking another quick look to admire his curiosity. "Because you smell like the woods and a different sea. Like how I imagine Washington would smell. And you always look like you're ready for the rain."

He hummed and his lips quirked up, approving. "Maybe so."

Pausing briefly, I added another observation. "And you look a little like you stepped out of the nineties Seattle grunge scene."

His grin spread. "Don't diss my combat boots."

"I would never."

We let the silence sit for a while, just the rumble of my grandfather's old farm truck, plucking along down the plowed road. In the quiet, my thoughts were loud, and I had to get them out. "I'd like to visit there sometime."

"Washington?"

I shrugged and nodded. "Why not? I'd like to get away from the city, experience somewhere I haven't experienced before."

He didn't comment right away, giving weight to his response once it slipped from him. "Maybe I'll meet you there, then."

My lips twitched up involuntarily. "OK."

He didn't comment on the fact that I had just made a plan for my future, and I didn't comment on the I-know-something-you-don't look that had taken over his gaze. We made a plan like young lovers did, ignoring reality for a blissful moment, because it was too painful for the both of us to admit the truth.

There wasn't enough room in the kitchen for all of the food we bought, so Jack and I dug holes in the snow outside of the back door of the estate, filling them with items that needed to stay chilled. After, we set our motivation to the dining room.

It obviously hadn't been used in years, piled up with boxes and old books that had strayed from my grandfather's library. At one point my grandmother thought to at least cover the chairs with sheets to keep the fabric clean, but besides that, the room was dusty and abandoned. No one needed a large banquet dining room when it was just two people, let alone just one like it had been for many years.

My mother helped us, and it didn't take long for the room to brighten up. With the boxes moved away, and a duster and cloth taken to all the surfaces, the polished wood table began to shine again and a life returned to the forgotten space. I was on the table, dusting off the crystals on the chandler, when Jack spoke.

"What are we going to do for gifts?"

Both my mother and I gave him a curious look.

"Well, it's a Christmas party. We should have gifts for everyone."

"I'm not really sure we have the expenses for that," my mother offered, regret on her tone.

I sighed. "It's a good idea though. There has to be something we can do. What would Grampie have done?"

Jack smiled with my agreement, shrugging a little. "Well, I had a thought, that's why I asked." He waited for our curiosity again before continuing. "What if you gave everyone one of these books?"

There was a pause as we processed his suggestion. My mother reacted first. "It would be like they would all leave with a piece of him."

"That would be something Grampie would have liked." When I smiled in Jack's direction, he returned it smooth and soft.

We passed the idea by my grandmother, and while she was apprehensive at first to let the books go, she realized she didn't have the space for all of them anyway and finally agreed. We used the freshly cleaned dining table to go through the guest list and agreed upon who would get which books.

It took us a long time and an order of pizza delivered to the door, but we managed to pair up guests with their perfect books before we hit the wee hours of the morning. Wrapped and labelled with names, we stacked the presents under the tree, filling out the bottom of the scene.

This was the biggest Christmas I would ever experience. There was a bittersweetness with that realization. I tried not to linger on it though.

We hung out around the tree for a while longer, talking and joking, the four of us, until my grandmother was falling asleep in her arm chair and the coals in the wood stove were dying down to glowing embers. My mother got up and led my grandmother to bed, leaving me alone with Jack in the low, warm light of the disappearing fire.

"If you were a grungy kid from Seattle in your former life, then what was I in mine?"

"Do you believe in reincarnation now?"

I snorted. "Answer the question."

Jack didn't miss a beat. "An angel."

I turned my eyes to the floor to hide my blush. "Be serious."

"Who said I was joking?" He smiled with his words, but when I gave him a pointed look, he caved and played my game. "An art student."

"From where?"

"From everywhere."

I chuckled. "I do have a bit of wanderlust sometimes."

He nodded, grinning. "You were born under the stars and that's why your eyes dance with them."

I blushed further. "Are you talking about me now, or former me? Because I can tell you, I was definitely born in a hospital with my mother heavily medicated." I had to make a joke; he was leaving me too wonderstruck with his words.

"Don't ruin the fun," he protested teasingly.

"OK. Did we meet, in this former life?" I asked cautiously, knowing this make-believe was going to hurt in the end, but loving the bit of fantasy for the moment.

He nodded. "You were drinking a cup of black coffee and drawing the buildings around you. I asked if you liked Nirvana and you said, 'Only the state of mind.'"

I laughed. "I sound like I was an uppity asshole."

"It's OK, we both were." He chuckled as well, quiet and lazy, sleep invading his eyes. He wasn't too tired to kiss me though. When the silence had drawn on, he leaned over and brushed his lips delicately past mine. There was a certain intention behind it, like he was storing the details away. When I realized, something hurt in my chest.

I sighed when he pulled away, frowning a little as he rested his forehead to mine. "I wish that was the truth. I wish I had known you, when you were human." I stopped, shaking my head to correct myself. "No, I wish you were human right now."

His face shifted, a ghost of pain crossing his expression. "I know. I do too."

"I don't want to say goodbye…"

"I don't either." He frowned further, swiping at the tears escaping from my eyes. "I'm sorry, Violet."

"It's not your fault."

"It is. I never meant for this to happen. I should have stayed away."

I shook my head immediately. "You're one of the best things to ever happen to me."

He kissed me again with my words, until his lips strayed from mine and kissed away the salty streams on my cheeks. With his arms around me, and my face buried in his collar, I was able to settle my sobs and find my voice again.

"I'll find you, in the next life."

I heard him breathe out a laugh. There was pain it in that mirrored the stabbing in my chest. "I'll be waiting."

XXXVII

We got up bright and early on Christmas day to help my grandmother start the dinner. With how much food there was, it would easily take most of the day to prepare, so she had a schedule written out. We barely had time to rub the sleep from our eyes before she gave Jack and me orders like a drill sergeant.

I was able to get a cup of coffee for myself and Jack before being put on pie duty. I made and rolled the dough, and he cut out pieces for the bottoms and set them in the base of the pie tins. It was tedious work first thing in the morning, but I kept a smile on my face by reminding myself of why we were doing it. The night would be special in its own bittersweet way.

Grampie would be proud.

Jack didn't handle the repetitive task as well as I did. When my grandmother was distracted, he fought his boredom by bumping his hip against mine, or pushing my hair aside with his flour-covered fingers to kiss the tender spot below my ear, leaving me flushed and marked with white powder.

Eight pies later, and my grandmother gave us a break. We used it to eat lunch and finish setting up the dining room with the nice china and new candles for the candelabra. My mother tidied up some other things in between calls from relatives, who asked for directions or times and wondered if they should bring anything. With every new ring of the phone, my heart warmed. I didn't know there were so many people that knew my grandfather. All these people, who I was connected with through him.

I had felt alone for so long; it was strange noticing this tie to life again. I was hyperaware of my pounding heart and how it ached with every beautiful emotion. I wouldn't let go of this warmth again. I'd hold onto it this time, until my fingers were weak. My grandfather would want it that way. Jack would want it that way.

We returned to kitchen work after a while, although this time there was a lot more goofing around on our part and a lot less actual helping. My grandmother didn't seem to mind; I caught her smiling with a knowing look in her eyes whenever I caved to my laughter.

My mother joined us with a surprise; she had retrieved the record player from its resting place under a pile of documents in the office. She cleaned it up and put on Joni Mitchell. It wasn't Christmas music, but it was almost more appropriate. Mitchell's soulful voice filled the kitchen through the scratchy, unique quality of the record player's speaker.

My grandmother worked on a yorkshire pudding and next to her, my mother finished up the stuffing so we could fill the turkey and put it in the oven. Once the first song got into the chorus, my grandmother sung under her breath. My mother started singing along too, with the lyrics she knew, until the soft, relaxed mood of the room had them both drawling their voices aloud along with the record player.

The smile on my face was gentle and lazy, growing intoxicated with the mood myself. My heart beat so hard in my chest it hurt.

It stretched further when Jack kissed the corner of my mouth and whispered in my ear, "It's unbearable."

"What is?"

"How beautiful you are." He nuzzled closer to my neck when I turned away to conceal my blush. "I can hardly stand looking at you. You're so bright with life, you make my eyes hurt."

I noticed as I turned back that his eyes trained on me despite his words. "You don't have to look," I teased.

"I do. I'd risk going blind. I don't want to miss a second of you."

Jack had only his dark clothes and combat boots to wear, so we went into the attic to go through some old clothes to see if we couldn't find something more acceptable. My grandfather was a few inches taller than Jack, but perhaps an old shirt would fit in the arms at least.

While searching, I found a box of my mother's old wardrobe, and a creamy lace-back dress caught my attention. I held it up to judge its size, and curiosity got the better of me.

I began to undress to try it on, telling Jack to turn around as I did so. I watched him to see if he would peek, and he didn't. I was both charmed and a little annoyed with his genuineness.

The dress fit well, and after asking Jack to help me zip it up, I admired it through the glass of an old mirror hiding in the corner.

"You should wear this." He kissed my shoulder.

I scoffed. "Why? It's too fancy."

He shook his head. "You look like an angel."

"Stop…" His compliments were too sweet.

I considered his suggestion though. I wondered if my mom remembered this dress, if she would recall that it was hers. Maybe she'd appreciate seeing me in it. The idea brought another smile to my lips.

Unfortunately, Jack didn't wear a button up very well. We found one that fit his shoulders, but with it on, he still looked very much like a grungy kid trying to tidy himself up. His slumped posture and skinny limbs were hard to spruce up. It was a bit like trying to put a tree in a tuxedo.

"Sorry," he offered sheepishly, realizing he was a somewhat disappointing sight.

"It's just a formality. No one will care if you're a little unkempt." I laughed when he pouted. To comfort him, I combed his fringe back with my fingers. He caught my wrist and kissed my palm.

People began arriving around dinner time as my grandmother started to bring items out to the table. Aunts, uncles, and cousins I hadn't seen in years greeted my mother and me as if it was only yesterday we'd last seen each other. It continued to surprise me, how accepting everyone was to have us back into the family, like we had never went anywhere. How easy it was for people to forgive. Perhaps I could learn how to let the past go if I followed their lead.

A lot of wine was brought as dinner offerings, so we opened each of the bottles to let them breathe. I smelled each of them, but when my mother got me a wine glass for myself, I declined discreetly.

Jack caught the sheepishness on my face and teased me. "You know, it's OK if you want to have a glass. I'm still here, if you drink too much again."

I shook my head at his bad joke, despite my grin. "I've had my fair share of alcohol. I think I'll refrain until I'm legal, at least."

We joined the others in the den and participated in warm conversation after introductions. At first, I found myself nervous and timid, concealing my scarred wrist behind my back whenever I was approached by someone, forcing smiles and pleasantries. Jack hovered by my side though, and his presence helped loosen me up until I was able to flow into the conversations a little more naturally.

It was just when I had begun to let my guard down that I was taken aback by a question directed at me.

"What are you planning on doing after the holidays, Violet?" It was my great aunt, her smiling face innocent and naive to the seriousness of her question.

"Yes, are you finished with school yet?" Her husband added.

I had to clear my throat, nerves taking hold of me. "I was recently in the hospital, so I took some time off from school on doctor's suggestion."

"Will you be returning to graduate then?"

"A beautiful girl like yourself shouldn't become a dropout." And here?

I stumbled on my words, finding my throat dry. I looked at my mother across the room, nervous of her reaction if I spoke wrong.

She must have seen my cry from help, because she interrupted. "Violet's health is the most important thing to us. So she can take as much time as she needs. After that, I hope she'll let me help her with whatever she wants to do."

My heart beat wild in my chest, and Jack moved a little closer to help me hold in the tears that threatened my eyes. I nodded in her direction, knowing she understood. Injected with a little more confidence, I glanced at Jack, taking his hand before speaking again. "I've been drawing a lot lately."

"She's a natural." Jack offered, squeezing my fingers when I blushed.

"It's something I'd be interested in pursuing maybe. One day."

I knew this was news to my mother. She had never seen any of my drawings. Regardless, she smiled and nodded. "We can look into art school together, if you'd like."

It was almost like the others in the room had completely disappeared. Forgiveness could do that, I guess.

"Yeah, that would be nice." There was no need for formal apologies, it seemed. Somewhere along the line, our actions had accepted each other back into our lives.

I worried for my heart. It was already sore from swelling so much, and the night wasn't even half over.

My grandmother called us for dinner, and she got some of her sisters to help her bring the rest of the food out to the table. I'd never seen a ham so big; it was almost the same size as the massive turkey. I had been concerned about the amount of food, if it was going to be enough for how many people who RSVP'd, but seeing it all on the table made my concerns disappear.

My grandmother stood at the head of the table to make a toast, and everyone quieted down to listen.

"It's wonderful to see you all here today. It makes the reason for our gathering bittersweet. You know, I had a whole long list of thanks I wanted to say but, my husband was always impatient for the meal on Christmas day, so maybe I'll save formalities for after you all have full bellies. Let's dig in."

Everyone laughed and cheered in agreement, clinking glasses and pulling the chairs closer to the table to hunker in and get to work. With the good food and wine loosening people up, the chatter came. While food on our plates dwindled, the volume in the room rose as we talked over each other. It was at this point that people started offering their own speeches.

Each person at the table had their own wonderful stories of my grandfather. I locked them away in the back of my head so I could hold onto their descriptions of him forever. A few weeks ago, I might have felt hateful and jealous, that these people got to have time with my grandfather that I was robbed of, but in the moment, I was nothing but thankful that I got to hear their beautiful memories of him.

Then we returned to the den and my mother handed out the gifts to everyone, having them all open them at the same time. No one was expecting gifts, so their reactions were amazing. We tried our best to pick books that fit the person, and it showed as they opened them. I heard someone say it was like my grandfather had given them the book himself.

I smiled at Jack to thank him for his wonderful idea, and he kissed my forehead.

We continued our anecdotal stories well into the night, until most of my relatives were red faced from the wine and slurring on their words and emotions as they shared. People started slipping away from the crowd to go upstairs and pay their respects, returning with tears in their eyes but a warmth in their heart that I could almost reach out and touch. I could tell the night was everything it was supposed to be. It was wonderful.

I would have been lying if I said I didn't cry. Somehow, I managed to be discrete, Jack helping by offering his sleeve for me to dry my lashes on, but my eyes were constantly filled to the brim with tears. They made the warm lights of the tree and the fire shine in a special, sparkling, surreal way.

I rested my head on Jack's shoulder as I sniffed to try and gather myself a little. I was drained from the emotions filling my chest, I could barely keep myself upright any longer. He wrapped an arm around my shoulders and pulled me closer, lips in my hair.

I sighed in content, and after a moment, he nudged my cheek with his nose and asked into my ear, "Tired?"

I nodded, shutting my eyes as he kissed one of my eyelids.

"You want to get out of here for a bit?"

I sighed again, relieved. As much as I hated to miss even one story of my grandfather, my heart needed a break from its rapid, happy pounding. I nodded, and he took my hand and led me with him as we snuck away. He was always so good at leading the way, I followed like it was nothing.

XXXVIII

I didn't want to be seen sneaking off into my room with a boy, so instead, we bundled up and escaped the loud buzzing of the house into the cool, quiet night. The snow on the ground reflected enough moonlight to show us our path, bathing the way to the garden in soft, calming blue. The snow sparkled like stars, mirroring the glimmering specks in the navy sky, and I felt a certain, wonderful magic swell in my bones.

There was something about nights like this. It was one thing to have a boy tell you he's Death, to show you the things he can do, things that could only be explained by a word like "magic," but that wasn't the magic I felt. It was this melancholy, of knowing you're alone and yet feeling the world around you as if it's present. Even though the trees were stripped bare and the animals were cozied up in their burrows, there was a life to the air as it blew past my cold cheeks: a caress that told me wonderful things about the world I had yet to see, waking a part of me that was dead for a long time.

Weeks ago, I had been no more than the flesh and bones holding me together, ready to embrace my death as it loomed on the horizon. Now though, even just an inhale of the fresh, crisp air brought my senses to life. I could practically feel the warmth of my own existence coursing through my veins. This was what living was like, and I was becoming addicted to its flavor.

With my elation came a sorrowful regret though, knowing that this new adoration for life meant I had to give up one of my other favorite things.

As if he felt me thinking of him, Jack wrapped his arms around me from behind and buried his face into my hair. I leaned into the attention, savoring it, trying to not let the sadness of our ticking away seconds bring tears to my eyes.

Jack fended off my negativity for a little longer. "I have a gift for you. I didn't want to give it to you in front of everyone else. It's not for them." He kissed my hair with his words, until I hummed and melted into the comfort of his attention. I didn't need gifts, all I needed was him, for a few seconds longer.

He gave it to me anyway. Still wrapped around me from behind, he shifted to retrieve a rectangular present, in the same wrapping paper and similar size to the books we had spent the previous evening wrapping. I took it in my hands, lifting an eyebrow and giving him a look out of the corner of my eye.

"When did you get this? And with what money?"

"I wasn't working for your grandmother for free, remember? And I might have slipped away for a second the other day, while you were digging through the frozen turkey's trying to find the biggest one." When I gave him a playful glare, he nipped at my ear and whispered, "Open it."

"I didn't get you anything," I commented, feeling guilty, even though I imagined he wouldn't be able to keep something even if I had.

I felt him smile. "You're stalling."

"What if I don't like it?" I teased.

He growled playfully into the skin of my neck. "Open it."

I sighed as if finally giving in was a bother, flipping the gift over to tear at the tape holding the paper on. Once I had an opening, I removed its brightly wrapped cover. My heart picked up a beat as my fingers touched leather; a sensation I recognized like an old friend.

It was not my journal, but it was exactly the same, minus the age and wear. The binding was fresh and untouched and the wrap that held it closed was tight still. The leather smelled freshly sealed and was comforting in my palms.

I had no words, so Jack spoke for me. "I thought you could use a new one."

He had no idea.

"The old one was running out of room."

It was jam packed full of all my darkness and pain, so of course it was running out of room.

"Do you like it?"

I sputtered out a laugh through the tears threatening me. "Of course I do."

"Look inside."

I turned to give him a questioning look, but he tilted his head to encourage me to see for myself instead. I unwrapped the band and let it sling from the back, then peeled open the front cover, hearing the leather flex, a satisfying noise.

I lost my breath a second time.

"Something to remember me by," he whispered, kissing the skin just under my ear.

I exhaled slow and pet a set of shaky fingers over the inside of the cover. Carefully secured on the paper backing was a pressed violet, and under its stem was sharp, pointed handwriting that read: "A Violet For Violet."

I couldn't hold the tears back anymore. I shut my eyes to keep them from falling down my cheeks. My words came out as barely a breath. "It's perfect, Jack. Everything. This gift, the party. This was exactly what everyone needed, what I needed. Tonight has been perfect, because of you. Thank you." I closed the journal and held it close to my chest, turning to bury myself into his embrace.

He let me find my composure before speaking again. "I'm glad that I was able to help. I've spent so long causing pain to the people left behind. It's been beautiful to influence joy for once."

There was something in his voice when he said this, like something had settled in him after tonight. It reminded me of crossing things off my list, a feeling of satisfaction, no matter how bittersweet. I think I understood. He wanted to build something up instead of tearing it down for once, and he had succeeded.

My grandfather would pass on tonight, but the foundation that Jack had managed to construct around his death was influencing change. There would still be pain, but from that pain would come something new and beautiful for my family.

It meant the world to him, that he made a difference. I could tell. Could he tell it also meant the world to me though? I put the journal into my sweater pocket, then buried my arms under his jacket to wrap around his thin body. I heard his heart, and felt mine copying its rhythm, like tiny, teasing clocks in our chests. I gripped at the fabric of his sweater as pain bloomed in my chest.

"Of all the moments I've wished for time to stand still for us…" I begged my heart to pause for just a second, but it kept pounding hard and fast, defiant as always.

"If even Death can't have his wishes granted, what hope do you think you have?" He tried to hold a joking tone but there was something defeated underneath it. "Time is a merciless God."

How terribly true. I cursed it by reaching up and taking his lips. If time would not give us our eternity together, then I would fill each second with eternity. Perhaps if we lost ourselves thoroughly enough, we could find a place outside of time to stay forever.

I couldn't reject Time as much as I wanted though, because it had been merciful, after all. It had allowed me long enough to find my strength before making me do the things that would have otherwise broken me before. It allowed me to keep from Jack my secret pledge to live, so that we could spend a few more precious seconds together. Time had been on my side, but it couldn't delay the inevitable forever just because I wished for it. The longer it waited, the more the pain swelled in my chest, threatening to break my ribs apart to make room for it.

My attempts at kissing him until my brain turned to mush failed rather quickly, dissolving into shaky breathing across his lips as I held down the aching pain in my chest. This secret would kill me if I let it fester any longer. I couldn't keep pretending. I knew the truth, it pumped heavy and wild through me, and he needed to know too.

"I have to tell you something," I whispered, leading him closer as I leaned back against the wrought iron gate of the garden.

"Tell me," he sighed back, his voice barely there, but encouraging nonetheless.

I shook my head and shut my eyes. "I'm scared that you'll disappear if I do." Reaffirming my fear, I tightened my arms around him, terrified to let go.

He took my face in both his hands and kissed me again, long and deep and slow, until my heart was in my skull, beating a pounding pulse. He spoke to my lips in the middle of a kiss, "I told you I wouldn't disappear anymore. I'm not going anywhere. Not yet." As if to solidify his words, he removed his hands from me and gripped the bars of the gate behind me instead, trapping me there. I wasn't going anywhere either, it seemed.

"You promise?" I croaked out the question somehow. I had to be sure.

"I promise, Violet."

I nodded, reassured, but the notion still hurt. I swallowed past a painful lump in my throat, trying to gather the words. "I got rid of my note."

He didn't catch my meaning at first. "What note?" When I didn't answer, he pulled away to search my face, reading my soul.

What I wouldn't have given to stare into the gray of his eyes forever. I wasn't allowed a rest of my life with those eyes though. I waited anyway, a fraction longer than I needed, to remember every vein of blue and silver, etching them away into the back of my skull where my darkness used to sit. If I ever found myself seeking out my dark thoughts again, I hoped I'd find him instead.

"My suicide note," I said finally on a sigh, the pressure in my chest hitting a peak. Tears welled and his face became a blur. "I ripped it up and put it under my grandfather's bed with my journal. I promised him… I promised him I'd live. I'm not going to do it. I don't want to disappear anymore." I tried to smile to fend it off, but that pain burst in my chest and overflowed around my heart into a violent ache. This was a good thing. It was good news, and yet it hurt so badly; I kept forgetting how painful it was to be alive.

Jack attempted a smile too, but it ended up as a tormented line between his brows. He gave a strangled laugh, before smothering something aching by bringing our lips together again. When he found his voice, it was on an exhale. "I'm glad you're finally admitting it."

I frowned, confused. "What is that supposed to mean?" Was he joking? "You knew?"

He sighed, pressing his forehead to mine again and petting his thumb over my cheek. "I knew before you did."

I blinked, lifting my gaze to show him my curiosity. It had taken me so long to decide; it was impossible for him to have known when I hadn't. "How?"

To my surprise, he breathed out a bit of a laugh. "It's hard to explain, but you've basically been buzzing with life for weeks now."

"Buzzing?" I lifted an eyebrow.

"Like a live wire. It's like you're overcharged with life. Kissing you is like licking a battery." He paused, realized what he said, and corrected himself. "In a good way, of course."

Somehow, I found a laugh as well. "A battery?"

I gripped my fingers around the collar of his jacket and tugged a little, admiring the grin playing at the corner of his lips. He hummed confirmation, following my subtle suggestion and kissing me with that smile again, soft and easy, forgetting for a brief, blissful moment that we were supposed to be sad.

When the emotion crept up on us again, I sighed and leaned my head back against the garden gate. An important question slipped past the melancholy and onto my tongue. "If you knew all this time, that I wasn't going to kill myself, then how are you still here?"

The tiny smirk that lingered on his face faded away.

"Because I was never here for you, Violet."

My head was slow and foggy with sadness, so I didn't understand right away. Things clicked into place after a long silence, and my heart found an extra beat. "But if you're not here for me then…" I turned back to the estate, as the pounding in my chest turned into the phantoms of mechanical beeps.

My grandfather. All this time.

Jack didn't confirm my suspicion. He didn't need to. He saw that I understood. Instead, he let out a breath that shook from his lips. "I told you I'd let you know when I had to leave."

I stared at him, until the tears made the outline of my vision go blurry again. I shook my head, silently begging him not to say it.

His gray eyes shined apologies.

"Tonight. I go tonight, Violet."

XXXIX

We decided we would stay there in each others arms until Time intervened. I trusted it to know when I was ready. I trusted it to tell me when I would have the strength to face my coming fate. It let us have a brief moment where I wondered if the world had forgotten about us altogether, a moment of just our hearts and breaths and the voice of life itself in the air, then it forced us back onto the timeline with the sound of my mother's voice.

"Violet. We've been looking for you. Everyone has said their goodbyes. It's time, when you're ready."

My stomach twisted up in regret. I didn't feel ready, but I tried to trust my fate.

We returned inside, and Jack hung back as I joined my grandmother and mother in saying goodbye to everyone. Some took their cars and others called cabs, but gradually, everyone left after offering their condolences and extra long hugs. There was a sadness in the air, but it thinly veiled something else. Perhaps just like myself, everyone else knew that, while letting go was hard, it led to a better place. I hoped closure was as good as everyone made it out to be.

Jack slipped upstairs while everyone was distracted. I wouldn't have noticed if he hadn't brushed his hand past mine, so gently I almost didn't feel it. I watched him as he went, giving a nod of understanding when he paused outside my grandfather's door. Whether I wanted to or not, I would have to join him.

He slipped into the shadowy room, leaving the door ajar.

As the last of my relatives trickled out of the house, the quiet, familiar noises started coming back. The ticking of the grandfather clock, the snaps and sparks from the wood stove, the mechanical beeps of my grandfather's last few heartbeats. When we finally closed the front door, the house empty save us three women and two not-quite-alive men, I gave a sigh that added to those barely there noises.

My grandmother took me into her arms and held me for a long time before pulling away to take my face into her hands. Her eyes were red, but she managed to keep them dry. She parted her lips, like she thought to say something, but nothing came. Instead, she kissed my forehead and started up the stairs to her room. My mother gave me a sad smile and a nod before following her, leaving me with my own pounding heart and shaken breath. The task of being the last one to say goodbye weighed heavy on my shoulders now.

Perhaps I shouldn't have asked for the duty, but if I hadn't, Jack wouldn't have been able to help, and I owed my grandfather that much. He waited for long enough for us to be ready. He at least deserved an easy walk to wherever Jack would lead him.

I inhaled to try and prepare myself, quickly becoming aware that there was no more preparing. This sadness would not fade any further. I was just prolonging it by rooting myself to the floor like this. My feet felt heavy, but I willed myself forward and managed my way up the creaking stairs.

In my grandmother's room, my mother's voice hummed the same lullaby she'd sung to my grandfather, *all the pretty little horses*, the sound of a brush stroking long and smooth through hair as my grandmother sobbed.

I turned away, to the other end of the hall.

The room fell into darkness as I closed the door behind me. My hand searched for the lightswitch on the wall, but then I decided against it. The moon offered cool light from the window, outlining the shape of my grandfather in his bed and Jack leaning against the wall next to me. Anything more would have felt abrasive. It looked like my grandfather was sleeping, and I felt the strong urge not to blind him with artificial light.

I stood there and stared at him in the bed for a while, trying my best to ignore the sterile smell that still triggered something to clench with nerves inside of me. When I exhaled a long breath, it trembled, and Jack's hand found mine.

"How is this going to work?" I asked him, squaring my shoulders a little to try and fend off the emotions filling up my chest.

He squeezed my fingers, coming a little closer, sensing my growing weakness and encouraging me to stay strong. He looked at my grandfather, then back to me. "If you want to say goodbye, you should now. Then, you can turn off the machines, and I'll take it from there."

"Will he be in pain?"

He shook his head immediately. "Not anymore. I'll make sure, I promise."

"And then?"

He sighed, understanding what the question had meant and being apprehensive to answer. I squeezed his fingers just as he had with me.

"Then it's my turn to say goodbye."

Emotion stung at my nose, but I swallowed it down. My heart pounded wildly in protest, but I kept my mouth shut, simply nodding instead.

I untangled my fingers from his and stepped towards my grandfather, sitting carefully on the edge of his bed. I didn't need the photograph of him this time. Even though he was more gaunt than I remembered, in the forgiving, dreamy light of the moon, my grandfather looked very much like he was simply taking a nap.

My fingers shook as I took his hand in mine. Thoughts came, but words failed me, tangling up in my throat and creating knots instead. I wanted to tell him I was thankful for everything, even if my mother hadn't allowed him to be there as much as either of us had wanted. I wanted to tell him he did a good job, even while laying in this bed, at keeping his family together. I wanted to apologize for us being selfish and needing just a little bit more time with him, and that I hoped whatever suffering he was going through would end quickly now.

It was all too much though. My mouth didn't want to form the words. I didn't have the strength. I squeezed his hand instead and whispered, "I love you, Grampie. We all do. So much that we simply couldn't let you go. I'm so sorry. We're ready now though. We'll miss you, but we'll be OK. I'll be OK."

There were tears in my eyes before I expected them. My words broke, and I fended off the sobs that threatened in my chest for a few more seconds by taking some deep, shaking breaths. When I found a sense of composure, I turned to Jack, who stood in the shadows, waiting.

He came over next to the bed, giving me a tiny, sad nod. I closed my eyes and counted the beats of my heart to settle my shaking fingers, then found his gaze again and nodded back.

I reached over to my grandfather's life support machines,

pausing just briefly before flipping every switch off. The tiny lights that always blinked or shined were now off, and as the last button was flicked, the mechanical beeping I had become so painfully familiar with disappeared, and the room fell into utter silence. All that was left was my own deafening heartbeat in my ears.

Jack gave me a last look, a final confirmation, most likely because he remembered too vividly my reaction the last time he tried to take my grandfather. I nodded again, through the tears welling in my eyes, and watched as he leaned over the bed.

That look that I had seen before took over him, his pupils dilating with an unfocused stare, as if he was seeing past the things I could see. He outstretched a steady hand, and as he laid it over my grandfather's eyes, he said, "Don't be afraid, I can take the pain away."

I silently sobbed, holding my breath to hold down the hurt. I squeezed my grandfather's unmoving hand tighter, silently apologizing for the additional pain I had forced him to endure. I hoped he understood. I hoped he heard it all and knew how sorry I was.

Jack let out a breath, like a tiny laugh, and it broke me from my thoughts momentarily. I sputtered a word past my tears. "What?"

"He asked me if that was an angel speaking."

"You?" I imagined how having a ghostly boy hovering over my deathbed and speaking about taking away my pain could make me think I was meeting an angel also.

Jack made the sound again, and then I watched him blink his eyes and come back to my side of the veil. "No, you."

My heart stopped. "He heard me?" Before Jack could confirm I moved closer, squeezing his hand tighter. "It's me, Grampie. It's Violet. I'm here."

Jack's gaze returned to wherever my grandfather's consciousness was, and a tiny smile pulled at the corner of his lips. "He says to remember your promise."

A fissure of pain split in my chest, and I shut my eyes tight against it. Jack didn't know about what I'd said to my grandfather, about the promise I made him.

He had heard me that night. He heard me all this time.

"I will. I will, Grampie." I couldn't get any more words out. My throat was swollen. I pulled his hand up and put my forehead to his knuckles and nodded instead as the sobs shook through me.

Jack's smile faded and his unfocused gaze drifted shut. A second passed, and I felt a chill shake through me, the room going bone cold. Then Jack sucked in a hard breath and removed his hand from my grandfather's face, opening his eyes as if coming back to consciousness.

He was unsteady on his feet, bracing himself with a hand on the edge of the bed.

"He's gone now?" I asked, needing to know for sure.

Jack's tired gaze found me, nodding.

"He's not in pain anymore?"

He shook his head. "No more pain, Violet."

I sighed, trying to swallow down the ache, to little avail. I didn't mention that just because my grandfather was no longer in pain, didn't mean mine was gone. It was alright though. He had already suffered so much; I didn't mind taking some of his pain if it meant he got to move on. I was strong enough now. I knew no matter how hard I cried, I had the strength to put my pieces back together all by myself, even if I didn't want to.

"What about you?" I asked, after I had found another scrap of togetherness to get a few words out.

He skipped over my question. "Do you want to stay here?"

I inhaled and looked at my grandfather, now just a empty vessel, the dread of death filling the room and mixing with the hospital smell that I hated. Feeling that he was no longer here, the room was terribly uncomfortable.

I shook my head. "No. I think I just want to go to bed."

He nodded, then stood on his obviously weak legs and took my hand. "Come with me."

I tried to get a hold of my quiet, shaking sobs, standing when he guided me to my feet. "What about you?" I repeated myself.

Goodbye, he had said. It was time for goodbye. So why wasn't he saying it now?

"Just a little longer…" Something read pleading in his voice when he spoke. As if he was begging, and I wasn't sure if he was begging me, or something else.

We stumbled to my room in our mutual exhaustion, practically collapsing into the bed, and each other. He held himself to me as I tore open and sobbed; his grip around me so tight that the pieces of me I felt shattering stayed in place thanks to him.

When I was too tired to sob anymore, my body settled to a numb quietness. The exhaustion was taking over, and in between my sniffs, heavy breaths, and hard, beating of my heart, I found myself drifting off. Jack must have been also, because I heard his inhales shallowing with sleep. It was this realization that made Jack finally speak.

"I can't stay, Violet." The words felt more like they were for himself than for me.

"I know," I whispered back to the skin of his collar.

"I wish I could." His voice shook.

"Me too."

I felt him swallow hard. "Maybe I can just rest here with you, for a few more minutes."

He did his death fingers thing, so he must have been exhausted.

"Just a little," I said.

He pulled closer and buried himself into my neck. He held me so close that if I didn't already know what would happen, I'd have sworn he'd never let me go.

"I love you, Violet. I always will."

I held back the tears. It hurt too much to cry. I had nothing left in me to sob anymore. I nodded instead, tightening my weak limbs around him also.

"I know. I love you too, Jack."

I fell asleep to the pound of his heart, and I woke to a cold, empty bed and a chest that felt just as vacant. As much as my drowsy self wanted to hold onto hope, I knew that Time had come for us finally.

I didn't know how long I cried, trying to stitch up the two gaping wounds in my heart. I lost track of time, of reality, of myself. For a moment, I wondered if a new darkness was growing inside of me. I wasn't strong enough to fight it if it was.

I twisted in my bed, and my swollen eyes found a familiar face on my bedside table; the violet Jack left me sat innocently in its pot, looking as lively as ever. I wondered, did he give it one last bit of attention before leaving, just as he had me?

As I focused through the darkness of my room, I saw a new addition next to my violet, and despite the tears dripping down my cheeks, a smile spread across my lips.

Propped open next to the violet was my new journal from Jack. I saw the first page, with the pressed flower, and his handwriting: *A Violet for Violet*.

Something to remember me by, he'd said.

My heart pounded morse code against my ribs.

A-live. A-live. A-live.

Maybe I was strong enough, after all.

About the Author

Danielle Koste is born and raised Canadian, but currently lives with her significant other in the equally snowy and cold Stockholm, Sweden. While working a day job and learning the language of the locals, she spent her free time honing the craft she always had a passion for. Movies, music, and video games are among her favorite time-wasters.

WHAT THE FLOWER SAYS OF DEATH is Danielle Koste's second published book. You can purchase her first novel PULSE, or find more of her work online at one of the following locations.

www.daniellekoste.com
www.facebook.com/DanielleKoste
www.patreon.com/DanielleKoste
or @DanielleKoste on twitter